AF431832

IT FEELS SO GOOD TO BE A VICTIM

Emma Newman-Holden

DREAM BOY
BOOK CLUB

Editor: Lili Kouzehkanani

Dream Boy Book Club
USA

ACKNOWLEDGMENTS

I want to thank my mother, my father, my step-mother, and my friends for keeping me alive and for making me live. I want to thank everyone who reads and engages with my stories, especially those gracious enough to champion my words, answer my questions, and reach out to me from a place of genuine compassion and curiosity. Finally, and most importantly, I want to thank my editor, Lili Kouzehkanani, and my publisher, Jonathan Blake Fostar, for not only believing in me but for making this book the best it could be. Lili and Jonathan awarded my work with the care and precision you gift a newborn child, and this is a kindness I get to cherish forever.

TABLE OF CONTENTS

AUTHOR'S NOTE

My favorite dynamic to write about, a serpentine thread of this book, is the irresistibly complex relationship between two sexual women. Whether or not they're vying for the same man doesn't necessarily matter; the fact that they're both vying for men at all puts them in a heated competition that can't break off until someone falls dead. In an attempt to counteract what you're rest assured is misogyny-based resentment, you actualize this perfectly ordinary woman into a deity. You befriend her, you love her, you want to fuck her like you've never wanted to fuck anyone before—all to make her someone besides your opponent, in the name of modernity or distraction. Every woman has faced this obstacle, and it never gets easier or less interesting.

My short stories speak on sex work, mental illness, substance abuse, parasocial relationships—and I hope I navigate these subjects in a manner that is, above all, true. This book is for fangirls and fat old sex workers. This book is for grieving mothers and autistic sons. This book is for that one person who slept with everyone at the SLAA meeting. This book is for functioning alcoholics and cigarette chain-smokers and adult women with self-harm scars. This book is for the Instagram influencer as well as the man who pays the Instagram influencer for pictures of her feet. This book is for everyone who knows that a soul is not a finite destination, but keeps on looking anyway.

I'm proud of this book, and I've never been good at

pride. I typically only feel pride in the moment. That's how short-lived my pride is: a moment's length. If I try to feel pride after the fact, it feels like a charade, like I'm boasting about a person who is no longer me, which makes it a completely different emotion. Adoration, maybe. Nostalgia, at its worst. But this project has forced me—allowed me—to extend pride's boundaries outside of the present. I am proud of these stories not because the past version of myself wrote them, but because the present and future versions would as well. These stories are so incredibly me that they speak across all my possibilities. So please enjoy this book, if for no other reason than I, myself, deeply enjoy it.

*Or you can dine and whine on stuff that's bound to give
you boils*

Hot dogs direct from Cruft's

Done in diesel oil

Or the burger joint around the bend

Where the meals thank christ are skimpy

For you that's how the world could end

Not with a bang but a Wimpy

— "Psycle Sluts," John Cooper Clarke

The Woman

I've been fucking my sister's boyfriend. My sister doesn't know. It doesn't stem from rivalry, we actually get on quite well. He's perfect. He is a perfect person, truly. I've never met a perfect person before, so I could not let this opportunity pass me by. And I have the right to experience a perfect person, I do. What I'm saying is, it could've been anybody's boyfriend, my wanting him has nothing to do with his girlfriend being my sister. The thing that's special about all of this is him, not her. But, of course, it does complicate things.

Adrien has the flesh of a ripe nectarine. His skin is always moist, like dewy grass—refreshing, thick. He smells of lemon shortbread, which seems like a feminine scent, but he wears it quite valiantly, mystically. As if in a past life, he was a calloused French assassin with a penchant for baking—it's niche, a virtue. He loves chess. He could play it all day if provided the tools and a source of light. He beats my sister every time, so I never dared challenge him. He blushes very easily, very starkly, the rosiness of his cheeks like blaring traffic lights. This prevents me from flirting with him in front of my sister, but not him. My sister will be in the same room, washing dishes or cleaning the cat's anal glands, and Adrien will have his fingers playing with my bra straps like a stringed instrument. He doesn't care about getting caught, or maybe it turns him on—I don't care either way. I just don't want to be the reason we get caught because this would place Adrien very low in terms of power, and I never want to make him feel that way. Of course, he has the perfect length—6.5 inches—and the perfect girth—4.4 inches. I won't tell you if that's erect or flaccid because some things I'd like to keep for myself. He has never made me cum—not that he doesn't know how, trust me, he knows how. He's just purposefully edging me. It's all foreplay. When he rests his hand on my lower back when my sister isn't looking, it's foreplay. When he takes a massive shit in the bathroom and warns me "not to go in there," it's foreplay. When he sticks his dick inside me and cums on my face, it's foreplay. He's just waiting for the perfect moment for me to release.

My sister and Adrien met at a weed shop. He works there, my sister was picking up raspberry-flavored indica, and she complimented his biceps in a half-ironic way. They've been dating for three years since then, on and off. The main reason they're still together is that stupid fucking cat. They adopted this seventeen-year-old cat when they first started dating, and that fucker is still going. She's an obese red tabby, and they call her Deez Nuts. They quickly became tired of the joke, but the cat would only respond to that name, so it had to stay. Anyway, they've both grown very fond of Deez Nuts, and I think the obligation each of them feels to Deez Nuts is keeping them together, like a child or tax breaks.

My sister is the real breadwinner—she works as a nurse at a senior home and has very long hours. I'm an AI content writer, teaching machines to think and feel and so on. Plus, I'm living on the inheritance of our dead father, but neither really covers the bills. She's paying for the roof over my head, and I'm fucking her boyfriend—bad person, I told you. Anyway, her long hours are the real reason Adrien and I have been sleeping together. We live together, we spend our free time together when my sister isn't home, it was only a matter of time before we fucked. It was all going fine until Adrien got me something: a bouquet of peonies. I mentioned I liked the smell of peonies once. Such a gentlemanly and unexpected gift—it changed everything forever. Once you are given a gift, you either have to give a gift back, fully knowing that this precedes an unending chain of niceties, a prison sentence of sorts, or live with yourself knowing that you are a horrible person. I already did the latter, so I decided not to give a gift back. But then he stopped calling me "cunt" and "whore" in bed—it was unnerving. I don't like it when people change the rules without saying so outright. Like, when we first got together, he made the first move. We were watching a reality dating show about anorexic midgets getting paired with non-acting pedophiles, and he put his hand on my thigh and said, "Miranda, I like you. I really do," and then he kissed me and then we paused the episode and then we had sex. No opportunity for misinterpretation. So what was this? It's not fun getting what you want; it's not a relief. It just causes more problems.

I wasn't gaining feelings for him—not yet, at least. But there he was, being kind to me, anticipating the feelings I would have before I could. And then I started thinking: it's so selfish that I get what I want. It's so selfish that I expect to be deliriously happy every day. Why can't I accept mediocrity? It's because there's an important part of my soul that is bored and unsatiated. Souls aren't allowed to be bored, but mine found a way. It hit me last Tuesday afternoon, I was home, watching a documentary about a mother's contaminated breastmilk—who had a botched boob job performed in a van in Tijuana two years prior—producing a child that could hear up to sixty thousand Hertz and say the alphabet backwards, and Adrien was working at the shop, and my sister walked in. She was exhausted, saying she had been working the past three days—basically no sleep to be had. And then she offered to make us dinner. I remember it exactly, she said, "Spaghetti? I'll make some spaghetti for us." I broke down. Sobbing, shaking, catching my breath, my sister holding me. This poor sleep-starved and actual-starved person is having to coddle me because I have yet to learn how to accept my mistakes. She keeps asking me to talk to her, over and over again, as if we were ever the kind of siblings to "talk." I tell her it's my period, then I let her make us spaghetti.

Today, I'm at home, at work, like usual, writing a persuasive essay arguing for a federally mandated tax that allows women to take off work during their luteal phase for the invisible people in my computer to plagiarize. It's been five and a half weeks since the affair started. One week since he's been sending me "good morning" texts. Today's message came with a red heart emoji, a tongue emoji, and a merman emoji. I text back a colon and a right parenthesis. I refuse to give in. I feel bad and send a green heart emoji two minutes later. Women would kill for a chance like this, to be treated by a perfect man like this. What an insult—the speed at which our bodies grow accustomed to comfort. Deez Nuts has been purring quite aggressively at me all day. It's really fucking annoying. I "take care" of Deez Nuts when nobody's home, really just putting tuna in her bowl when I get the chance to remember. But the thing is, I hate cats. I really fucking hate Deez Nuts, and she hates me too. I hate her like a child I don't want, and she hates me like I am evil incarnate. Maybe she knows my secret. Cats are intuitive like that. Just another reason to hate them. She's been really bad the past couple of weeks. Peeing on everything but her litter box. It seems like my stuff is more of a target than my sister's or Adrien's. She's already ruined a new pair of running shoes and my Apple watch: the universe telling me not to get into working out.

"Heyo!"

I instinctively shut my laptop. It's Adrien. He's home about six hours too early. But really, I would've been able to tell from the footsteps alone. His are light and quick like a rabbit, my sister's are clunky, intentional, like clogs on a moving platform.

"Hello, pretty lady."

I turn around and stand up. He's all red—his cheeks, his eyes. Sometimes he gets high at work. I don't care, I really don't. Honestly, his weed use usually makes him zone out while fucking, meaning he'll be able to eat me out for hours. I don't know if that's problematic or not.

"Um, hey. Hi. Why are you home—here?"

He snakes his hand across the back of my neck. He knows I love this. I love feeling like my head is only standing up with his support. He taps his fingers down my spine like piano keys.

"Gas leak in the building. So no work for the next coupl'a days."

He's rubbing circles with his pointer finger now. Right behind my left ear.

"Oh—well—are you okay?"

He laughs, runs his spare hand through his sweaty hair.

"Yeah, yeah. I'm totally fine. I was thinking on the ride home, though—we should go somewhere."

I laugh. I tickle his left oblique—it's really a tic at this point. He laughs a painful laugh.

"Where?"

His hands drop to his side and curl into fists. He takes on an analytical look—his chess face.

"I mean, I can't take us anywhere fancy, you know that. But, I have a friend who works at this pretty cool hotel not too far from here."

He's pacing now.

"A-And I think he can get us a pretty good deal. Pretty sure there's a hot tub? Either way, wouldn't it be nice to have one night to spend together? Like, sleep next to each other, like, at night?"

Deez Nuts meows, and it kind of sounds like she's saying "wrong." Or maybe "raw." Intuitive. She rubs the top of her head against Adrien's bare calf. She's always favored Adrien.

"I mean…it sounds great—"

"Right? Just for a day or two, since you can work anywhere and—"

"But how will we…you know…"

He smiles, his cheeks wide and taut like water balloons—his winning face.

"Yeah, so, I'm going to say I'm visiting my parents. You say you have a work conference nearby. You don't have a car, so I have to drive you places anyway, so, and I'll say I'll drop you off on the way. We should get back home at different times, though—I don't know, we'll figure that out. But it's kind of *full* proof."

I think about this with as much clarity and reason as I can muster. He's getting close now. He's definitely getting too close. This will end horribly, which is fine—it was always destined to—but will it even be enjoyable in the moment? Will I suffocate, will I shrink away? Will I lash out, will I hate myself? Is there a hot tub or not?

"Yeah, let's do it," I say.

We tell my sister that night, and leave the next morning. The drive is a little less than an hour. We play "I Spy," and then I give him road head, trying to seem spontaneous and carefree, but then he chastises me and I suck the saliva back into my mouth and we go back to playing. He wins every round, of course. We arrive at the hotel, and it's much shittier than anticipated. It's tiny, made up of beige brick, surrounded by dying birds-of-paradise and shrubbery the color of biscotti. He says hi to his friend, daps him up—I say nothing. There are no concierges. We have to carry our stuff inside to our rooms by ourselves. There's one bed, four bedside lamps. Who needs four bedside lamps? The throw blanket is this pneumonic kind of green, and the sheets have the texture and smell of insulation. There are exactly two drawers and a television that could date back to the eighties. There's a painting of a faceless naked woman opposite the bed, which catches Adrien's attention straight away. But the view makes it worth it. The far wall has great big windows. No bodies of water, no cities, just houses, rows and rows and rows of them. I can see a cul-de-sac, can see a young father teaching his daughter how to ride a bicycle. Her little face moves quickly, scrupulously, from expression to expression—I can't tell if she's crying or laughing.

"So, what do you think?"

He's standing, strong and tall, illuminated by the view now behind me. His beautiful shoulder-length hair, scratchy and greasy, like a country singer's. Green eyes, chestnut skin, his cracked front tooth, his entire forehead pinpricked with beads of sweat. I touch it: feels cold, smells salty, almost fishy.

Of course, it has nothing on the lemon shortbread. I nod and make out with his face. I almost forgot he was perfect. I nearly forgot he was a perfect man. That's why I'm here in the first place, isn't it? A perfect man who kisses perfectly and grabs the right parts of my body with the perfect amount of pressure. I push my tongue down his throat and tickle his left armpit—he slaps my hand away. He then throws me on the bed and eats me out for twenty-eight minutes.

We spend the next couple of hours getting drunk on the room's overpriced shooters and playing hide-and-seek. This was my favorite game as a child, especially whenever I was in a hotel, so he concedes. When my dad would go on his "work trips," he'd bring me along, because he knew how much I loved hotels. I love performative comfort—manufactured homes. Because nothing surface-level can ever truly disappoint. He never brought my sister. She was old enough to know what was going on. My dad always found me within the first ten minutes. The last time we played, I was eleven years old. I hid in my own room—I thought I was so smart for an eleven-year-old—but he never found me. I really thought that I finally beaten him. That was until I found him, two hours later, passed out in his room, only dressed in nipple clamps, smelling of whiskey, alongside a fat epicene prostitute counting twenties. I remember thinking his dick looked like a hairless hamster. The prostitute told me that they were my daddy's masseuse. I didn't know what masseuse meant, so I pretty much assumed the worst anyway. Anyway, I win the first round, quickly, easily. Adrien's on the seventh floor, hiding behind the trash can next to the vending machine. Amateur move, really. Next, I hide. I hide behind a cluster of houseplants in the lobby. No one ever thinks to check the lobby. He ends up getting frustrated and has to text me asking where I am. Men can't lose in vain, you see, meaning that if they do lose, you must immediately do something they can win to balance out things, assuage their ego. So, I finally concede to playing chess with Adrien. Of course, he brought the game. Of course.

"No, you can't move that one like that."

He's had to remind me that about twelve times so far. Each time, he takes on a really indignant tone as if I'm purposefully cheating. I try moving the one that looks like a lobster claw forward a space. He slams his fist on the bed, and his face heats an autumnal orange.

"Miranda!"

I laugh, but he shakes his head. Sometimes it's best to be frivolous when he's angry, but sometimes not. I can't tell which time this is. I move a random piece across the board and yell "Checkmate!" as a joke. He doesn't laugh. He analyzes the board and pulls at the end of his left earlobe habitually.

"You can't do that," he states gravely. His jaw is clenched, his lips dry.

"Oh, no, I know. I was just kidding."

"Well, were you kidding about the bishop, then?"

"The what?"

Now, he's laughing. Not a good laugh, though. The kind of laugh a parent laughs before they smack the shit out of you. He walks around the room, grabs a tightly wrapped doobie from his luggage. Shuffles inside his man-purse to find a box of matches and lights the joint. I stand up, coolly walk to him, stroke his bicep, play with the hem of his skinny jeans. His skin has that kind of coarse bounce you can only find on your cousin's old trampoline, his muscle tauter than a green apple.

"Look, I'm sorry…I told you I didn't know how to play."

"I want you to suck my dick."

His eyes are a reptilian yellow, surrounded by cherry red veins. His undereyes are a cold purple, and so are his lips. I swallow my laugh.

"What?"

"I want you to make it up to me by sucking my dick. Now."

He's stone-faced, which isn't ideal, honestly. He thinks the stoicism helps his case, feeds into the dominance, but it just reminds me how hyperaware he is of his own performance. We're both voyeurs for his fantasies of manhood.

"Um—"

He pushes my head down—that, for some reason, brings me into it. I think because hands aren't performative in the way faces are—they can't be. Hands are truth, powered by impulse rather than vanity. I follow the weight of his palm, lower to my knees. I unbuckle his pants, force his dick in my face. Tastes of brine and black licorice. Immediately, he lets out a squeaky whine. Then he coughs and switches to deeper groans and grunts. The length, the width, they perfectly coat the perimeter of my mouth, it almost feels like a sensory toy, a relief like chewing gum. His tip clashes into my throat, making my eyes well up every now and then, and I like it, I do. Perfect, I think—he is a perfect man. How come I keep forgetting this? After an unknowable amount of time, he pulls my hair, yanks me upward. I wipe my mouth, and he smiles.

"You're beautiful."

He carefully sets down the roach and throws me on the bed—he always does this, but now I'm thinking about it. Now, I'm paying attention to the beating tendons in his forearms, to the red sweat of his face, to the largeness of matter above me. He's strong, he is. He's strong like a man who doesn't know his own weight, his own power. If I no longer felt like having sex, would that realistically mean anything? Would it have any bearing on what would happen next? I don't know, but I can't think of this. I have to think of what's happening. His soft tongue inside my ear, now my mouth. His knee chafing against my clit. My hands running through his waxy hair, to his shoulders, to his waist, to his dick, which I begin to guide until I realize.

"Wait—we need condoms, do you have—"

"C'mon, Louise never lets me go raw—"

He takes his dick from me, as if it's not rightfully mine when it's being used against me, and pushes himself inside.

"What?"

He laughs, which quickly transitions into another squeaky whine.

"What…"

"You're still fucking my sister?"

One pump, then two.

"Uh, are you kidding? Why wouldn't I be?"

Five pumps, six. His eyes are fully closed now, his voice sounds unaffected, automatic. After twelve pumps, he pulls his dick out and cums on my shirt. There is nothing more embarrassing than the few seconds before a man cums. He's looking for a place to do it, he feels unsure what the optimal location is (face? tits? bedsheets?), and then he finishes himself off, all while looking as deeply unattractive as possible. Scrunched up face, mouth-breathing, shaking, no sense of coordination, no sense of rationale. Nothing is more unattractive than a man with no sense of rationale. He opens his eyes—first the left, then the right.

"Fuck, sorry. That was good, though. You're so fuckin' tight—like, really, you are."

I take my shirt off, and he lets his weight fall next to me. Isn't this what I wanted? What a horror, the way I find failures in the most likely of people.

"Um—well, I don't know. I mean, I don't know why I thought you weren't still fucking my sister. But I thought it."

I can't tell how my inflection is coming off right now, mostly because I can't tell how I feel right now. I wish there were someone who could tell you that.

"Wait…are you, like, mad?"

I shrug. My life flashes through my eyes, except that's not the right word—it's not quick, it's slow, insidious. And it's not images, it's really just words. Dead mother, mean father; boring sister. Ugly boyfriends, gay boyfriends, suicidal boyfriends. An endless string of nothing-jobs. It's like a recollection of events that led me to this moment, an attempt at explanation for my unhappiness. But my life would have to have reason in order to provide an explanation. So, of course, I come up short. He takes a deep sigh, stares at the popcorn ceiling, and begins speaking.

"I don't know, it's not like either of us has done this before. We're good people—this is new, so—"

"For you, Adrien, this is new."

He looks at me, his eyelids still dull with dopamine. The rose of his cheeks fading to a sandy beige. His mouth parts, as if he actually has anything to say.

"You think you made the first move, but I did, I did really. I-I would walk around the house half-naked, because Louise assumed we saw each other as siblings. I'd make fun of you like that because I…do this."

I'm in tears now, and it's not for the best—it's not a cathartic, relieving kind of cry. It's more like pissing your pants in public.

"What do you mean?"

"I'm never the woman. Never."

He wants to laugh, but stops himself.

"W-What?"

I'm not making sense now. I'm not forming my thoughts coherently. Images begin to surface in my brain in place of words. Nails painted teal in a coffin. Dad's cigarette case I stole. My sister's jump rope I cut in half.

"I do this thing—take people who are already owned by other people. I always want what I can't have, and each time I trick myself into thinking it's a special situation, and, and…"

Something hard is lodged in the base of my neck. I cough, but it remains. The wet heat of my cheeks after each mistake. The cracking itch in my stomach before each mistake.

"But worse than that—worse than that is, it's not a choice, it's a means of survival. I have to be the other woman because I am never the woman, the first woman. But once in my fucking life, I'd like to be the woman. Because both hurt in the end, but only one is allowed to keep their pride. Only one has the whole world on her side—or, is it something more? Yeah—yes, it's something more."

He looks scared, but he's listening. I feel grateful for that. That feels more real than the words I'm saying.

"It's something more, because, it started as an attempt to be the better woman. Virtually faultless, because she represents an oasis, see? But the real part of her character is—she's—well, she's temporary. She's invincible, but she's temporary…right? But I found a…but by being multiple men's other woman, I found a way to be temporary forever, and that's as close as I got to making a person of myself that can…"

And suddenly, I'm out of words. He says my name, or something close to it. His face squirms into an expressionless pose. Or maybe it's just an expression I'm not familiar with. It's not like I know everything.

"Are you high?"

He's shaking now. No, it's me who's shaking. No—it's both of us.

"No, I'm—no. I'm not."

I turn back to the window-wall, but it's all dark now. The little girl could still be there laugh-crying, but I wouldn't know. I wouldn't.

We leave the next morning. Earlier than anticipated, but necessary. I make us shitty coffee and he pretends to watch a news segment about a tanning lotion that turns darker when detecting a date rape drug, and the subsequent recall due to blackface allegations. I tally all the naked woman's flaws in the painting. Long toes, armpit fat, asymmetrical breasts, wide ribcage, cankles. Then we pack, and then we get in the car. It's bright and dry out, and I feel drunk even though I'm not. Everything feels strangely lurid and out of place. I walk up to one car and realize it's the wrong car. Then I find Adrien, not even realizing I lost him, and try to maintain eye contact with his bobbing head. I try opening the door before he unlocks it. He takes a minute fumbling with the keys before he does so. It's like both of us are sleepwalking. As soon as I get in the car, I feel starkly sober. Sober and anxious, as if I'm about to undergo a driving test, even though I'm in the passenger's seat. I cough to fill the silence. Adrien coughs too. I think of this as a truce, so I look at him, which is louder than anything I could say. His oily skin, plum-colored eyebags, flexing triceps. His smile lines are deep, his nose tense, his eyes squinted, like he's about to sneeze. But he doesn't. He starts the car and begins to pull out of the empty lot. I think about moving my hand to his right armpit. Just a quick flutter of the fingers. It's close enough, easy enough—all I need is the urge, and rest assured, I have that. Sometimes, you must do these things for the greater good. He spasms, almost crashing into a red Volkswagen, and smacks my hand away.

"Jesus, Miranda! Stop! Fucking—it's not like a cute, funny thing. Like, you tickling me isn't this cute, funny thing. It really makes me unhappy, okay? It's not, like, this whole cute moment—okay? It's *annoying*."

Sometimes you have this great big fight, and you think it could be the end. But, really, it's the inconvenience after the fight that ensures: yes, this is the end. He doesn't look at me. He just puts up an apologetic hand to the Volkswagen driver, who, in return, flips us off. His face is wan, sickly. Now, I feel sober beyond sober. I feel hyper-alive—it's sacrilegious, supernatural. I pretend I'm anyone else in the world until I'm able to fall asleep.

At some point, Adrien stops the car at a gas station. I wake up, but don't open my eyes. I can hear him getting out. Now I open my eyes. He's lighting a cigarette, calling someone on his phone. I roll down the window and listen. I hear my name.

"Nah, man, I mean—she was a fucking child. She *is* a fucking child…Yes, really…Ha, yeah…Yeah, I think so."

The smell of lemon shortbread is palpable—rancid, really. Or maybe it's the gasoline, tobacco, and stale post-sex sweat. I finally realize something I should've realized decades earlier: if he doesn't find me special, it doesn't consequently make him more special. It doesn't make him anything at all. And by the way, there wasn't a fucking hot tub. There was never going to be a hot tub.

I expected to return home to my sister sobbing that Deez Nuts died, belly up, in a puddle of her own puke. It just seemed to be one of those weeks. But no, that fucker was still kicking. Not literally, of course, I don't think she was ever capable of that. We walk in, and they're both on the couch, sleeping, arm's distance apart. Louise must've called in sick to work. A rom-com is playing on the TV. It's about two estranged brothers falling in love, and there are also werewolves involved, but I don't remember how. We loved this movie growing up. It was funny, and the gay brothers were hot. Adrien goes straight to his room. I kiss my sister's forehead and head to my bed in the basement, open my laptop.

My next assignment for work is a multiple-choice "test." AI gives me three different sentences, and I must choose the one that most accurately represents a young person's lexicon. The topic is the link between GMO consumption and autism diagnoses in children.

> 1. *Bruh, my little brother ate that canola oil the fuck up, and now he neurospicy as hell, for real!*

> 2. *Oh, yeah, sis—she's got a touch of the 'tism. The tea is as piping hot as the formation of the double-strand breaks in the cells' homologous recombination repair systems inside her soy beans, queen!*

> 3. *Dude, my MILF didn't check the label on my tofu, now I'm straight tweaking, fam! Genetic engineering is sus, but, no cap, that stir fry was high-key bussin'!*

Before I answer, I think about any person saying any of these phrases. I never do this, but I've done it, I've already done it. It's best to never imagine an actual human saying the things a machine says. At first, it will be funny, but I've been at this job for two months—I've surpassed funny. Two months since I got this job, since I had to move in with my sister, since I met Adrien. There's only denial and cynicism left—that's it. I hover my pointer over the second sentence. What makes this one better? Because it's longer, because it's feminine? The machine knew I'd pick this one—it knows me better than I know it. Another virtually useless and debilitating line of thinking. As all of this job is, as all of all of it is. The stillness of my hand, of the room, makes my despair transmogrify into rage. I click the second sentence. Then I click on the second sentence for the next question, and then I just keep on clicking. Click, click, click, click, throw—now I've thrown my laptop against the wall, and it hasn't broken, but it did wake my sister up. Now she's running down the stairs telling me to be quiet because apparently I'm screaming, and apparently I'm sobbing, confessing—well, not really confessing, just saying the word "Adrien" over and over again, and she's there, no, she's here, and she's holding me, firmly, clutching my neck as it falls against her bosom, as if lessening her grip never even crossed her mind, telling me she knows. "I know, I know it hurts, my love, I know, I know," and my useless body can do nothing but what it's already doing, and at some point, my "Adrien"s turn to "Why"s beyond my control and I can feel her looking at me and she whispers "I've killed you a thousand times in my head. I can't do any more than that," and we continue standing there, crying and muttering now-unintelligible words to each other, a secret language, a shaking, hot, pathetic mess of things like matches choking on their own flame. Adrien knocks on the door, asking if we're okay, and I laugh so hard that I vomit in my mouth, and Louise kisses my forehead, and she laughs, too, and although I want to take this as a truce, I know it's not, I know it can't be, and I could look at her right now, to see how she's feeling, but even if I did look, I wouldn't know. I just wouldn't.

All I Got Was This Poor Gag Reflex

My son died. My son died and the grocery store clerk doesn't say sorry. She didn't know him or know of him, but that's no excuse. She smiles as I hand her the cash, making fun of me. She smiles because to her, a world without my son is not only a joke but a respite. I buy orange juice, paper towels, and tins of sardines. She's smiling because there is no apple sauce, no Cheez-Its. She's smiling because my grocery list is severed, just like the rest of me. She's smiling because I'm not, and because one of us has to smile or else the world will fail to exist. I suppose it's a kindness. I suppose it's a necessity. I suppose a stranger is not a symbol of latent malevolence. I try to smile back, but all I can produce is a belch-infused cough. She frowns.

My son died. My son died and the car won't start. The car won't start because if you have a bad day, the universe is only allowed to make it worse, as is its right. Oh—there we go. My son died and the car is starting because one must always be doing something, especially when they're incapable of doing so. I drive, I steer, I stop, as if these things mattered, as if the world would stop spinning, as if I would feel worse if I rammed into that tree, crashed into that police car, ran over that girl on the scooter. The girl hits a bump and falls face-first. She cries as if she is truly hurt. I speed past and picture my son's face crying instead.

My son died. My son died and my husband is making salad. Salad is the least-food of all foods, and that is why he is making it, because once life stops happening for you, you aren't allowed to enjoy anything. The salad is green and brown, and I add sardines to it because nothing on top of nothing equals nothing, and that's all I can bear to stomach these days. I chew and swallow, but I could just as easily puke it up or spit it out, or better yet, not put it in my mouth at all. My husband stares at the plate as if it will start moving and living and breathing for him. He's got the right idea. He looks up at me and laughs, and I vomit green and brown and gray onto his plate.

My son died. My son died and I have sex with my husband. I have sex with my husband because when the world fails to exist, you must suck a dick. You suck a dick in hopes that a fog of stillness manifests, one that brings back former selves. Selves that can burp and laugh and fuck without consequences. His penis tastes of lemon water and his lips of rock salt. My son once slipped on the ice outside before my husband could tend to it. He broke his fibula. Everyone in class signed his cast, everyone except his crush. I signed his cast to make him feel better. He yelled at me and crossed my name out. My husband's body remains soft like the rest of him, and I turn off the bedside lamp.

My son died. My son died and I wake up. My son is crying because he wants pancakes and a strawberry milkshake instead of oatmeal and orange juice this morning, but, of course, that is not actually the case, because that would be too easy. This is the thirty-ninth day I've woken up. This is the twenty-first day I've woken up to white sheets. I find a stick and pee on it. My son died and the pregnancy test is positive. I grab onto the closest person, scream silently into his stomach, hoping I can pass the illness through breath. I try to cry, but nothing comes out. I try to cry because a baby can be rotten if it's not the one you had in mind. My husband tells me he's going to be late for work, and I let go of his shirt.

My son died. My son died and I walk to the convenience store. The cashier says hello because he wants to know what it's like to fuck nothing. I buy Smarties, and then I eat the Smarties. I buy Smarties and then eat the Smarties because you must do good things in order to feel bad about yourself. If I did bad things, then I'd feel good about myself, and that is simply not on the agenda today. I packed my son a case of Smarties with his lunch every day. One day, he told me how he gave the special needs kid his Smarties because the older kids were making fun of him. I told him I was proud of him and he told me that it was whatever. I steal a bottle of Pepto-Bismol. I take a swig and tell the cashier goodbye as if that means anything these days.

My son died. My son died and I stop at my neighbor's house. I stop at my neighbor's house because when your son dies, you must suck a man who is not your husband. His penis tastes like grains of sand and his cum like expired milk. My son drank expired milk once and used it as an opportunity to miss school. He said he felt sick, but I knew he was lying. We went to the dog pound that day—I thought dogs might make him feel better. He misunderstood me and thought we were adopting one. He sobbed a dry sob the whole way home. That was the first time he told me he hated me. I vomit the expired milk onto my neighbor's balls. It's pink and bubbly like a strawberry milkshake. My neighbor turns soft like my husband and begins to yell like my son. My son died. My son died and all I got was this poor gag reflex.

Scout's Blessing

The room to my left is reserved for an ongoing food fight. Refined in the way that the ammo includes beef tartare and Beluga caviar, and unrefined in the way that there are no limits when it comes to the bodily harm you're allowed to inflict. A food *war* would really be a better word for it. The room to my right contains something more clandestine, reserved for snorting ketamine in the nooks between Instagram influencers' toes and fingering any wait staff who are itching for a big tip. And in the center of the room I am assigned to, the one I'm standing in right now, sits a giant ice sculpture of a buxom naked woman. This is supposed to be the polite room. A room for bodies to drink blue-dyed gin and rehearse lines about crypto and sound baths. For young trophy wives to find their new plastic surgeon while getting groped by the bisexual pyramid-scheming girlbosses. For the nepo babies to pitch their thirty-thousand-word Google docs, which they are all rest assured will be the "Next Great American Novel," to anyone with a halfway-working ear. It sounds like I hate these people. I don't hate them. They're fine. I am currently holding a platter of glasses fizzling with champagne while letting people talk at me. I am wearing a chartreuse suit and a pink tie, a uniform for the waiters to easily stand apart from anyone else in the world. I am not happy, but I am easily distracted, and that's all anyone seems to want for at this time. Some tuxedoed man with rosacea is assaulting the already-melting cavern that represents the ice woman's vagina, trying to humor his buddies. I have to give him a talking to. I let a coked-out Mommy vlogger finish her spiel on the dangers of "cortisol face" before walking over.

"Excuse me. I must ask that you, the ice sculpture, refrain from it—from touching it. It is purely for decoration."

I have said this so many times within the last hour that I am uncertain if the words are still coming out in the correct order.

"Oh, you must? You *must*?!"

His teeth are coated in an indigo sheen. This only exaggerates the ruddiness of his complexion. His buddies laugh and casually disperse.

"I understand your frustration. Champagne?"

He huffs pugnaciously, then takes two glasses.

"Very well, sir."

I don't hate my job, but I do wish it weren't my sole source of income. To afford this town, you really need at least three jobs, and it's ideal if two of the jobs are slightly illegal, but I have yet to earn the confidence necessary for this career move. Someone squeezes my butt. It's Adeline. She doesn't take this job very seriously since she has her two other slightly illegal jobs to fall back on.

"What's up, bitch."

Adeline thinks I'm gay, and I have no interest in telling her that that's not the case. She's Chinese. She's twenty-one and thin and annoying. When we first met, she told me she was a cutting bulimic and then she laughed and then I laughed and then she said "No, I'm serious" and then proceeded to laugh again, so I don't really know what the truth is. I know she sells her mother's Xanax to high schoolers. I know she extorts her father for money by promising not to tell her mother that she caught him giving a blowjob to a washed-up reality TV personality in their garage six years ago. The blue-toothed, red-cheeked man walks away with a whiny grunt.

"Nothing."

She shrugs, gives another butt-squeeze, then tries luring a plus-sized swimsuit model with her erect platter of specialty cheeses. We're pretty much inter-active statues. I'm only permitted to say fifty words, max, to a guest. I must have a straight back, must have a still platter, must be smiling at all times, but not the kind with teeth, never the kind with teeth. We are scheduled almost every night. Things get much easier after nine p.m. since, by that time, everyone is beyond plastered to the point that your mistakes are not only forgettable, but actually invisible. This is around the time my coworkers get completely wasted as well. I watch Adeline's butt sway as she leaves the model and saunters up to a group of racist tech guys. She has great child-bearing hips, which really helps when try-ing to overlook the emaciation. Her breasts are small, yes, but they're perky. And she—

"Hey, dude. I'll take one."

I turn to see a tall, lanky ginger with a shin-ing smile. I want to tell him that tooth-smiling is not permitted, and then I remember he is not staff. He's wearing baggy jeans with the red hammer and sickle printed on his pants' right thigh and a tank top that looks like it's made entirely out of paper clips. He has a tattoo of Amy Winehouse on his right tricep, which he flexes with great calculation. He has more rings than fingers and more feet than shoes. He nabs a glass of champagne by the stem and sips.

"Of course, sir. But I must ask that you, uh, wear shoes on the premises."

He points to his right sole, where lies a crim-son, rubbery-looking plaster that perfectly molds to the bottom of his foot, impossible to see from a bird's-eye perspective. Fashion seems all wrong nowadays. He pats my arm and winks. It's one of the nepo baby novelists—I'm just realizing now. His name is Lake. He's only nineteen. His parents were this gorgeous It Couple, and both died in a tragic car accident, making him one of the most sought-after men in the world by horny fourteen-year-olds. His last girlfriend was emblazoned on tabloid covers, her body peppered with large blue-green bruises. This began rumors of Lake being physically abusive. The drama was exacerbated by the girlfriend coming out and saying, "Yes, Lake was abusive." But because of his hot dead parents, he will never fully lose.

"Is that your girlfriend?"

He casually strains his neck in the direction of the racist tech guys—no, of Adeline. He smirks—his lips are obscenely pale, cracked. He licks them like a frothing animal.

"No, sir."

I mean, it is true that Adeline and I hang out a lot, but that's only because it's so hard to find friends in this town. We've made out a few times. She made the first move, though—said she wanted to "know what it's like to kiss a gay guy." I didn't want to refute that and discourage healthy curiosity. It's not creepy, though, because I'd never go any further than that with her. I've never felt an urge to fuck her. It's more like a game of patty-cake: rhythmic, satisfying, communal. It's a ritual more than anything else. Lake smiles as taut as his stringy white mouth will allow.

"Good."

I excuse myself to do a quick look-over. Make sure no one is ever sober enough to question why they started drinking in the first place. Make sure the ice lady is protected. Lorenzo is waving me down at the bar. Lorenzo is the bartender, an old Italian guy with a consistently aloof attitude. It's explicitly spelled out in his work contract that he's not permitted to speak a single word to the guests.

"Boss-man said new round of drinks. This one's called Baker's Blessing. It's basically just a Negroni, and this here, this on the stick here, that's a red velvet macaron. Here's the ingredient list, kid."

Lorenzo is pretty much always inebriated, but in a temperate way—in a way where he's still one of the best workers we've got. He fills eight macaron-adorned glasses with pink liquid and places them equidistant around my platter. He tucks the ingredient list in my right breast pocket. There's a tiny stage right next to the bar, one being used by a female singer with a deep, scratchy voice. It sounds like she's in pain, but the purposeful kind.

"And what do *you* need?"

He asks me this as he pours himself a heavy shot of bourbon. The singer looks at me. Her eyes are black and glossy. She has terrible posture, but I think it adds to the whole depressed shtick she's got going on.

"What do you mean?"

Lorenzo takes his slug and swats his hand in my direction—I take my platter and go. I spend the next hour repeating these steps: giving out drinks, expelling the least amount of words necessary, and returning to the bartender to resupply. I memorize the ingredients in case anyone asks. But no one does. No one actually cares about what's going in their bodies; they just care for the certainty and speed at which it's going in their bodies. Adeline is mainly serving the tech guys. I see they're making her laugh. We're technically not allowed to favor any guests, but Adeline never sees this as a promise. I know the Indian one made a dating app specifically for those with, let's say, esoteric animal-related fetishes. That's probably what he's showing her on his phone right now. She looks impressed, and he looks horny. I catch Cameron in the corner of my eye. He's vaping into his sleeve and zoning out on some nondescript pop musician's ass. First time I've seen him tonight. He's chronically late, but his dad is the boss-man, so he could shit in a guest's mouth and it wouldn't matter. Well, that's a lie—that would actually matter quite a bit. Forget I said that.

"Cameron. Cam!"

He's pretending like he can't hear me again, so I walk to him. I really kind of hate Cameron if I'm being honest. I think I hate him because he's trying to get with Adeline despite having a girlfriend, which is messed up for everyone involved. He also constantly smells of onion rings. He's almost too good-looking, which is off-putting for a man. I once heard him call me a "spazz" to Lorenzo. Actually, I don't want to talk about this anymore.

"I'm going on my first break."

I hand Cameron the platter. I try stuffing the ingredient list into his breast pocket, but the paper falls loose from my fingers while on the journey to his chest. I pick up the list from the ground and hand it to him normally before walking outside to the staff parking lot.

I sit on the curb, right next to my car, and let feeling return to my toes. I think about getting in my car, where there are heated seats, but the last thing my body needs is another enclosed setting. The whole point of the outside is to provide a necessary foil to the inside. I need cold earth and cold silence and—

"Hi!"

A little boy is walking around with what I assume is a bicycle until I see the two auxiliary wheels hanging from the sides. It's yellow with iridescent streamers sprouting from the handles.

"Hi."

He stops in his tracks, looking pensive, or possibly constipated—it's hard to tell with children. I think about ignoring him the same way you do with homeless people or street Evangelists, but something tells me that he's not the ignoring type.

"You know, kids at my school say the word 'faggot.'"

I accidentally laugh. He may have been mistaking me for a teacher or a person of authority.

"Oh."

"Do you not care?" he asks, almost angrily.

There's not much to see out here. The dilapidated beige of the neighboring building, the empty green dumpster, all the wet trash bags lying next to the empty green dumpster. No streets, no trees. Even the moon is hidden. Not its light, though, of course.

"I guess not, no," I say.

"I get bullied because I have a girl's name or whatever. They call me 'faggot.'"

He's not wearing a helmet. He's walking around in circles now. A car honks, and he points in the opposite direction to where the sound is coming from.

"I'm sorry to hear that. They don't sound like very good friends."

He stops mid-track and slams one tiny foot on the pavement. Hardly any sound is made, but I understand the implications.

"I never said they were my friends!" he says, loudly.

I smile.

"What's your name?" the boy asks.

I can feel the heat of the twitching street lamp on my face. It feels acidic. Hot curdled milk. The moon only shines on the little boy, it seems. A spotlight.

"Scout."

He laughs an ugly, high-pitched laugh. I can see why he gets bullied.

"But that's a dog's name!" he argues.

I should probably ask where his parents are, but that might ruin the mood. No one wants to think about their parents more than they have to.

"Yes, well, it can be a person's name too if you really want it to be."

He blows a raspberry at me, his tongue a deep turquoise with blue FCF.

"That's just silly."

He drops his tricycle and walks away, like that was the last straw, like he's so offended that he's now finished with material possessions. He's heading east. Something squeezes my shoulder blade. It's Adeline. She sits down next to me. We are supposed to wear slacks, but today she went for fishnet tights and a mini skirt.

"Hi."

"Hi. Are you going on break, too?"

She either ever smells like an abandoned bookstore or polyurethane varnish. I like the bookstore more, but today it's the varnish. Most days it's the varnish.

"No."

She's holding two iced drinks. Her fingertips are an unnatural bright white. She's shaking. It would be pretty sexist for me to assume her temperature and take off my blazer and give it to her, so I'm not going to do that. But if I were her brother, I'd tell her to dress warmer in the colder months.

"There's a lot I don't know about you, Scout. Old Scout-y boy."

We've never talked about me before. Besides kissing, we mainly just go to her parents' house and watch movies and talk about things that aren't necessarily important enough to be talking out loud about. She stabs my thigh with a knife. It's a fake knife, the plastic kind that retracts. She laughs. Every time she laughs, she snorts. It's objectively ugly, but also pretty because it makes her stand apart from the girls with the normal laughs.

"What's that?" I ask, mostly because I don't know what else to say to this.

She tucks the knife in between her bare hip and her tights.

"Have it in case any of the old rich guys try anything funny."

"But it's useless," I argue.

She smiles.

"That's what you think."

"No, I—okay."

I thought we were about to talk about me, but maybe that was my mistake.

"Oh, here's your drink, by the way. Lorenzo made screwdrivers."

She tries handing me one of the iced drinks.

"Oh, I don't drink. Thanks, though."

"Wait, wha—Really? How did I not know

this?"

I shrug.

"It's not like I'm against it," I tell her, "I just… don't like drinking."

She nods. As I was saying earlier, she also has very full, wide lips. It's good for a woman's mouth to be bigger than most men's mouths. She has silky, bubblegum pink-dyed hair and swooping side bangs, which is a smart tactic for women with square-shaped faces. I like women with square-shaped faces, it toughens them up. I wonder what she thinks of my face shape.

"Some people think living a life sober is easier. It's not. It's just a different kind of hardness. Just a kind of hardness where you remember what day it is." Sometimes she likes talking abstractly, but she doesn't say anything to this. She just smiles, gets up, and walks inside with her iced drinks and her white fingers and her full lips. As soon as I hear the door slam, I press my hand to part of the curb her bony butt was sitting on. I don't know what I'm hoping for, but whatever it is, I don't get it.

I step back into the venue, and the mood has changed drastically. Less awkward small talk, more genuine laughter. There's an Albino magician on the tiny stage now. He's doing a trick where he cuts a beautiful woman in half, but not the kind you're thinking of—the incision is *vertical*. People are actually watching, they look happy with shock, giddy with disgust. It's almost like every room gets better the moment I step out of it. I see Cameron talking with Lake, and he is platter-less. They're laughing at something on Lake's phone, and Cameron squeezes Lake's balls—more like a firm tug, really. Lake laughs so hard at that an opaque liquid sprays from his nose. I don't entirely understand the way men act toward one another. It makes me feel left out, but then I remember I wouldn't very much like grabbing a man's balls, so I think it's fine. I see the rosacea-ed man is once again molesting the ice woman's lower half. I puff my chest out and walk over.

"Sir. I don't have to—want to have to call security."

Everyone stopped when I told them to. Everyone but him. Doesn't he know that a meaning is diluted when it's said twice? Doesn't he know that something goes from funny to sad when performed twice? I'd like a list of things he knows and a list of things he doesn't know—now, that's what I'd like.

"Listen, you tell me this again, and I'm going to have you fired. I'm not joking—you think I'm joking? I'm not kidding, buddy. I've paid enough money to be here—I have. You think I'm joking? Let me show you my wallet, see how much I'm carrying on me at any given moment. You'll see—then, you'll see, buddy."

His face is almost purple now, that's how red it is. Before he can fish out the two hundreds from his wallet, I walk away. Leaving immediately is always protocol when a guest unnecessarily embarrasses themselves, and I apply this logic to outside life as well. Lorenzo is waving me down. He's pouring martinis. It's nearing nine o'clock. I walk over, platter at the ready. He places the drinks, pushes in the ingredient list.

"You don't say much, do you, kid?"

Lorenzo has thick eyebrows, a thick beard, and nose hairs that paw his top lip. He exclusively drinks dark liquor and smokes Marlboro Reds. Sometimes, I hear him fighting on the phone with his ex-husband, his ex-husband who wants sole custody over their nine-year-old daughter. Sometimes, I catch him swiping Grindr in the dark nook of the bar and feel a sadness that could not be made outside of this place if it tried.

"I don't know. I...*think*. I have a good internal narration—I don't know."

He scoffs.

"Yeah? And what's that s'posed to mean?"

I shrug. I never truly learned how to gracefully leave a conversation. I usually just go when a moment of silence is available, so that's what I do now. I offer people martinis with my close-mouthed smile and linear posture. They're the kind that are murky yellow in color, drowning blue cheese-stuffed olives on a stick. Pretty disgusting if you ask me. I've grown so accustomed to this room, this place, that none of the details actually compute in my brain. It all just *is*. But I take a moment to take it in. Dripping black tapers stuffed in gold candlestick holders, bunches of red valerians budding in fine china centerpieces. Round tables cloaked in ruffled skirts, plates made out of pink glass, periwinkle mood lighting. Sparkling silver chairs and violet couches made of velvet. One of the most beautiful chandeliers I've ever seen. No—the *only* chandelier I've ever seen. Hands made that chandelier. Hands made that chandelier, and those hands don't even get to enjoy that chandelier. A hand stamps my back. It's Cameron.

"I'll take one, buddy."

His cheeks are a warm coral, and he's smiling in a way where you know he finds everything funny right now.

"Shouldn't you be handing out appetizers?"

He laughs. He tries playfully slapping my shoulder but misses and hits my armpit—it tickles.

"Yes, I just was, *actually*. I just was. Can't I take a two-minute break? Jesus, dude. I *just* was."

He finishes his martini in three gulps. He stuffs the stick of olives in my breast pocket.

"I think you're wanted in B7. Yeah—Adeline was asking for you."

Cameron says this before walking off with his empty glass. His shirt is unbuttoned and loose from his pants, but I can't worry about that now. B7 is the sex room I was talking about—the room where people have sex. I've only been there once and that was because someone was choking on a melon and prosciutto skewer, and I was seemingly the only person on the premises who knew the Heimlich maneuver. And why is Adeline asking for me? Wanting to make out during work hours? Just a horrific lack of professionalism. It's not like I take this job *that* seriously, but c'mon. I'm not about to stick my tongue down her throat three feet away from a failed Disney actress turned crackhead doing the same to a pedophilic casting agent. I will not pretend like I'm one of them, I barely like pretending like I'm one of me. I mean, I'm flattered—of course, I'm flattered.

"Hey. I'm Faye."

I turn. It's the sad singer. She looks older, but the kind of older where she made extremely healthy lifestyle choices. Like she's actually thirty-six but passes for twenty-three. Of course, except for the horrible posture, but this only humanizes her. She has clear skin and a heart-shaped face and a curvaceous figure. I'm excited by the prospect of seeing what her ass looks like.

"Okay. Hi, Faye."

"I was wondering if—do you ever want to go out?"

She has a manly voice, but this is good for a woman—toughens her up. And it's a nice juxtaposition to her sweet personality.

"Okay."

"Okay?"

She's looking for an answer, that's what she's looking for. But that would require me knowing an answer. Her breasts are so perfectly circular. Kept upright in her tight denim V-neck. I accidentally look at them for too long.

"No, I'm sorry. Not allowed."

And I walk away. That's what I do—I walk away. Jesus Christ. In moments like these, I actually, disgustingly enough, have great admiration for people like Cameron. Things would have gone astoundingly different had he been the subject of that conversation, and that can only fill me with envy. I'm walking toward B7 now, that's where I'm going now. Her face wasn't even sad when I left, but uncomfortable. The only thing worse than making a girl sad is making her uncomfortable. I found a woman beautiful and that beautiful woman asked me out and I reacted as if she kicked me in the shins. But none of that matters now, I have to get back to my job. Come to think of it, Adeline may be asking for me for a work-related reason. And I've been flirting with this random girl, leaving her hanging! I open the door to B7 with my left hand while gingerly clutching my martini-filled platter with my right. God damnit, I didn't even get to see what Faye's ass looked like.

"Come 'ere, mate!"

An older Englishman is the first to corral me. I'm guessing he's a big-time music producer or a gangster movie director. The thing with this town is, you must judge a book by its cover. The cover wants to be judged. The cover pays millions of dollars in hopes of being judged. He has a gold hoop in his left ear and a nose that is completely deformed, flattened into his face, with one nostril practically sewn shut. He has a half-naked lightskinned girl under each arm. One of them has her hand down his pants. I hand him a martini without making eye contact.

It's very dark in here, making balancing the platter a bit trickier. Orange-lit lamps and leather loveseats and grass-green carpeting. A bit '70s because the only time period better than the time period you're currently in is literally any other time period. Glass tables holding an array of clean-cut, white-powdered lines. A cacophony of drunk laughter and sex grunts that blend to make a sound like a dog crying on its deathbed. Lots of making out, some oral sex under cocktail tables, and a healthy amount of breast-squeezing. I see girls who look unreasonably young, but I convince myself that this is just an illusion of the limited lighting for I do not have time to deal with that right now. Must find Adeline.

The room is long, narrow, slithering. It's really just a decorated hallway. The farther I go, the murkier the air gets. I'm getting to the smoking section—doobies, cigarettes, and something that looks like a crack pipe, all aflame. And the people get more naked. Men without underwear, women without tops. The robust stink of it all. It's hard for me to comprehend this being someone's idea of fun—of relaxation! I pass a girl on a plastic yellow couch, making noises like sneakers squeaking against linoleum. She's with Lake—he's fingering her. Poor thing. In an attempt to stop possibly nonconsensual contact, I lean my body in, platter-first, offering beverages, not that she needs any more, and I probably knew, let's be honest, I knew the whole time, but that's when I see. I see it's Adeline. She's the one getting fingered. I trip over someone's foot, maybe my own foot, I don't know, and the platter comes crashing down. Spilling on me, on Lake, on his red hammer and sickle, which washes away like a firehose to a blood slick, then on the floor. Of course, the carpet makes for a soft landing, but I am still met with the harsh smack of belligerent grunts. I thought that your mistakes were unrecognizable after nine p.m., but maybe that was a rule confined to the polite room—I guess if your mistake interrupts a sex party, then it's a catastrophe like no other. Adeline pulls Lake's hand out of her orifice. Her tights and skirt hang around her ankles. I am currently making eye contact with her bush. I wonder what would give me a bigger adrenaline rush, this moment or slamming my hand with a car door.

"Scout?"

I am now picking up the empty glasses. I am putting them back on the platter. I should probably say something out loud.

"But what about the knife?" I say.

Her jaw hangs open. She looks confused.

"What kni—what do you mean?"

She gets down on the ground and begins helping me, bush still out and exposed, asshole pointed towards the British coke fiend like a loaded gun. I try swatting my hand to her, signalling to fix herself, that I'm good, I swear that's all I was doing, but I accidentally end up hitting her in the face—slapping, really. I slap her face. She yelps. I was wrong earlier: there's something worse than making a girl sad, and there's something worse than making a girl uncomfortable, and it's slapping a girl in the fucking face. I really wish I were in the food war room instead right now—wouldn't find drama like this in there.

"Dude, what the fuck?!"

Lake says this, but I won't allow myself to look at him yet. He doesn't understand anything that's happening right now, not a single thing. If he gave me a list of things he *thought* he understood right now, I'd cross every one off, big red X to each one, that's what I'd do. Adeline's eyes are big, it almost looks like they're sinking down her face. She doesn't slap me back or curse me out or play it off. Those are the only three options I can think of. Instead, she just looks scared. I take my platter and speed-walk out of the room.

I return to the polite room, and the lights are now violently bright. It feels like everyone's eyes are on me, like they know what I did. How did this place go from a work conference to a frathouse to a courtroom so quickly? Places are evil in that way—frighteningly malleable. And that asshole is still terrorizing the ice woman. He's not fingering anymore; now he's fully licking her genitals. Some people are uncomfortably laughing, some people are watching because they feel like they have to. But no one is telling him to stop. I catch Cameron in the corner of my eye, looking barely conscious and flirting with some new prospect, and I hand him my platter, and I walk toward that asshole of a man.

"Sir, please."

I stay calm. Calm but strong and inevitable, like the ocean. Can oceans be described as calm?

"I am going to call security. This is your final chance."

He's in a deeply unflattering position—he has to squat to get his tongue on her taint. It doesn't seem like he cares. He's practically on his knees, and he thinks he has all the power. Maybe that's why men get on their knees to propose marriage. Maybe it really is a pose of dominance, and no one told me this whole time. He doesn't say anything, he just keeps licking, people keep watching, keep laughing. Those rich laughs, they're singular, unnatural. Instead of being described as laughter, it's more like *laugh, laugh, laugh*. It's not right. He lands on her clit, he performs little circular motions, his rotten, stained teeth scraping her labia. He winks at me. That asshole winks at me. Her being is dripping, her skin is water, she's open against her will, and he believes this all to be so funny. Doesn't he get that she represents a real person? People don't take symbolism seriously enough for my liking. I feel an anger I haven't felt since I was a child. Like when you really hate your mom, but it's all so irrational, which only adds to the whirlpool of emotion you're feeling. Everything is suddenly hot, how your face gets right before you cry, except it's my entire body. I wish I had slapped him instead of Adeline. I wish everyone hated him and I wish he were dead and I wish I could go to his grave and spit on it and then I'd laugh, laugh, laugh.

"Look, look!"

"Is that fucking piss?"

"Oh my god, he's peeing his pants."

I look down. They're right. I've pissed my pants—the chartreuse turning a delightful sage green. Now it doesn't just feel like everyone is looking at me, but it is aggravatingly clear that everyone is looking at me. I see Faye walking out of the bathroom. I run to the parking lot before she can take notice of the scene I'm creating.

The autumn breeze pinches the sour piss into my slacks, into my skin, causing a sensation not unlike a rash. It smells like nickels and oyster sauce, and I am certain that both of those scents are coming from me. I want to cry, and I want to scream, and, yes, I want to laugh, because someone who pees their pants—well, that's funny. The yellow tricycle is still on the ground, handlebars flickering under the cream of moonlight, streamers flapping in the stressed syllables of wind. And the little boy returns—again, seemingly, from nowhere. I need to get better at noticing beginnings. He holds a Sprite in his left hand and a bag of Takis in his right.

"Hi."

"Um. Hi."

Urine has trickled all the way down into my socks. Some leaks onto the pavement. I'm getting used to the cold itch, like a ringing in the ears.

"Sometimes I have accidents, too," he says, staring at my crotch.

"Okay."

If I were him, this would be the point at which I'd be walking away.

"What are you going to be for Halloween? I know what I'm going to be."

He's doing that thing children do when they're uncomfortable, but they want to keep talking. They flail their arms, look at the ground, and kick their feet in the air. I wish I knew what shape the moon was in right now. Waxing gibbous, for example. Yes, that'd make me feel better.

"Um. That's weeks away, I don't—"

"I'm going to be Batman. Is that good?"

His teeth are very tiny. I can't tell if they're still his baby teeth, or maybe he just has small adult teeth. He has wide-set eyes, which is good for a guy to have—it adds an air of mystery, makes it easier for women to fall in love with you.

"Yes. Yes, that's good."

"Yeah, I think it's good."

I can still hear the fuzzy echo of people laughing their non-laughs inside. They're intent on me knowing that I'm forever just too far away.

"What's your name?"

I ask this because I realize I haven't asked this yet, and because I don't want to talk about my piss and I don't want to talk about Halloween. And wasn't he talking about his name earlier? How is it that the actual name never came up? Why must everything be talked about instead of talked *of*?

"Aubrey."

Oh, yes. The feminine name in question. This will be bad when he's younger and good when he's older, like most things that you're born with.

"You know Drake? The singer? His name is Aubrey."

He looks confused. Or uninterested. I forgot that with children, you have to get to the point right away.

"He probably got bullied for it too. But, like, look at him now," I say.

He kicks at a green shard of broken glass on the ground.

"Are you saying this 'cause we're both black?"

I am unsure. I shake my head no.

"No," I clarify, "because you're both named Aubrey."

He nods. He opens his bags of Takis and eats two. Then, he hands me one, which I take and which I eat. We continue this pattern—he eats two and gives me one—for a few minutes.

"You can't have my Sprite, though," he says.

"That's okay. Thank you."

We keep eating until the bag is empty. He licks his fingers with precision before stuffing the plastic into his pocket. Then he cracks open the Sprite and finishes the can in one mighty gulp. A sound like a foghorn on helium exits his mouth. We laugh. The moon now lands on me, along with the streetlamp, turning my hands a fungal yellow. I have small hands. Small-baby hands. Good for handing out drinks, bad for those who don't necessarily only want drinks from you. A rusty creak sings, and a warmth manifests beside me. Adeline.

"Hi."

I can't tell if she's talking to Aubrey or to me. Aubrey waves. Adeline waves back. I don't say anything yet.

"I know that was an accident. It just—it scared me, you know. But I know it was an accident. It's okay."

She doesn't smell of varnish any longer. Or maybe the varnish smell is still there, but it's being overpowered by new scents. New scents of funnel cake, of gasoline fumes, of cheap vodka. She smells like a carnival.

"You know, he, like, hurts people. Like his ex-girlfriend, he hurt her. I feel like that's important information for you should to know—for you to know. Should know."

Aubrey takes the piece of broken glass from the ground and draws circles on the cement around his tricycle. Neither Adeline nor I tell him to be careful or to stop holding dirty, broken glass. I put my piss-wet foot to the space she left between us. She sticks the fake knife in the tender bit of my neck. I mime my hands to signify that blood is spurting out of my arteries and I'm in horrible pain. She laughs. I smile.

"Yeah, well…I'm in love, old Scout-y boy. It doesn't hurt for me to be this way. Not everything has to hurt. And I'd like it if you liked him, you know."

It all reminds me of a movie Adeline made me watch with her the other day. About a man and a woman. The woman would stick forks in her calves when she was sad, and the man would pull hair from her skull when he was angry. She said it was a romance movie. I'm not sure what it was, but I'm pretty sure it wasn't that. I look at her body, up and down, lingering on her white heartbeat.

"It's honestly…it's just embarrassing, Adeline. You should really change."

She opens her mouth to say something, but all I can hear is the groaning night breeze and the scratch of glass against rubble. She pats my thigh, gets up, and heads inside, taking the warmth and the carnival with her.

I tell Aubrey to go home, go to bed. Who knows if he'll do as told. I don't wait to see which direction he heads off into, and honestly, it's weird for me to be talking to unsupervised children at all. To make friends with a child is to admit to yourself that you've run out of options. I head inside to see the party fading, or maybe the party has just switched rooms. That's all parties do, they move—they're like energy, never destroyed nor created. I see the ice woman is all alone. That man played with her vagina so much that her nether region now resembles a gaping hole, a man-made crater in between her legs. Receding pubic bone, labia long gone, and the clitoris remains a mystery. Just emptiness eating into her, bottom-first. Thinking about this cold, exposed woman melting here all alone—well, it sends a shiver down my spine. I could take her home, but she wouldn't much appreciate my heated seats. And I really have no space for her, no means of keeping her erect. I go to the bar. I see Lorenzo is texting a profile picture of an uncircumcised penis.

"Give me a Baker's Blessing."

He clicks his phone off and raises his eyebrows. He likely knows me better than anyone else here, and I wish I were more comforted by this fact.

"Are you sure? I can give you a stiffer drink—"

"Baker's Blessing!"

Lorenzo nods and does as told. I didn't mean to get upset, but I hope he knows that my temper is warranted after the night I've had. I hear that ugly-pretty snort. Adeline is in this room too. She's speaking with Lake and Cameron in the corner, and they're laughing. She's holding a platter of martinis, which is good. But she's kind of miming handing them out, like she's ironically playing the role of server. This makes Lake and Cameron laugh more. Lorenzo hands me the drink. I shove the pink pastry down my throat—a little of the ganache comes back up, but enough stays down. I try sipping, but all my mouth can do is gag. I spit icing and Taki powder into the glass, making a foamy, crumby froth of a drink, and continue watching Adeline in my periphery. The Mommy vlogger is suddenly beside me. She says my drink looks good and asks what it is. I ignore her. Adeline puts the platter of drinks down on the closest table, then does a little spin and puts her hands up like *ta-da*! Cameron pulls her on his lap, Lake slaps her butt. They're all still laughing. I didn't like her, but she didn't exactly give me the chance to like her, did she? I could've if I really wanted to. If I had more time—that's all a person needs for love, more time. I feel two acrylic nails tiptoe along my neck.

"Whaddya say we—let's go back to my place, my baby—baby boy. Huh? I can pay you nicely. What would you say?"

The Mommy vlogger is extraordinarily drunk, her complexion matching my suit, each thought punctuated with a close-mouthed burp. I carefully remove her wrinkly hand from my person. Her wedding ring gets caught on my collar. Lorenzo fails at muffling his laughter.

"Um. I think, no. I think I don't want to do that—no. Sorry."

Blonde split ends, lazy green eyes, enough makeup to rectify the age spots. She's probably someone's version of beautiful. Not mine or Lorenzo's or really anyone's I know, but someone's. She says something that I can't make out and walks away. I probably should have said yes, honestly. Make money as a prostitute, quit this job. It's not like dignity is in fashion nowadays anyway. I'd just be trading one humiliation ritual for another. I hear that familiar nasal whine—boss-man is out here now. He's yelling at Cameron and Adeline, telling them to get back to work while Lake laughs at them. It doesn't make me feel good, though. Doesn't he know that they were just taking a break? I want to see what face Adeline is making, if she's crying or laughing or doing nothing whatsoever, but a body gets in the way. It's Faye, and she's next to me now, her eyes still black and glossy. Something primitive in the way she looks through me. She has puffy, dark hair—it crowds her being like one big thought bubble. She has a bit of runny egg on her cheek, a morsel of meat tucked behind her ear, but I can't think about that now. She smells like cigars and wet laundry. And she has the smallest hands I've ever seen. This is my second chance. In terms of my entire life, this is about my nine-hundredth chance. I must say something perfect. No messing around, no second-guessing, no room for ambiguity. If you want to fall in love, you have to convince yourself that you need it. In order to be loved back, you must speak first. She bites her lip, hunches her back, and picks the skewer of olives out of my blazer pocket. She holds the stick up and laughs. I stuff my hands in my pockets and pray my words come out suitably enough.

"Would you like to come to look at the moon with me?"

Everybody Has A Secret, But Not Everybody Knows It Yet

"I wish they let you have vapes in psych wards. And razor blades."

A Hispanic boy with bandaged forearms laughs in the corner. Her delivery is good, that bitch. I can tell she tries hard to be funny, but it doesn't make her any less infuriating. Plus, she's obviously pretty. Anorexic-skinny, so she still has white teeth. Platinum hair down to her waist. Self-harm scars purposely placed on her cleavage, begging for men's attention. The thing is, if you're not the best in the psych ward, you're nothing at all. This specific logic rarely applies to anyone but women. I continue my crossword as she colors a cartoon dog purple, like the interesting girl that she is. Four-letter word for "urge." She leans towards me and squints her left eye. The Hispanic boy stares at the flabs of her breasts that are now slumped against the table.

"Goad."

God. Fuck her. Fuck her and her goad. I tried to be nice—you can't say I didn't try. I pick up my crossword and pencil and excuse myself from the lounge. I don't go back to my room, I go to Ryan's instead. He's doing push-ups on the dirty tiled floor. Sweat soaks his forehead's acne scars and dandruff-ridden hair plugs, seeping into his bloodshot eyes. His calves are tight and ripped with muscle, clenching with each movement downward. His arms are trembling, rashy, and swollen in sporadic areas. I like to imagine that's what his penis is like as well.

"Hi."

He hops to his feet. A tiny boner is poking into his sweatpants pocket, but I know it's just from the workout. He always says exercise is his porn.

"Oh. Hey, Sarah."

We arrived on the same day. In our first group therapy, we had to explain our reason. His was that he had a manic episode for four days and believed he was the Messiah. His neighbor called the cops because he was walking around the block naked and asking people to follow him. I don't know where he would be leading them, but I'd follow him, I know that.

"Dinner is soon if you want to walk together, or whatever."

He puts a finger up to his mouth, miming the shushing sound, and points to his roommate, an elderly cross-eyed man with a button nose: Sam. The poor man lost his wife and rarely leaves his bed. I haven't heard him speak a word. He's been here five months. Ryan walks out of the oblong hole representing the door, and I follow.

"So, how are you liking the new girl?"

I shrug. I was afraid she would catch his attention.

"She seems very intelligent for her age. Very intuitive. I was talking to her about distress tolerance and—"

"So how's the letter coming along?"

Ryan is crafting a letter to give to his abusive ex-girlfriend. She's twenty years younger than him and often made him cry by insulting his body and mind. He cries just talking about her. He's crying now.

"Oh, God, sorry. You know, like what Marta said, I might not even give it to her. Might just throw it in a fire. But it's nice to write out my feelings. So, yeah, I'm not done with it yet. I still haven't gotten to the part where she called me 'faggy' when I wore leather pants on my birthday, so."

Marta is one of the attendants. She always

gives Ryan and me extra brownies for dessert. We're her favorites, and rightfully so. We pass the lounge room, then the showers, then the phone. The girl's there, leaning against the pitted cement wall and twirling the cord between her fingers.

"Okay. Yep. Gotta go. Love you. Bye."

I pick up my pace, hoping Ryan will follow suit, but he doesn't. He slows down, in fact.

"Ryan! How's the letter coming along?"

Her fake animated disposition seemingly lights the world on fire. Nurses smile, patients gawk, and the ward priest never fails to touch the small of her back when they're in the same room. Ryan inflates his chest and walks inappropriately close to her.

"Thank you for asking, Avery. Really well. Really, really well, actually. Maybe you could read it over for me? I don't know."

She's tall, too tall—taller than him. He probably likes that, though.

"I'd love to, Ryan."

They're too close, it's awkward. I don't know why she's doing this to me. What have I ever done to her? Marta pushes through the two of them: my savior.

"DINNER!"

Marta is so beautiful. Slicked-back black hair. Defined cheekbones and full lips. Deep-set brown eyes. I feel no jealousy because we're not in the same class—no competition. She's more like a statue I'm fond of looking at.

Dinner is a platter of cold beans, a bowl of white paste that looks like oatmeal but tastes like ketchup, and, of course, the two helpings of brownie. Ryan usually sits next to his roommate during meals, and they talk quietly, probably about things that only men above forty could understand. Not today. Today, he sits next to her. "Avery." Her narrow frame, in contrast, makes him look mighty and strong. She hunches over, making herself even smaller. He smiles at this. I'm close enough that it feels like I'm also sitting with them, but not in a natural way. I feel like a bus pervert jacking off to a teenage girl in pigtails who can't decide if she likes it or not. Joining their conversation does not feel appropriate, so I just listen instead.

"Are you a natural blonde, Avery?"

I stifle a laugh.

"Mmm, well, yes and no. I'm a natural blonde in the sense that I couldn't point Lithuania out on a map if you asked me to."

Fucking hell. I fantasize about smashing her jaw into the cold porcelain of the floor until her mouth becomes more laceration than anatomy. Ryan laughs—so much so that a spray of spit exits the back of his throat, some of which coats the left side of my face. I can see two helpings of brownies on her plate through the specs of spit in my eyes. I leave my tray of food for Marta to clean up and head to my room before I can hear Ryan's pithy reply.

My roommate, Abby, is reading Veronica Roth's *Allegiant,* sitting criss-crossed on the floor, too close to my side. Abby's a fat Jewish girl who tends to monopolize our bedroom's thermostat. She needs it to be sixty-three degrees or else she sticks her head in the toilet and the attendants yell at me. I hope Tris' death crushes her.

"Hi."

She doesn't answer. The corners of her mouth are hoarding white clusters, agglomerations of food and spit. I lick my lips in hopes it will prompt her to do the same. It does not.

"Kind of an ugly day, isn't it?" I say to my bed before lying in it. It's raining out. This is what people say when it's raining out.

"You can't do that," Abby affirms, eyes glued to her book.

"What?"

She groans.

"That's my bed."

I scoff. I then make sure where I am. I scoff again.

"No, it's not. It's mine."

She sighs, as if explaining this universal truth to me is futile, but she will try anyway.

"*No.* No bed is anyone's. I want that bed. I want to switch beds every night. George said I can."

George is another attendant. He is bright yellow-green in complexion and has so much filler that he's more chemical than person. He has a gay voice and appearance and mannerisms, but always talks about his elusive "wife" and how much she likes to "bake"—which is exactly what a closeted gay man *would* say. Abby is his favorite because she taught him how to crochet and they can talk about past *Survivor* seasons together—joining the mental healthcare workforce is truly such a selfish act. I don't know what it is: the fact that my bed feels like the only sacred thing, the only thing I have ownership of in this place, or the fact that she used George's name as if referencing a deity instead of what he actually is, an alcoholic twink with a Botox addiction, but I feel a sudden surge of spite for the mentally ill.

"Fuck you, Abby."

I only catch a glimpse of her face before I storm out, but it is pure horror. I walk through the halls, buzzing, feeling even larger than Marta. The lounge room is crowded with the Hispanic boy who laughs and the teddy bear of a widow. The phone is once again overtaken by her. Ryan is using the shower, made obvious by his distinct shower-cries that echo throughout the building. I guess there's no other choice but to attend a group therapy.

There are three people, along with an attendant at the head of the room—Ethan, an Asian man who only speaks in monotone. A pear-shaped old woman wearing a bile-colored sweater is speaking. Her hair is a cloud of burgundy. Her tits fall to the tops of her thighs, long and skinny like utters. I remember her arriving the day after me. She called everyone she met "honey" and yelled at an attendant for me when they said that they ran out of tampons. Is Wanda her name? Yes, Wanda, that's it. The whiteboard behind Ethan reads **SEXUAL DYSFUNCTION?** I tune in.

"They're these sorts of dark fantasies. I'm myself—my age, my appearance. But I'm a pilgrim on the Mayflower headed to the Promised Land. And I have a newborn child. The trip is treacherous, the morale is low. And my child has pneumonia. The only satisfaction I get is from feeding my baby boy from my breasts. It's the only thing that seems to heal him. At first, it's a normal satisfaction—maternal. But then I have these, uh…these premonitions. Premonitions that my baby boy will grow into the man that I marry. It's weird…but freeing. Knowing I'm raising—crafting—a man to love. And it makes me look at him differently, and, well—I don't see my baby sexually, but I also don't *not* see him that way, you know?"

Ethan stays silent, mouth agape. The other two people in the room react similarly.

"Yes, well, it's dark. Like I said."

I sit in the empty seat next to Wanda while Ethan uncomfortably rambles on about "emotions being valid" in an intonation that would make a suicidal person seal the deal. She has skin like melted toffee, a wide nose streaked in grease, lips tough like a calloused bunion. I hover my hand over her thigh, her downturned nipple within reach of my pinky. She grunts and walks out. I follow.

"Hi," I say to her back. She turns.

"I just wanted to say that that was really cool— for you to be vulnerable like that."

She sighs.

"Yeah, well."

She winks at me, or it could be an eye-twitch. I wink/eye-twitch back. I have sex with her pretty much immediately. I'm not a sickly English infant with mommy issues, but I'm the closest she's going to find in this place. Plus, she has an empty bedroom since her roommate was sent to the other side of the ward after punching George square in the dick. I don't have to worry about someone walking in on us: the attendants carry a very lackadaisical attitude throughout the night. It's actually quite frightening. One could easily be raped or killed. But that hypothetical has yet to happen to me, so I don't worry too much.

"How's this?"

I'm fingering her. Her insides feel like dry rubber. Even my fingers hurt from the contact burn, I can't imagine what her vagina feels like. But she seems to enjoy it: she whimpers and whispers words in a language I'm not entirely familiar with. I'm imagining I'm inside Ryan, but then I remember Ryan doesn't have a vagina, which takes me out of it. I then imagine I'm doing this to an orifice Ryan actually does have, like his ear or his mouth, and then I'm back into it. I don't have to worry about anyone hearing us either: the thunderstorm is now roaring outside. The rain's tempo quickens the faster I go. Maybe I'm in touch with the weather—spiritually connected. I think I understand the omnipotence Ryan felt when he flashed his neighbor. After five minutes, I get tired and stop. It's enough for me, though, and enough for her. Enough to have the validity of having happened.

"Thank you, honey."

I wink goodbye and walk back to my room—the halls are still a gaudy white because night isn't allowed to exist in a place like this. Abby is sitting in my bed with a sort of evil smile, which I deftly choose to ignore. I walk into the bathroom to wash my hands, and I see it. The toilet—as well as the floor surrounding the toilet—is blanketed with stones of shit and puddles of orange piss. I look back to see Abby laughing, her double chin like a scar lining her neck, her yellow teeth like rows of tonsil stones, her pube-like eyebrows raised as if her face is just an extension of her cunt. In one swift motion, I crank up the heat and yank the thermostat off the wall, using all my might to do so. I've never felt anger like this before—it produces effective results. I crawl into her bed and soothe myself to sleep to the sound of her breathy sobs.

When I wake up, she's standing over me, spit agglomerations at the ready.

"George fixed it."

I shrug, and she closes her eyes and smacks the air, obviously imagining my face while doing so.

She takes a deep breath and walks back to my bed. I change into an oversized sweatshirt, baggy sweatpants, and legwarmers. I feel a stubborn urge to make myself as small as I possibly can today—sorry, a stubborn *goad*.

I pass the lounge, and there Ryan is, staring at me through the laminated glass. He's smiling a creepy smile. It almost feels sexual. We're having sex with just our faces. I'm about to smile back when I realize he's actually just looking at his reflection. He's fussing with his hairline, making sure every shard is in order as if they're not surgically cemented into his skull. I walk in.

"Hi."

He turns to me, and the smile fades.

"Oh. Hey, Sarah."

I sit down opposite him, leaning against the glass. I push my hands through my billowing sleeves so they're almost entirely hidden, hoping to look practically invisible. Ryan takes little to no notice of this.

"Yeah, so I had sex with Wanda last night."

He looks as Abby did yesterday: pure horror. Not the response I anticipated. Maybe an eyebrow raise, a smirk, a high five. Not this. I thought I remembered him telling me he had a thing for bisexual girls. Maybe I misheard him.

"Oh, okay. And…why did you feel the need to do this?"

God, this is my least favorite trait about him: his need to therapize everything. I try to respond, but all that comes out is a noise that sounds like a shudder. He solemnly nods and looks back at the glass, longingly.

"Do you know where Avery is?"

I get up and leave without saying anything. I thought we had an understanding, but perhaps I was mistaken. Or maybe we do have an understanding, and today is just an off day. I hope Avery's mind heals and she gets out of this place tomorrow, that bitch. George spots me from down the hall and speed-walks in my direction.

"Hey! No more messing with the thermostat."

He doesn't even use my name, just barks orders at me.

"You don't want to go to the other side of the ward, do you?"

I shake my head no like an obedient soldier, and he licks his lips into a sarcastic smile. As he walks away, he reconfigures his balls in a way that he thinks is stealthy but is actually painfully obvious. I'm glad he's still hurting. Marta walks past him, screaming into his ear as she does so. My savior.

"BREAKFAST!"

Avery isn't here today. Ryan is sitting next to his roommate—back to the old ways. Wanda catches my gaze, giddily tapping an empty seat beside her. Abby looks at me with another evil smile. I pretend like I don't see either of them and head for an empty table. This morning's meal: scrambled eggs that smell like tuna and feel like Wanda's vagina. I look over to her to see if she's thinking, "Wow, these eggs have the same texture as my vagina," but she houses them down, seemingly oblivious to this thought. A young girl with puppy-dog eyes sits opposite me. She's still in the paper blue scrubs they make you wear in the emergency room. Her top has a V-neck, though. Mine didn't have a V-neck. Her breasts are squeezed together as if she's wearing a push-up bra. But she isn't, she couldn't be. Her body is a crime against nature. And she's a natural blonde, with big blue eyes and rows of freckles. Booby the blondie. I have no intention of learning her name. I hear a yelp, then a scream.

"I can't do it. I won't—I can't! Don't make me! Don't do it—please."

It's the roommate-widow: Sam. He's sobbing into Ryan's sleeve. Ryan clutches Sam's head as if he's breastfeeding him and uses his free hand to continue eating his eggs. Sam's snot seeps into his mouth, into Ryan's shirt. He keeps screaming the word "please." Please, please, please. It seems as if one of his eyes is looking at me.

After breakfast, I go to the lounge. Avery is there. She's coloring a cat bright green with a pink tail. I grab a crossword. It's another Bible-themed one. Four letters. "Place for the wicked." She clears her throat. It sounds like she's trying to swallow a jawbreaker.

"I'm really…struggling. I call my mom about ten times a day. It's just…hard. It's really hard in here."

Her face squirms into a frown, one that shows off her premature smile lines. Through the laminated glass, I see inaudible screams materializing from an elderly woman. The woman is stout, her head an erratic nest of white hair. She punches her fist in the air as if she's throwing something, but nothing comes from it. Guards pin her down to the ground before sliding her out of my view on the sticky linoleum floor. A sprightly prepubescent boy dancing the "nae nae" takes her place. I look back to see Avery crying. I clear my throat as well.

"Sometimes, well…I kind of think everyone is actually normal and just not telling me. Everyone out there. I don't know."

She laughs, but not in a way like she's making fun of me. She just laughs.

"No," she says resolutely, breathing in the snot, wiping away the tears, puffing out her striped breasts, "no, not at all. Everybody has a secret, but not everybody…knows it yet. That's…what I think."

She is intelligent—she is intuitive. Booby catches her attention through the glass—she's talking to Ryan, breast-first. His letter is in her hands. A tiny boner grows in his pants pocket.

"Ugh, I don't know why, but—I just—I just hate her, don't you?"

I smile. It's the first time I've smiled since being in here.

"Yes. Yeah, I do."

Transcribed Message Of A Flu-Ridden Therapist's Newest Patient Caught On Her Sony ICD-UX570 Recorder

"Well, I—the thing is—I'm an only child. But it's also confusing: I never really know how to answer that question because—well, my parents had my sister, right? Before I was even a thought. And she died when she was two years old. And then they had me. So, you see? It's tricky. Answering that. But I—I just want to clarify, like, I usually say no. I usually say no to siblings because…obviously. Bless you. Bless yo—bless you. Wow, three in a row! That's good luck, right? Want a tissue? Look, I'm not trying to fish for sympathy, but, like, I might as well tell you all of it, right? And it's—Well, I know I should be, but really, should I be? I never met her. I'm sad for my parents, I suppose. I'm sad they had to experience that grief. But I wouldn't say I'm grieving, no, and I—Sorry, woah—I completely forgot for a second. But, Abigail. Abigail was her name. But they usually call her Abby, for short. What? *Is* her name, then, I don't know. It's like—here's it—here's the thing—she could've been this beautiful person and I could've been this great big brother, and my parents could still be together, but why even fantasize? She simply doesn't exist, which sounds harsh, a-and people don't like hearing that, but it's the reality. In truth, I rarely think about her. I've seen pictures, and of course, my parents love to talk about her, and they feel this resentment when I don't share this love—I know they do. Because I can see it! See it in their silence to my silence, in their aggressive-passive side glances. It's sickening. They have no empathy for my natural disconnect. I'm not going to get her name tattooed on my ribs like my mom or write a self-help book like my dad—it's fine that they did that, that's fine, but their tragedy is not mine to partake in. I can't love a ghost, I can't. As a kid, I loved her, sure, because she was more of this fairytale, and honestly, grief is a much less complex thing to digest before puberty and—Oh, wow, another sneeze—God, you really don't look good, should we—okay, okay. She is, of course, the star of the family in many ways. Everyone talks about her. "My Abby would love this." My grandmother says that constantly. As if she actually knew her. As if Abigail was able to reach the cognizance to become a person to know. It's perverted in some ways, feasting on your fantasies through a dead baby. See, that look! That's the look my mom gives me. Just disgust, like I-I'm a monster. Oh, that was just you about to faint? Alright then. I can get you a glass of water or—fine, fine. I mean, have I thought about how different my life would be if she were still alive today? Sure. Of course I have. It's natural. But it's mostly selfish. It's mostly me thinking about the subsequent attention I would receive from family. Which is funny, because her being alive would seemingly draw more attention to her, but it wouldn't, it would not—think about it. Death is this gross spotlight. Gross as in, well, all of its meanings, really. There's nothing people love more than a dead daughter—it can make being a living son very difficult. I know I sound…whatever, but you're my therapist, so I can sound like a dick to you, right? That's why people go to therapy, to finally say the fucked-up things out loud—Right? Thank you— or bless you. In all honesty, I don't know what that sound was. See, I had this girlfriend, really hot girl. Smart—likely smarter than me, which is—I'm not saying that lightly, I don't say that lightly. But she could be cruel. She once told me that having a dead sister made me emotionally stunted. She said I was subconsciously feeding into my parents' fantasy of having an immortal child, and by doing so, I had a "precarious" sense of identity. Said I averted responsibility at all costs, which couldn't be farther from the truth. And she said having a dead sister made me *mean*. Mean! She said that I didn't respect women because of all of the pent-up anger I had for my sister, which is truly just absurd. She really was such a bitch. Jesus! That one scared me. I'm starting to think it's not good luck that you caught. Do you have a mask you can wear, or, um, that I can wear? Okay, well, so, this "girlfriend" ended up breaking up with me, right. I missed her birthday. It was my sister's death anniversary—lucky coincidence. Yes, I told my girlfriend I would go to her birthday party, but that was before I remembered about my sister's death thing. And of course, it had been twenty-five years, of course, so my parents want-ed to do this whole thing. They wanted to go to her grave and when you go to a baby's grave that's when you really remember—because even their gravestones are miniature—it's that—everything about a dead baby is wrong. It's a paradox or an oxymoron or some word insinuating that it shouldn't exist, should nev-er exist. But, yeah, so we go to her grave, and I feel emotional, I do—no one wants to think about a dead baby, and is it my fault that I forgot to text her saying I can't make it to her little party? Fuck, shit, dude! You got snot in my mouth! Your mucus is molesting me! Please, your nose is a fountain of death at this point— it's actually quite unprofessional. What? No, I do not think that my acknowledgment of your spraying flu-ids is a sign of latent issues with my father. Nice try, though. Anyway, my girlfriend refused to sympathize with me. She said that I was supposed to be meeting her friends and paying for dinner and she said that this was symptomatic of a long pattern of neglect, and not once did she acknowledge the fact that *my* sister *died*. My fucking sister died! I haven't talked to her in a few months, the girlfriend, but I see she's already dating this new guy, one who probably feels more than comfortable entertaining her verbal abuse and doesn't have any dead siblings to psychoanalyze. So wild to think about—even in death, even decades after her non-existence, my fucking sister fucked up my fucking life. So to answer your question: basically, no. No siblings. But it's really not a big dea—Achoo!...God fucking damnit."

Count Three Beats

"I've had so much hatred for you. At times."

He stops mumbling half-words. Not immediately, more like a casual fade-out, as he lowers the volume with an easy swipe of the pinky, as if his brain and the car radio were one unit. And maybe they are.

"Well. I've had a lot of pity for you."

He always does that, copying my template of insult. It's frustrating because he gets all the glory of having the last word. And he gets to make his more incisive by going second. But really, I did all the leg-work.

"At times," he spits out, reflexively. No, not reflexively—it was with a measured nonchalance. He probably counted to three before saying that. The perfect amount of beats before twisting the knife.

He continues singing under his breath—his low volume really just a facade, a means of plausible deniability for if he gets the words wrong. I don't know the words myself, I don't know the band or the genre. It feels like a lifeless tune, like every song in the world combined. He turns it up: pinky swipe.

"Anal, possibly?"

He doesn't look at me, but he almost does—a satisfying twitch in the neck, bend of the brows. I love it when I'm able to stump him. Rare, precious, almost spiritual.

"Excuse me?" he laughs, trying to maintain dominance through forced jest.

"Well, we've tried therapy. We've tried opening our marriage, threesomes, and, of course, the divorce. But we haven't tried the very obvious—anal."

He analyzes the rearview mirror, glares at the road, clicks his tongue. I feel my body glow with pride, my being as incandescent as the snow melting off the windshield. Perhaps all I'm looking at is my reflection.

"Um…"

"I know, I know. I never wanted to. But I think I'd be open to it now. Could be an…eye-opening experience for both of us."

He glances back at the rearview mirror and sighs. A sigh can be an automatic defeat or an automatic win—it's tricky, yet useful like that. It all rides on what he says next.

"And what about anal is so *obvious*?"

I shrug it off, reflexively, lamely, as if I'm bored by his curiosity, his lack of insight. But really, I'll have to wait for the answer to come to me. Rusted green rock thick with icicles, slate gray trees, sky the color of raw bone. The roads are entirely brown with sludge, impossible to see any pavement markings. This doesn't seem to concern him.

"Remember what you'd say? Whenever I caught you spiraling about one of my friends—colleagues—who were women?"

My head spasms in his direction—an accident, of course. It's rare for him to go first. I feel I have to even the playing field, reward him by participating.

"You'd tell me to stop being jealous."

He laughs with the cadence of a man satisfied, sufficiently accompanied by his own inside joke.

"Yes, yes, and then you'd say: *I'm so good at it, though.*"

He giggles, no—chuckles, no—not that either. He does whatever the word is for laughter that is very contained and very masculine and could just as easily be mistaken for a series of coughs. This doesn't feel like a win. It doesn't feel like pity, either. It feels like something much worse than either of the two, which could only mean he's complimenting me.

"I always found that very cute. It's not like there was anything going on with these women, but I did love hearing you say that. Because it was true: you were good at it. You do well with jealousy. It sharpens you."

Mind games, but it's okay, I've grown accustomed. The first marriage, I learned, is about love, and the second marriage is about who is the best. A race would really be a better word for our arrangement. I bring my knees into my chest and hold my feet, my toes still outrageously numb. He doesn't even have the heat up that high, and look at him, wearing a short-sleeve, goosepimple-less. That is, unfortunately, a point for him. He clicks his tongue. A necessary prelude for men who feel they have something to say.

"I remember you accusing me of doing it with my boss, saying she probably took it up the butt because—"

"Yes, well. You've always been good at making me jealous. It was a dynamic that suited both of us. I'd get to be angry, and you'd get to be right."

Interrupting him is collateral damage for me. Petulant and distasteful. But I'm willing to take that loss. A noise, almost imperceptible, echoes in the back of his throat, maybe somewhere even deeper—warm and thick and cunning and, once again, nameless.

"I don't think there was any right or wrong…"

Funny how only people who know they're right say this. I place the tip of my nose to the window: barren trees now replaced by woolly pine bushes, doused in shavings of hail. Everything is replaced when you care to look hard enough. I count to three.

"No. Probably not. Probably just a game, for both of us. Victimless."

The song is still going. It feels like hours since it started. I can't even tell if it's a man or a woman singing, can't discern the instruments. I think it's supposed to be a happy song. It's loud, and that alone makes me think it's happy. A fourteen-wheeler slightly veers to our side of the road. I flinch, but he calmly steers out of the way, as if he had been preparing for it. There's a black heap up ahead, impossible to tell if it's a rock, snow, or a dead body—he simply runs it over. I let the car's impact jolt my body backward and forward—his posture remains as straight as an arrow. I lick my lips, pinch my toes pink, let words rise from my throat like steam.

"Anal is obvious because I think you'd like to fuck yourself in some way."

When I first met him, I wanted to become his whole world, but that didn't work out, so my next plan was to become *the* whole world; that way, he'd be forced to see me whether he liked it or not. Everything I say now feels like an extension of this plan.

"What the fuck?"

It's no longer forced jest. It's compulsory anger, defensive doubt, something too unintentional to have any real meaning. I've got him by the balls. His grip on the steering wheel grows white.

"If you're fucking me up the ass, then you can imagine it's your own ass you're fucking, and that seems like your dream."

He checks the rearview mirror once again, and I follow suit, craning my head to the backseat. Our son sits, seemingly unbothered, a grin resting on the right side of his face. He's still wearing his noise-canceling headphones, still watching his true crime documentary. His cheeks red from the slopes, his eyes bloodshot from our fight in the resort lobby, his body wrapped up in a thermal blanket like a finger in a bandage. I turn back, cradle my knees, let my chest turn sour with heat. The first establishment we pass is a diner, offering holiday specials in bright red letters. As always, I will go first, as per the rules set in place by some cruel god above.

"Happy Valentine's Day, by the way."

The right side of his face smirks, hard to tell if the left side is matching. He winks at the rearview mirror, a wink which could mean a million things, a wink like a promise, like a secret code, only kept for my son, who probably doesn't even see it. He zones in on the icy road, turns into the parking lot without asking. At some point, he's stopped singing along. Or maybe the radio is turned off, I can't exactly tell with this new harangue of ringing in my ears. He puts the car in park, and his chest sinks in, his body hunches over. He begins crying, silently, with quick breaths, his concave chest shivering. What's his strategy here? Where is he going with this? He's all machine, and the rare times he's not, he's all melting plastic. His mouth looks like a smile, but it's really just trying to contort in a way that can produce words. I count three beats. I count to three again. Then one more time. He says nothing.

Is It Thursday?

She is always itching and almost always scratching. Mostly her neck and her calves, those are the problem areas. She isn't crazy, it's not like she thinks there's an implanted microchip she'd find. But she does think that her body, and her body only, has this kind of poison bubbling within the skin's surface. Something that, if she scratched hard enough, would seep out through her pores, or maybe even flake off. Not deep enough in her body to be deemed a futile effort, but something just barely within her reach: an eternal mind fuck, a seemingly Sisyphean struggle. People do cardio to sweat out the bad feelings—this is her cardio.

He despises the look and feel of flesh, especially anything pink, because pink means vulnerable. Gingiva, nipples, labia: his worst nightmares. Obviously, he is a virgin, and he feels no shame over this. In fact, he feels second-hand shame over people who proudly have sex. It's all so foul, a sensory horror, to be that close to someone's insides, unnecessarily. It feels like, to him, a socially acceptable form of medical malpractice. He dresses as if it were winter all year round and chronically wears latex gloves, even outside of work.

She grew out her nails, specifically to attain more high-quality friction with her skin. Most of her body is chronically sunburnt red and as dry as sandpaper. But she knows she has to keep scratching until something escapes. It isn't a parasite, no, it's something her body naturally produces but doesn't actually need, something that makes her sick with anguish. She just needs to find the right spot, apply the right pressure, and she'd be able to cleanse her body of the sickness. Once that was taken care of, she'd finally be able to start living.

They've lived in the same town their whole

lives, went to the same schools, go to the same grocery stores, and even have some friends in common. But they've never spoken to one another. At most, passing glances. She feels a likeness to him, and he feels a discord with her; both of which deter them from interacting with the other. He works as a chemistry lab assistant for one of the world's leading cosmetic companies, and she as a daytime stripper and a part-time birthday party clown.

He knows his job is a cold, callous one, testing potentially harmful products on animals. But he doesn't see animals as emotional creatures, he sees them as things. Their "flesh" is not actually flesh, it's more like waxy silicone, like vinyl Halloween masks. A chewy fabric meant to be injected with chemicals until it grows sufficiently inflamed. Today, he is using a pipette to funnel a seafoam-colored liquid into an albino rabbit's left eye as his advisor Leonard jots down the subject's stats. He will have to keep close watch on the accretive levels of discharge, opacity, and redness over the next week.

She knows her jobs are undignified and lackluster, but not everyone is cut out to be a doctor. Her body is shaped like a child's: shrunken breasts, distended stomach, short stature. This attracts a very niche audience, one not favorable enough to land her the night shift. Today, she is wearing her pink panties with the word "Tuesday" engraved on the butt. Three bald men sit and watch as she swaddles a metal pole between her legs. The one with the gray beard tosses a twenty at her feet, the one with the black beard calls her a string of slurs, and the one with the orange beard simply watches. She will have to keep close watch on the bald ginger.

He washes his hands for two minutes and thirty-four seconds, re-gloves, says goodbye to his co-worker Leonard, and clocks out. He drives home and pops a TV dinner in the microwave for four minutes and fifty-six seconds, giving the meal forty-five seconds to cool before eating. It's very generously called *Mexican Delight*, and is supposed to be two enchiladas containing beans, cheese, and chicken, but the bread has been reduced to paste and there's hardly any chicken. There are also mysterious cubes of hard white. He takes a bite and wonders what it might be: rutabaga? Cauliflower? Parsnip? A genetic modification that sustains the flavor profiles of all three? He picked this up because it presented an alluring sale of three for the price of one. He can't tell if he likes it or not, and he feels more unsure if that even matters. The contents of his grocery hauls are always directly dependent on that week's discounts. He isn't poor, but it seems like just as respectable a factor as anything to base your meals around. He scoops another bite of the bread-drenched white cube with his spoon, but before he can eat it, he is interrupted by a knock at the door. Then, three knocks. Then, a high-pitched scream.

She gets her weekly check from the manager and changes into her sweats. The newbie, Allison, walks on stage dressed in nipple pasties and three-inch pumps. Her moves are smooth, masterful, but her face is puckered with insecurity. She waves goodbye to Allison, and Allison waves back, a smile cracking through the fear. She walks out from the shadows and neon purples, and into the daylight, white like foam. As soon as she is out of view, she scratches her cheek, her ear, her chest—a perverted habit must be done in private. She gets in her car and continues scratching like a living person inside a wooden coffin ten feet underground. The bald ginger eyes her. She stops scratching. He's opposite her, in a venous blue car, one riddled with marks and dents. He honks, waves, smiles. She smiles and exits the parking lot. He begins to follow her. She makes a left, and so does he. She makes a right, and so does he. She makes another right, now going in the opposite direction from her house. He's so close to her, she can see his hot ruddy cheeks in the rearview mirror. She makes a quick left, parks, and runs to the closest house, the one with the dark green door. She knocks. "Let me in!" she screams. "Let me in!"

He opens the door to see a person with a child's body and a woman's face. She looks vaguely familiar. "Sorry, someone was following me. I couldn't have them know where I live. Can I come in?" He looks outside to see nothing except what he believes to be the woman's car parked in front of his yard. He shuffles the woman inside, the heat of her body feeling far too close to him—claustrophobic, manipulative. "But now they know where I live," he argues, locking the door. She's sweating, flushed, her entire face swimming in reds and pinks, her chest heaving as if it were carrying something very heavy. "Yeah, but if he tries to come here and rape me and sees you, then he'll leave. Probably." She turns her attention to the living room, to the plate of food. "Is that soup?" He nods his head yes and swallows the spit that's been accumulating in his mouth since she walked in. She steps closer to the food. "Oh. I have that at home. *Mexican Delight*, right? I think you heated it too long, though." He shrugs. "I like the turnips in it," she says. Turnips. He nods in agreement as if he knew this the whole time. Her body almost looks atrophic, making her head seem huge, but it's actually probably the same size as his. "How old are you?" He felt that if he didn't ask this, he would explode or possibly go to jail. She laughs. "Twenty-six." She sits on the couch in front of his dinner. He sits next to her, a normal distance between them. "Cool. Me too." She laughs again. "I know." She begins to eat his food, and he lets her. "Jude, right?" she says with a mouthful. He nods and realizes—Iris. "Iris?" She nods. Her body tenses up, her eyes scatter the room—she looks like she's about to puke. She thanks Jude for the food and runs out the door. He goes after Iris, but she's already getting in her car, speeding away, and clutching her chest.

She is let into the house by a tall man with worried eyes. The man looks pasty, flushed—almost ill. She explains her situation to the tall, ill man. Her toes are prickling, her calves throbbing. The man almost looks dead, and she can't tell if she's in his house or her own. Is she in shock? No, because you're only in shock if you don't know you're in shock, so she's fine. His hands, gloves. His hands are gloved. Jude. It's Jude, she knows this now. She breathes in and pretends as if she knew this the whole time. Is he a doctor? Something like that. The world tilts slightly to the right, so she sits on the couch to avoid falling. Her chest is burning, her jaw shaking. She needs to scratch. Not with Jude around, no. Her mouth fills with saliva. She eats the food in front of her. Did he make this for her? She thinks, probably, yes. It's mushy and cold. She swallows it all down. "Iris." Did she say her name, or did he? Her entire body is fire, rumbling and aching and pleading. The food tastes like the food she has at home. Is she home? No, she's with Jude. In Jude's house. Her heartbeat is now everywhere, it's in her bones and flesh and hair, it's in the room itself, the walls and floor and Jude. She needs to get out—she needs to scratch. Why did she leave her car in the first place? There was a reason, but she can't think anymore. All she can do is feel. All around her are shapes and air—that's it. She runs out of a blurry rectangle and climbs into something that feels cold, metal. She claws at her chest and breathes a sigh of relief. The world is now clear, in focus, upright. She's in her car, under daylight like foam. She continues scratching and drives away, only then remembering the bald ginger.

Jude injects a butter-yellow liquid into a rat's bloodstream. He rubs a cotton candy colored balm into a shaved patch of a guinea pig's abdomen. Is Iris okay? It's been three days now—or was it two?—but he couldn't help but feel guilty, worried. He could ask Olivia or Darren if she was okay, but he didn't want to cause a stir. He checks the albino rabbit's eye, adds more seafoam liquid. There's a yellowing of the fur, reddening of the cornea. Enhanced sensitivity, little swelling, and about a gram of discharge. He writes all this down as Leonard is not here today; he hasn't been for the last few days. He's on vacation—or is he on sick leave?—and turned reign of the lab over to Jude. What did Iris do? What could she have done to prompt a stalking? He washes his hands, re-gloves, and clocks out. As he drives home, he wonders if Iris will be there waiting for him. He knows this to be a preposterous thought, but is disappointed nonetheless to find his dark green door uncrowded. It's not like he wanted to see her, but she had made him complicit. How could he live with himself, not knowing if she was raped and killed? Even if she were raped and killed, he'd feel better knowing that this was fact rather than fantasy. He hears a familiar high-pitched scream.

Iris shows up in white face paint, a red nose, and a purple wig. She has her costume on and a bag full of balloons, bowling pins, and disappearing scarves. The man on the phone said it was Sophia's seventh birthday and she had a thing for dancing clowns. The only dance moves Iris knows are related to a metal pole, so she will have to improvise. A woman opens the door and leads her to the party in the backyard with screaming children and drunk mothers. There is only one man here, and it's *the* man. The bald ginger. A little blonde girl tugs at her pant leg and begs for a trick. Her neck is like a gurgling railroad, one that needs the solid presence of a heaving train. Her calves are like two heads counting down the seconds until the guillotine falls. Her body is all wanting, all waiting. A boy with glasses asks what's in the bag before opening it up himself. Of course, Iris can't stop him because she's now on the ground, pushing her body back and forth against the shards of grass, and scratching the areas the grass can't reach. The boy asks for a balloon in the shape of a snake, and Iris tries to produce the closest sound she can to "Okay." Some mothers believe she is having a seizure, others believe she is engaging in some perverted sexual kink, and one accuses her of witchcraft. Iris believes them all to be fair assumptions. The boy is crying now, saying he never gets what he wants, as Iris chafes her cheek against an ant hill. The bald ginger is holding a scared little girl and reassuring her that this is just the clown's way of dancing. Why is he the only man here? Was this all a setup to get close to her? Are these all paid actors? She sees white and feels a cold palm like death on her writhing shoulder.

Jude carries Iris back to his house. He heard the scream and knocked on his neighbor's door to find the cause for concern. He found the seizing clown and then recognized that seizing clown as Iris. She's lying on his couch now, her limbs occasionally twitching, her eyes glazed, her face febrile. She was scratching her skin raw when he found her, but she's stopped now. "Why were you at my neighbor's house?" Her heartbeat is fast, fills the air, makes Jude's own heart quicken. "Stalker," is all she can manage to say. Jude washes his hands and puts on a new pair of gloves. He hears Iris talking, and he lets her. He sits down next to her big clown feet. Her makeup is in disarray, smudges of rouge and white and dirt, and her wig fell off at some point during the carry. Her nose is still attached, somehow. He wants to laugh but stops himself—now is not the time to laugh at things that aren't supposed to be funny. Her fingers are trembling, her nails long, creamy ovals. She's crying now, opaque tears swimming down her neck, her makeup like an interactive painting. "I could never have nails like that," he says, just to say something, "Would rip right through my gloves." She sits up and uses her nails to scratch his cheek. He winces until his jaw locks and his abdomen shakes with pressure.

Iris sees the bald ginger laughing and the next moment she sees Jude's ceiling. She smells his house— scents of mouthwash and mold. She props herself up on her elbows and sees Jude washing his hands. She thinks he touched her at one point—was she dirty? "Thank you." Her voice sounds squeaky and far away: a floating plastic bag. Her body feels misty, fading from her grip. She always wanted to rid herself of herself, but not like this, no. "What happened out there?" Jude's voice sounds large and stoic and concrete. It sounds closer to her than her own heartbeat. She doesn't know where to begin—come to think of it, she wouldn't know where to end, either—so she says, "It seems like life is taking me a bit longer to figure out than other people." Jude sits next to her feet. She can see the pulsating tendons and veins of his hands through the gloves. He stretches his fingers and looks at her, pensive. "I wouldn't worry. That's how everyone feels." She laughs, which reminds her that she can laugh and that things can be funny, especially things that aren't supposed to be. "That's what people say when they have life figured out." He says something about her nails, and she pets his face, slowly, softly, as if his body needed the opposite treatment to hers.

Jude's face retracts, his body backing away before his mind even thinks to. A woman crying in a clown suit is a new visual for him, and he doesn't know the appropriate feeling to attach to it, but he feels guilty that, so far, it's largely positive. She asks something, and he nods yes, out of bodily instinct. Iris throws her nose to the ground, unzips her clown suit to reveal her bare breasts and pink panties. She kicks off her shoes, lies on the couch. He does as he's told, because this is real, this feels realer than work, and speaking of work, did he close the rabbit's cage? Did he write down the rat's stats? Everything that isn't Iris has been a blur, so all he can do is focus on the now and worry about the rest later. She's on her stomach, her legs kicking in the air. Her back is smooth, concave, and her calves are slender and flaky like pastry. He reads her butt. "Is it Thursday?" he asks Iris. Her head shakes no. He scratches her, every part of her, in a fast, rhythmic motion, like a pubescent boy jacking off. He starts at her feet for three seconds, then calves for four seconds, all the way to her back for five seconds. He scratches her large scalp for a full minute, and then he repeats the process three more times. She's moaning and sighing with pleasure as he turns her entire body a warm pink. This is worse than sex, and in that way, better than sex, for Jude at least. It doesn't bother him, no, because he's been given a task and in that way, she is a subject, her skin like waxy silicone. Waxy silicone that he is slowly falling in love with—that can't be right. How can a woman make everything so clear and so complicated at the same time? She flips over, her makeup almost entirely erased from sweat and tears. He can't tell who leaned in first, but their faces touch, specifically the lower halves. He does what he thinks is right with his mouth, trying to swallow back any saliva that wants to come out while attempting to apply the perfect amount of pressure on Iris's lips. She tastes of deli meat and wheatgrass. Iris retracts; she looks at him with a silent knowing. A perverse kind of knowing that means she is no longer in the same room, same house as him. She's somewhere else entirely, and he can't do anything about it.

Iris stops petting his face once his body starts vibrating and his eyes begin to water. He backs up as if she were dangerous, as if she had a virus. Does he know? Does he know about the sickness within her? He seems shocked, afraid—but he's a doctor, no? Maybe he's concerned, maybe he can help. "Can you help me with something?" He nods, timidly, but emphatically. She strips, tossing the clown accessories far from her body. His eyes widen like a schoolboy's, his skin white as a ghost's—he will have to get used to that. Or maybe she will. She lies down, facing away from him, because this has to be done in private, of course. He asks a question, but she doesn't hear—she's too focused on the potent heat of his hand hovering over her left heel. The touch of his gloved hand on her feet is almost orgasmic, a type of real feeling that is too real. It surpasses reality; it stands on a fine line between fantasy and horror. He scratches, he scratches her body so hard that his nails pierce through the gloves. He scratches as if it were a job—he scratches almost as well as she scratches herself. It's a high that can't be described in words, only in nail grooves. His fingers are dexterous and well-timed, like those of a pianist, and she is just happy to be played. Everything is pink and warm, and Iris believes this to be love—or the closest motor response that she is capable of feeling. Once he covers the entire parameters of the flesh she cannot reach, she flips around—she needs to reward him. She leans in, kisses his crumpled lips. They feel wet, unsure, pressurized. He retracts. He looks at her, confused, maybe disgusted. And why wouldn't he be? She tries to imagine what she must look like. Nobody wants a depraved clown, a child of a stripper. She is everything wrong in the world, somehow, she is all of it. His eye twitches, his mouth crinkles inward so no pink is left. He has a kind of sickened boredom that she can't remedy. All she can do is leave with a dignity that she dreams of one day deserving.

When Jude gets to work the next day, Leonard, with tense brows, presents him with a tuft of fur with two shiny buttons for eyes. It's the albino rabbit, and it's dead. Its bones stiff like metal, its tiny rabbit mouth wet with foam. He had forgotten to refill the rabbit's water supply. Or did he put the wrong mixture into the pipette? Either way, he killed the rabbit, making the experiment null. Leonard tells him to pack up his things, and Jude can't seem to muster the energy to argue. He gets home, makes his *Mexican Delight*, and eats in silence and solitude. He can see shreds of dead skin under his fingernails—parts of Iris within him. And the couch still feels warm from Iris's abdomen, from her stretching and burning. She's everywhere but can't be seen, like a virus. His body has never felt the kind of warmth that her body felt, and it's not a luxury he'd like to risk, only watch. He's interrupted by a knock at the door. Every muscle in his body contracts, willing his door to produce Iris. He swings the door open. It's his neighbor, the bald one with the ginger beard. The neighbor asks Jude if the clown is okay. Jude tells the neighbor that the clown has a name and that name is Iris and he has to go now. He shuts the door and continues eating his dinner, letting tears and snot stream into turnips. He uses his bread-wet spoon to carve his face, imagining Iris sitting beside him, scratching the waxy silicone of his cheek, much to his dislike. And he'd say thank you.

When Iris walks onto the stage, she sees the bald guy with the black beard and the bald guy with the gray beard. No ginger today. She swings around the pole, shakes her ass, and plays with her tiny breasts. And why isn't he here? Did even he grow tired of her? It upsets Iris to think that hate is weaker than love. She rips off her high heels, takes off her panties. Her entire body is still red from yesterday's scratching. She hears the men whispering about it, surmising it's a rash, something contagious and malicious. The black beard grunts out of disgust and leaves, muttering obscenities on the way out. The gray beard drinks his beer and scans the room, looking for something else and finding it: Allison. Her face is now lit up—large and toothy, it takes in the entire room like an inhale. Gray beard tosses two twenties at her feet. Iris has no idea what her own face looks like—that's not a luxury she's ever been gifted. She grabs hold of the metal pole, remembering that you can turn an object into whatever you want, and cradles it. She lets the cold metal touch her calves, her neck. Her face, her chest, her thighs, her everything. She breathes in the cold as if it were a body, hoping that this is a way to be reborn. Maybe scratching isn't what she needs, maybe it's the cold, maybe she had it all wrong. Maybe she needs to make more of herself instead of less. She will ice her skin back to health, undoing all the scrapings of years past. And once she lets go, she'll finally be able to start living.

The Procedure

The first thing I did when I found out the news was chug a seven-dollar bottle of rosé. Then I smoked a cigarette butt I found hiding in my trash can and fucked my downstairs neighbor. I figured it was fine, considering my plan and all—that being said, I didn't tell him I did any of that.

I was, in many ways, naive for thinking I'd have the power just because I was older. That was never the case with Gabe. We were in the same Race in Film class. I remember when I found out about his early graduation and obscene SAT score, thinking, *Why would you choose to study something as fucking stupid as movies with a brain like that?* I never asked that. I was sure he had gotten that question enough from other hook-ups and, selfishly, I wanted to stand out. He was precocious—a term I'd never thought I'd use, never wanted to use, to describe a lover of mine.

He looked like some strain of Balkan and was possibly Jewish. I never asked about that either, not out of a desire to seem aloof, but it just would not have mattered to me either way. He was big-eyed, big-nosed, and small-mouthed. Every part of his person was a different shade of beige or brown. He was the kind of person who looked easy to draw, but you'd never get it quite right if you tried. I made the first move, of course.

It was on the day we watched Colin Farrell's *The New World*. In the discussion afterward, most people were just echoing things our teacher, Ms. Diaz, had already said, talking about "white savior complexes," "historical inaccuracies," and "calculated microaggressions." Once a lull entered the conversation, Gabe, very coolly, raised his hand as if he didn't really care if he was called on or not, as if people didn't need to hear his thoughts for them to be valid.

"Yes, Gabe, what would you like to offer?" Ms. Diaz asked.

He cleared his throat and leaned back.

"Well, people are reading her broken and forlorn nature as a metaphor for her racial otherness, but I see it as the opposite. Her race is a metaphor for her internal otherness: she's *emotionally* Native American. In that way, and honestly, in all ways, this is a love story. A love between a broken girl and a lonely man, and I don't think enough people are recognizing that."

I didn't agree with him, or at least, I don't think I did, but I found his refusal to acclimate to the rehearsed liberal culture of the class admirable, sexy even. And it was definitely unexpected—such a romantic response. I momentarily fantasized about us doing role-play in bed, me, Pocahontas, him, John Smith, pumping behind me and pulling my long, dark hair while whispering sensual words in my native language. But then I felt bad and stopped thinking that. Ms. Diaz, of course, didn't like this and called his observation "grossly negligent to the entire point of this class," but I mostly stopped listening after that.

After class, I went up to him. Tapped his shoulder, said his name in a confident tone as if we were already friends, and told him I liked what he said. He said it was mostly a joke, and I laughed like I knew it was. We found a seat on a nearby bench and talked for a bit, with mostly him talking, chiding our "woke" peers and verbally masturbating over the main actress in the movie. Our class was at night, and by the time our conversation reached a natural conclusion, it was nine o'clock. I coyly suggested he walk me home since it was a city and all—just to be safe, of course.

He didn't even need me to invite him in; he showed himself around my apartment as if it were rightfully his. He said he knew the guy who lived below me, told me that he was an absolute asshole—I told him I used to date the guy in response just to make him jealous. He made courteous small talk with my roommates as I poured us two glasses of red wine. I filled mine substantially higher than his and took a large swig when he wasn't looking. We went to my bedroom and talked—he asked about my family, I asked about his ex-girlfriend, he asked about my major, I asked about his favorite sexual position, only after my third glass of wine, mind you. But, of course, after that, there was nothing to do but fuck. He was the perfect amount of toned: not too small like a twink, not too thick like a gym rat. He had a big dick and no concern over whether or not I was getting off—it was hot. He routinely called me a "dirty whore" and slapped my ass, or lack thereof, without me needing to ask, which I appreciated. Afterward, he patted my stomach, kissed my forehead, and made his quiet and respectful exit.

We spent the next eight weeks like that: hanging out after every Thursday night class to talk and drink and fuck. Once, I suggested that we hang out on a different day, but then he got really serious and stern and told me about the "importance of emotional boundaries," so I did not try again, which I was fine with. I was more than used to casual sex being the standard. That was just college for you, and city college at that. He did open my worldview quite a bit, though. He got me into reading Slavoj Žižek, got me into saying the word "retarded," and got me into unprotected sex. It was on the ninth Thursday night that

I realized, lying alone and naked on my bed, granules of his cum marinating inside me after another poorly timed pull-out, that I hadn't gotten my period.

I stole a pregnancy test from my roommate's bathroom. As I was waiting, I looked in the mirror as if I were watching a character in a movie and thought, *do something poetic, say something memorable, cry for fuck's sake*. I did none of the above.

I hate to admit it, but I had willed this to happen. After every hangout—I don't know if it was post-nut clarity or something more sinister and less inevitable—Gabe would grow detached toward me, and it always seemed so cruel and so certain. I never felt sure that there would be another hangout until he walked me home the following Thursday, all smiling and joking as if nothing had changed. Because of this, I wished to get pregnant. Well, wish isn't the right word, but it was a concrete and consistent intrusive thought. I did not want to trap him with me through pregnancy; I just wanted the assurance I'd see him again, and an abortion would, most likely, assure that.

After getting drunk and letting my downstairs neighbor—who actually turned out to be a very lovely guy— cum into my recently used vagina, I called my mom and asked her to schedule it. She only did this after sobbing wordlessly on the phone for three minutes to the point of dry-heaving. I let her indulge in this comfort, only speaking to say, "It probably would've been retarded anyways."

I stayed up all night doing "research" on the "topic" and kept coming across the word surgical. Surgical...really? That seemed a little dramatic. It's not like I was getting my appendix out or doing something actually morally depraved, like getting a boob job. One site said to seek professional medical help if I "still feel pregnant" a week after the abortion. What does that even mean? I did not even feel pregnant now. What would I have to compare it to? I only noticed that time had passed through the sun rising between my blinds. I got ready—picked the dried mascara off my undereyes and sprayed either dry shampoo or deodorant on my underarms. I called Gabe on my way to my seven a.m. Horror Film class.

"Hi."

"Hi."

He sounded unaffected. I could picture him scraping dirt out from his fingernails and flinging it at the phone screen.

"We have to talk."

There was a smacking sound—either he was clicking his tongue or slapping his thigh. I didn't know which I preferred.

"Listen, now is not a great time. You can't just call me and—"

"Shut up, Jesus."

I had no time to shower so my crotch was itching with semen and spit, the latter of which wasn't his fault but made me angry nonetheless.

"I'm pregnant, Gabe."

He coughed. Then laughed. Then went silent.

"But you're on birth control," he argued.

"No, uh—no, I'm not. I never said I was."

He coughed again. I thought I could hear a girl giggling in the background.

"But I pull out every time," he affirmed.

I couldn't believe how stupid he was being for a supposed smart guy. It sounded like he was trying to stifle a laugh, and then I weakly made out someone saying "bitch" in the background. I hung up, texted him the address and time for the appointment, and sprinted to class to keep my body from crying. I fell asleep ten minutes in and was awoken by a pale man with one green eye and one blue eye. He kindly tapped me awake and I asked where everyone had gone upon seeing an empty classroom. He, strangely, just muttered, "You're beautiful." I told him, "Not now," and left. When I got home, I masturbated to his face, took an Ambien, and fell asleep for twenty-two hours.

The appointment was the following Tuesday. I would have to miss a midterm on 1960s gialli for it, which I didn't mind too much. I didn't abstain from drugs or alcohol or cigarettes or sex or whatever that weekend—I was simply doing my due diligence to help the doctors move the process along. Saturday, I went to a Greta Gerwig-themed rave, rolled on molly, and ate out a forty-year-old woman dressed as Lady Bird. Sunday, I went to a frat party and let a married guy give me head in a nearby porta-potty and stole the host's unopened bottle of Fireball. Monday, I skipped my classes and drank that Fireball while chain-smoking in my bedroom and stalking Gabe's Instagram. I saw that two blonde sluts had recently followed him. I blocked both.

I kept peeing, once every hour, it seemed. Every time I'd get the tension in my bladder, I'd forget my current circumstances and have the terrifying thought of, *Wait, am I pregnant?* and each time, I had to force myself to remember. But by Tuesday, I had fully remembered—I guess the word would be "known"— that I was pregnant. My breasts seemed monstrous, my brain wanted to kill me, and the smell of my roommate's prosciutto made me want to barf. I'd never seen her buy prosciutto before. I think she did it on purpose.

When Tuesday came, I walked to the clinic to see Gabe standing outside, looking guilty, which was not a good look for him. He hadn't reached out to me since I called him. He was wearing a suit and tie, and his hair was gelled back. I suppressed a laugh.

No geriatrics wielding graphic photos of dead babies loitering outside. No unemployed men calling me a "dirty whore." Just Gabe, who was definitely thinking it. As I filled out forms, he kept straightening his posture, straightening his tie, looking around. I wondered who he was trying to look good for.

As they took my vitals, I let myself wonder things I knew I wasn't allowed to wonder outside of that white room. Approximately how many babies did they kill per day? Would my vagina be the ugliest vagina a baby would ever die in? Could bits of the dead baby get caught on my vaginal walls, and just how long would that take to pee out? The lady doctor laughed like she could read my mind. Once things got going, she started talking me through it, but I tuned her out the same way I do with Ms. Diaz. I didn't *actually* want to know what was happening in my body. I wanted her to be in control, and it felt selfish of her to put any more than she had to on me. I tuned out most of what was happening, actually. All I really remember is the cold of the salad tongs inside me, cold of the crunchy sanitary sheet below me, cold of the bubbly nurse's stare through me. Cold cold cold.

Afterward, Gabe walked me home—it was the first time I'd ever seen him nervous and uncomfortable, and I sort of wished he had the abortion instead of me so I could be the nervous, uncomfortable one.

He always got the best roles.

"So," he began, with no clear indication of where he was going.

"So," I mimicked.

"Do you ever want to have a kid?"

I couldn't believe he had just asked me that. It was not right timing. It was not right.

"I don't know. I don't…think so."

His hands were in his pockets. I felt an urge to fish one out, hold onto it. I put my hands in my pockets too.

"I think I do. I can definitely see myself with a daughter."

I cringed at the thought of him being a father to a daughter. I cringed at the thought of him being a father.

"Me, too," I heard myself say. I continued.

"I always thought if I did have a child, it would be a girl. I think I could be a great mother to a girl. It would be hard, but…I think I could be really good at it."

He remained silent, but not even in a rude way, he just seemed preoccupied. He looked around as if he was seeing everything for the first time, garishly clear at the sky, the sidewalk, me, his shoes. Or maybe that's how I was seeing the world and I was just hoping he saw it that way too.

Once home, I downed three Advil, and Gabe tucked me into bed. He put two tall glasses of water by my bedside, plugged in my phone, and placed a towel underneath my butt "just in case." He left shortly after that, which was for the best—we didn't need either one of us getting attached just because of this.

It's not that I had felt "full" before, but I felt

strangely empty, an unprompted kind of emptiness, an emptiness that feels mountains heavier than its former counterpart. I don't like feeling things that I didn't know were possible to feel. It's annoying. I bled brown goop and cramps would occasionally surface, but I remedied with strategically placed maxi-pads and the rest of that Fireball. I thought about that movie about abortions we had watched last week in my World Cinema class. *4 months, 3 Weeks and 2 Days*. The girl who got the abortion had to fuck a mean guy in order to get it. And so did her friend. I didn't have to do that. I just had to fuck a mean guy in order to need it. I hadn't realized the luxury of that. I pushed the empty Fireball off my bedside table. It didn't shatter. Just rolled around, mockingly.

I don't know what it is about cinnamon-flavored whiskey, but I felt inclined to check my blocked accounts and unblock the prettier-looking blonde: Hannah. Her most recent post was with Gabe—a high-resolution photo where he was topless and, for some reason, soaking wet, and she was kissing his cheek with a beer in hand. Her breasts were spilling out of her black satin dress, much bigger than mine, even when I was somewhat pregnant. If she ever got pregnant, she'd have all the men at her feet.

I asked one of my roommates—the one that actually liked me, or maybe pretended to—if she was pretty, along with a refill on my glass of water. My roommate said that she looked like me. I appreciated that, not only for the comparison to a woman who has achieved my crush's affection but for saying it like that: "She looks like you," instead of "You look like her." The implication that I came first, whatever that means, was something I treasured for days. I checked

Hannah's more provocative posts' likes and told myself, "If he liked it, you should kill yourself." I'm not actually suicidal, not everything I say to myself is true in a surface-level sense, and these kinds of thoughts have proven inevitable during times of severe insecurity, best to hear them but not listen to them, which is the same attitude Gabe held toward me, guess we had that in common. Anyways. He did, of course, like every one.

She was also a film major, but a successful one: a rarity. She was doing a paid internship at MUBI and was self-funding, directing, and starring in her third film, a slice-of-life short exposing the abject underbelly of white feminism through the perspective of a myopic white woman. Her bio read "Gen Z Lena Dunham." Her profile picture featured her smoking a blunt in a thrifted wedding dress outside of a 7/11. I hated her, but I wanted to be her, and I hated myself for thinking the latter.

I thought about her dying, not graphically, not viciously, but the absoluteness of it, the entrancing concept of her just not existing. But if anything that'd be worse, he'd mourn her forever, and she'd become this sexy dead girl, this idyllic idea of young tragedy and a fuzzy symbol of lost love, and I cannot compete with that. He'd have to actively reject her for me to be happy, but that seemed too far-fetched, so I resorted to thinking about her dying—graphically and viciously. I felt a hot zap in my stomach, as if a finger was scraping, trying to find its way out. Hannah and Gabe. Hannah, Hannah, Hannah. I had always thought Hannah would be a really pretty name for a daughter. Oh well.

The Photoshoot

I remember the burping acid in my gut, the cold itch in the back of my throat, the fucking shake of my fingertips. Something about her voice always made me feel like I did something wrong, as if she knew I was spoiled before I even got the chance to find out. Every text from her was like a roundhouse kick to the jaw, threatening and aching, because, to put it simply, she was fucking hot.

I replied with a thumbs-up emoji and took an Uber to her apartment. I had a camera that a girl left at my place; she had told me she lost it, and I had told her that's too bad. Anyway, I didn't know shit about cameras—still don't. But Monica asked me if I could take her picture, most likely tasteful nudes based on her line of work, so of fucking course I said yes, and so would you, don't even deny it. Once I got there, I realized I was desperately early, so I smoked two cigarettes and half a joint before going up. It was always a game of roulette with weed: either made me feel like a god or like a eunuch. High risk, yeah, but high reward.

To be honest, my attraction to her felt largely chemical and obligatory, so it might help if you read the description of her while rolling on molly with your dick pumping inside a scooped-out cantaloupe. Her shoulders were decked in tattoos of literary imagery, her head of natural brown hair, because she didn't need dye to make her cool, but I suppose this same logic could be applied to the tattoos, but she had such a pretty face, you forgot about this contradiction. She had model face. Big, fat, fucking forehead, black, wide-set eyes, so she was always looking at you even when she wasn't. Thin nose, freckled cheeks, tiny baby ears. Small mouth, but thick lips, chronically squeezed into a pout. Her body was one hundred per-cent bones, except for her breasts and her ass, which were one hundred percent perfect spheres, just as God intended. Scar on her left knee from a biking accident (sexy), abnormally long toes (useful), and a mole on her left breast (just pretend it's an extra nipple)—so, really, not one fault to be found, even when I tried. Her entire person said "fuck me," so don't blame me for being a little nervous.

I knocked three times, and after a few minutes, she opened the door, smiling. Lacy, black lingerie. Sheer, exposing her nipples like Tic Tacs, and tight, ex-posing that fabric of a bush. I usually liked girls who looked like they didn't want to be fucked, because, of course, those are the sluttiest girls. So what was she?

"Uh—hi."

"Hi, Thomas!"

The roof of my mouth and my tongue kept suc-tioning together, making my words sound phlegmy. I needed water.

"Do you have anything to drink?"

She headed to her fridge, allowing me to gaze at that beautiful, pale ass being flossed by a fiber of black. Not one dimple to be found. They were kind of like a pair of nippleless breasts.

"Oh, yeah, here."

She tossed me a bottle of water, which I coolly caught and then uncoolly chugged.

"Thanks."

Her apartment was really just one room, but it was huge—three times the size of mine. The wall far-thest away from me was all grimy windows, painting the place a faded white. Bare mattress on the floor—obviously just for the aesthetic. Decaying oak dining table. Oriental rugs, pictures of dead musicians, vintage clown dolls. Exposed brick, bare bulbs, no television. And it was a fucking mess. Sprinklings of dirty clothes scattered the floor, and unwashed dishes pooled in the sink. Scents like hot beef and expired milk. I breathed through my mouth.

"So where do you want to…"

She chugged a bottle of water herself as she pointed to the mattress. It had one pillow—blue velvet, in the shape of a heart. A photo of Fiona Apple's mugshot was taped above it, sitting alongside a hanging wooden cross.

"I know nothing about photography, by the way…"
Her feet were bare, slapping against the parquet floor, with her overgrown, unpainted toenails. She fell back onto the thin, stained mattress, her body taking the position of a star.

"That's okay. That's why I'm here," I assured her.

She reconfigured her body into a lying position on her side: one hand propping her head, the other on her hip, revealing the tangled forests of hair living inside her armpits. Her scar was a phosphorescent pink, seemingly moving with the light, like an optical illusion. If I knew anything about photography, I'd probably say this was a very cliché pose.

"Yeah—that's no good."

She nodded, gravely, like a diligent student. I grabbed the camera from my backpack and pressed random buttons until a light flashed red.

"Well, what exactly are these for? Or, uh—who are these for…"

I didn't know much about her job—all I knew

was that she was a sugar baby for multiple men, but "sugar baby" could have meant anything. I wasn't sure how this interacted with the therapy stuff. She had to be fucking them to get this apartment, but who knows—men can be desperate nowadays. They'll take whatever they can get.

"Uh, two guys, specifically. Mateo and Levi. Mateo likes artful, more tame. So I honestly think this might be best for him."

I breathed in through my nose—beef and milk—and shrugged as if saying *Well, fine, if I have to, but please know that this goes against my entire nature as a respectable artist.* I clicked a button and heard a satisfying noise. I did that three more times, moving around, trying to get as many angles as possible because more angles seemed more professional.

"And Levi…"

She unhooked her bra, pulled down her panties, and peeled off her stockings.

"Well, Levi is a freak."

I was a good-looking guy and did pretty well for myself, but I had not been in this scenario before. A beautiful, naked woman, and me, entirely clothed and unsure if I had the right to stick my dick in her or not. The eunuch effect began to kick in.

"Do you have anything to drink?" I squeaked, the phlegm-intonation returning.

"Um, well, your water is right—"

"No, like. Alcohol."

She pulled out a pack of cigarettes and a box of matches from underneath the heart pillow. She lit the cigarette in one go and tossed the used match over her shoulder.

"Oh, shit. Sorry, no. I'm sober, actually."

We met at a Sex and Love Addicts Anonymous meeting—I went as a joke, but she was pretty serious about it. I guess it would make sense for her to be sober from the other shit, too. Her lips puckered; they were the perfect shape and size for a cigarette. I wondered how she was with blowjobs.

"Oh, shit."

She inhaled, and her eyes rolled back, her head fell limp, her mouth exhaling a pleasing sigh. This was probably the highlight of her day, seeing as it was her only permissible vice.

"Yep. Around five years from heroin, and one-ish year from alcohol and other stuff."

I sat down on the edge of the mattress, pretending to analyze the photos I just took instead of looking at that statue of a body. Maybe she thought I was gay. I manspread to avoid this assumption.

"Damn, that's…tough."

"It's fine."

I looked out of the corner of my eye: no stomach rolls, even when she was hunched over like that. Spiky spine, pointy shoulders, and two sandbags glued to her chest. Her fingers were short and covered in scabs and chipped black nail polish. They trembled every time they left her mouth.

"So, have you gone to another meeting since last Tuesday?"

"Yeah, I mean, um—"

Honesty earns pussy. This has always been the case.

"I actually didn't tell you, but my friend and I went as a sort of dare."

She turned to me.

"A dare?"

I suddenly felt very nauseous with lust—the acid burps returning—or maybe it was the weed that made me sick. Something in my body was boiling, and the only way I felt I could remedy this would be by kissing her: her body was my natural antidote, and she was keeping that from me. I pulled my vape from my pocket and started blowing O's.

"Not a dare—just. It was supposed to be funny. Ronny, the short, black guy with me. And then our other friend, Noah, well—Ronny and I are, like, more promiscuous, I guess you could say, so Noah was like 'you need help' and it was this whole joke. Honestly, you just had to be there."

She cleared her throat and lay back on the pillow, two smooth poles of shins facing me. Narrow ribcage—could probably fit my grip around her torso if I tried.

"I *was* there."

I laughed. She remained stone-faced, pouty-lipped. This would be a great photo: her looking like a bitch, smoking, naked. Maybe I did know something about photography.

"No, not at the meeting. Look, all I'm saying is I don't—I'm not into the therapy shit like you."

"Oh."

She killed the cigarette's flame directly on the floor—she didn't even finish half of it. I coughed, trying to hide the sound of my intestines sloshing around.

"Don't you think there was a deeper reason?"

I turned my body to her. She leaned in, showing me everything, like a magic trick; her stomach like a metal slab, breasts like cotton candy, vagina like my favorite Fleshlight. Lips cracked from smoke and eyelids heavy with relief. Pink cheeks, pink like the best parts of her. She turned her head slightly to the right, pushing thin hair behind her hollowed-out gem of an ear. I wanted to fuck that ear. No, want and need were not acceptable terms for my feelings at that moment— in my head, I already had her, as this was the only way I could stomach looking at her.

"Don't you think you went as a way to actually get help, even if it was under the pretense of a 'dare'?"

She took my vape from my hand, hit it, and blew the smoke in my face. Finally, she laughed, making those beautiful breasts bounce as if they, too, were making fun of me.

"Can I take your picture or what?"

She nodded, stood up, and twisted her body into a backbend position, her face peeking through her calves, underneath the bush like an angel atop a Christmas tree, and tongue out, just inches away from her own asshole.

"How's this?" she slurred out, mouth open.

"Perfect."

We took more pictures in similarly compromising positions. Legs behind her head, close-up of her vaginal canal, like a picture of an infected throat: hot. We took one where I was behind her, and she was on her knees, her face looking back at the camera, toyingly. This was when I saw, or when I realized, she had back dimple piercings. The things I'd do, I thought, I'd take her from behind, pound her guts, scrape those long thighs, and rub those shining specs, carefully, attentively, as if they were part of her, like two back-clits, and she would probably get off on that, she would— even ask for more. I took three pictures before casually holding the camera near my crotch.

"Yeah, so, uh—I think we got it."

The next couple of weeks were like that: she'd text me, and I'd get a car to her place, camera at the ready. She wasn't always naked, and she started using more props: her clown dolls, classic literature, and really whatever the men requested. Surprisingly, no sex toys, though. One photoshoot had her dressed in nurse's scrubs, sensually licking a variety of exotic fruits: carambola, pitaya, gulupa. These dudes were fucking perverts, man. After that one, she texted me a hands-heart emoji, you know, the one where the hands are making a heart. The least sexual emoji. If celibacy were a text, it would be that.

In the meantime, I fucked bitches I didn't care about—bitches whose pussies made me gag and whose political views made me want to drag a sharp object across my inner forearm. I don't remember any of their names—Stacy? Lacy? Macy?—and all their faces and bodies blended together like beige soup. Clam chowder. I was fucking clam chowder and Monica texted me a hands-heart emoji. My life was fucking retarded.

I've been dodging her texts recently because, really, I should focus on finding work, and it's not like she's paying me. I'm the one who's paying her, really—she's making money from incels, and I'm losing money on all the Ubers. Anyway. My last job was as a busboy at some fancy restaurant, but I got fired because I fucked one of the waitresses who ended up being the main chef's wife. What I need is a job with all men or a job with all ugly lesbians, like coal mining or Planned Parenthood. Or maybe even SLAA—based on the kind of neurotic attendants I found at that one meeting, they seem to take just about anyone. One dumb ass old bitch who claimed sex could be abused as a distraction, as if everything in life is not a fucking distraction. She's just upset because she hasn't had sex in years and her Wall Street husband is fucking his daughter's best friend. I could do that—I could lie and vaguely reprimand. I type "jobs for horny men," and the Internet directs me to gay porn, a video of two black guys fucking, both dressed as policemen. The world doesn't seem like it was made with me in mind. My phone buzzes: two notifications. The first is from my mom, a link to a job opening, but it's the same exact job and place I was just fired from. The second, from Monica. I click on the latter.

Please, Thomas.

She ends the text with a teary-eyed emoji. Okay. Okay, I'll do it. But no weed, no nicotine, and eat before. I need to be clear-minded and able-bodied when I see her. I order a car.

"I really appreciate this, Thomas, I do. The guys are loving it."

She's wearing a lime green silk robe and caressing my bicep. Her face is puffy, her lips bitten and bruised, her hair knotted and greasy. Her freckles look gray, her nose scarlet, and her scar has seemingly faded—now it's just a ribbon of beige. This time, the apartment smells of sour eggs and wet cardboard. And the entire kitchen is now covered in food-crusted dishware, one browning, half-eaten starfruit within my reach. I look down; her floor is a minefield of discharge-stained panties and sweat-stained baby tees. I sigh.

"Do you, like, fuck these men?"

My body is stable, but my surroundings are not; a stripe of nausea rises through my chest and buries itself in the back of my throat.

"Well. I used to, um, but, well—yes. Yes, I've started to again, yes."

I say nothing. I take out my camera and pretend to adjust the settings. She begins biting at a hangnail.

"How are *you* making money?"

I make the faces photographers make: knit brows, squinted eyes, wrinkled lips.

"Well. My parents are lending me some money while I apply—"

"Ah. So can't exactly judge my situation, can you?"

I laugh, and she laughs as well, a laugh that stretches her smile tauter than it can manage, opening a scab.

"Fuck."

She wipes the blood from her mouth and motions me to the mattress. She disrobes and lies down, her bones creaking like porcelain. I kick aside a heap of clothes and make myself comfortable at the foot of the bed.

She's on her back, sinking into her elbows, her chest tremulous and bright, except for that beautiful black mole, like another eye, watching me. With the window's light, I can truly see the sagging turquoise of her eyebags, the flickering pupils, the red patches of eczema, the skin of her lips falling off in clumps. She looks like shit—it's all so vulnerable. Her legs open slowly, like a rusty door, and me, out in the cold, waiting to be let in. The sweet, sticky sound of her vagina dividing and opening to me, like a mouth telling me to come inside. The stench of rotting food disappears. No, it is entirely heavenly. Fresh and warm. Dandelions in an oven is all I can think of. She pulls strings of hair over her face, hiding any expression she might have. I click once. Then twice. I angle the camera so it looks like Fiona and the cross are sitting on her shoulders, like an angel and devil. I change a setting, just for the hell of it, which increases the flash, painting her garishly white. My hands are shaking now, my stomach speaking in tongues. Focus. I stare inside her. A pussy like cream, a pussy like breath, a pussy in waiting. I'm inside her now—yes, I am. I'm inside Monica. I'm so deep, but it's not good enough, she aches for more, for my dick to ride through her guts and pop out her throat. She claws at my chest and begs, sobs, really, because it's so fucking painful yet so fucking good, and she doesn't understand how both of those things can be true at the same time. I'm so fucking deep, I'm practically wearing her, she's simply an interactive accessory, a tube tailor-made for my pleasure, if my right hand had tits. I grab her ass, I find her piercings and rub them, yank at them, tweeze them like nipples. I finally pull the piercings out of her skin and it's not blood that sprays out of the two pinholes, it's *cum*. She moans, she thanks me, she tells me she's never fucked any other men, not even the sugar daddies, I'm her first, and she can't even believe it fits. I smack her face, tell her to shut the fuck up, and, for a second, everything is blue hearts and white stars and pink skin. She cries a long, squeaking noise, her fingers tremble, her eyes roll back, and her face falls limp against the velvet pillow. My vision sharpens, and I place the camera near my crotch.

"So, yeah, I think we got the shot."

Her head bobs forward. She licks dried blood off her bottom lip and opens her eyes wide.

"Really? That was quick."

Those slender branches of arms throw the pillow aside and lurch for the cigarettes. I sit on the edge of the bed and stealthily place the pillow on my lap.

"Yep. Uh, yeah, I got it, though. How's SLAA, by the way?"

She tries to light a cigarette. Once. Then twice. Her fingers are shaking too much. I do it for her, then light myself one.

"Thanks, uh. Yeah—fine. Whatever."

She coughs out a cloud of smoke. I inhale as if it's my last breath, despite the twitch behind my tongue.

"You seemed pretty serious about it, Thomas."

Another statement that makes me feel like I've made an irremediable mistake. And I wonder what the kink is—where the drive stems from. It's not being attracted to authority; it's something bigger and less meaningful than that.

"Oh, well. You know I take this very—photography is an art, really—"

"No. No, at the meeting. You didn't seem to treat it like a dare."

Her entire body is shivering now: a folded animal of shaking white. All I want to do is wrap her in a sturdy blanket and force-feed her chamomile tea.

"Your friend Ronny seemed a bit childish. Now, looking back, his story about being raped by his mom and dad seems made up."

"Yeah. Ronny is a fuckin'—"

"But you. You were nodding and listening. I mean, you came up to me after. Asked me about my pathological infatuation with gangbangs. Was that just to get into my pants?"

She laughs, and in one swift motion, she is all body, all cream and breath again. Is this how it feels to be dating—to be in love? To so quickly and completely and easily oscillate between seeing them as a tortured thing and a sex object? Am I in love? Is she?

"Fuck, dude—what are we doing?"

She laughs, this time out of pity, maybe confusion. The shoulder closest to me features a fine line tattoo of a bird with its head cut off. She told me the name of the book, but it's escaping me now. The shoulder flexes as she takes another drag, contorting the bird into the shape of a falling angel.

"What?"

I turn my body to her. Look at the eye that seems the most static.

"Why can't we just have sex?"

"Wha—"

"I mean we basically already are. What do you call what we just did?"

She tosses her lit cigarette to the other side of the room with a vibrating flick of the fingers.

"It was a shoot."

I stand up. Throw the pillow down in a dramatic fashion. Toss my lit cigarette on the mattress, hoping for flame. All it yields is a dusting of charcoal cotton.

"I'm gonna fucking *shoot* myself—are you serious?"

I take a deep breath through my nose—eggs and cardboard—as she stands up, her body coarse with hair and goosebumps.

"Thomas...baby..."

"Jesus fucking—"

I kick a pair of purple underwear, striped in brown. Eye the clown doll on the floor. It's white, with a red, sardonic smile. I imagine ripping off its porcelain head and fucking the hole beneath it.

"I'm not interested in you like that. I-I'm sorry."

She walks to me, slowly, awkwardly, as if every part of her body were broken, like a baby deer taking its first steps.

"Well. Actually..."

She assesses me. Starting at my hair, ending at my feet, lingering a beat on my mouth. She smiles.

"You're pretty cute. We can do it if you want."

Her complexion is almost green, her lips a muted lavender, eyes black as a raccoon's.

"What?"

"Yeah. The SLAA shit is just not working for me, so."

She holds out a rattling hand and presses the cold—colder than the metal in her back—into my lips. She uses the other hand to stroke my semi.

"But only if you can take pictures of me afterward—all red and flushed. That'd be sexy."

Not in a million years, you cold-hearted, anorexic, druggie slut. A whore. A whore with a dirty apartment and dirty armpits and nasty ass feet. Unemployed...something. Unemployed cunt—yes, that's it. Unemployed cunt who will probably die in an alleyway, naked, with five different men's semen on her tits and an infected needle in her arm. Big-headed-ass-bitch. Fatherless, probably. Sad. Just a sad fucking waste of nothing.

I don't say any of this, obviously. I have sex

with her and cum in under thirty seconds. Then I pro-
ceed to take pictures of her, although the pink never
returns to her cheeks. The next morning, I wake up,
naked, in her arms, head on her bosom, her fingertips
stoic and strong, brushing through my hair, pushing
into the flesh of my cheek, her eyes heavy and soft,
staring at my lips, as she asks me if I have any single
friends. I say yes and catch a subway to the nearest
SLAA meeting.

Transcribed Message Of An AA Member's Speech Caught On Her Court-Ordered Parole Officer's Voice Memo App

"I can't make myself cum because I have such low self-esteem, right? I have low self-esteem where I'm, like—like, I don't believe I have the 'authority' to make myself feel good. You know? Like, how can I alone decide what feels good for me—I can't do that. I'm not equipped to do that. But then I also have such a problem with intimacy, physical and emotional intimacy, that I never let anyone get close enough to the point of me cumming. So, really, I'm fucked both ways. Without being fucked at all, right? Ha. I bring this up because—why did I bring this up? Oh, yeah, because sex, or really, the idea of sex, is the sole reason for alcoholism. You get anxious meeting another person because you're thinking about them naked or because you know they're thinking about you naked, so you take a shot or six in advance. I'm only nervous talking up here right now because I'm thinking about having sex with each and every one of you. Sex, it's…everywhere. It's a plague. And I've abused alcohol so often during sex, that I no longer know what it's supposed to feel like. I've lost the concept of bodily pleasure, and that, among many other things, I will have to take my time mourning, a-and re-learning. But, and, sometimes I think I'm so obsessed with sex because it's— it's the only unrestricted hunger women are allowed to feel. Ooh, that brought a hush to the room, didn't it? Ha! I know AA is all about taking accountability, I get that, but also, it only makes sense, to me, for a youngish woman in this day and age to see sex as freedom, and by extension, alcohol as freedom. Oh, she's eyeing me right now—she doesn't like when I make excuses. My parole officer is here tonight, thought I should say. Hi, baby! Just kidding—she doesn't like when I say that. Because she's against lesbianism. That's a joke as well. Jesus. Tough crowd. But she's right, I've made more than enough excuses for one lifetime. Honestly, what it is—I learned, later than my peers in life, that life is not about other people fighting your battles for you. They don't want that, and, more importantly, you don't want that. I thought the use of other people was for protection. It's not. Everyone who isn't you actually means very little. Except for that sexy Filipino lady in the bullet-proof vest. She's my everything. Love you, hon! Hm. Anyway. Seriously though, solitude is the only true path to freedom. Solitude from people and substances and all the other bullshit. I know I said I don't know myself very well, but that doesn't mean—well—even my very limited understanding of my body in this world is still the most important thing I have. I don't know if I should share but—this is all about sharing, right?—well, I used to have sex with this guy. He was a real freak and to match his confidence, I'd have to practically black out before each hook-up. He would do really crazy things to me, like gag me with his shit-stained tighty-whities and stick an oversized foreign object in each of my orifices at the same time and make me call *him* 'Mommy.' He also did things like kick stray cats and steal money from his dementia-ridden mother. Funnily enough, he was perfectly sober. He'd do this thing where, like, for a minute before he ejaculated, he'd warn me. Although it was less of a warning, and more of an exclamation—*I'm cumming, I'm cumming, I'm cumming!* But it was never said while he was actually cumming, only right before. I was always so envious of that—of being a person well enough to know its mission, to predict its victory. Seems impossible. Anyway, the reason why—I thought I liked doing these things because alcohol conveniently makes you reassess your values and interests. I did not like his shit crumbs in my mouth, but drunk me believed it made me a rockstar. I felt this cheap sense of enlightenment, because risk—I so easily interpreted risk as progress. I was a modern woman. I was a modern woman because I conflated a man's desires with my own. See how funny and obvious it seems! God! I'm talking it out, that's what this is. Maybe one day I'll forgive myself enough to finally learn the difference between feeling good and feeling bad. That's the goal, anyway. Maybe I'll finally learn the undulations of an orgasm. People say it feels soft, yet bright. Dizzying—but hopefully not in the way alcohol makes you feel. I am scared of that in all honesty. But with it comes an intention that I never had with drinking. I forgot, but my, well, she was a friend, or—anways, she saw the color blue when she climaxed. I forgot about that, I can't believe I forgot about that. She loved the color blue. I hope I can love something so much one day that it follows me along like that. She also said it felt 'complete.' I'd ask her about it, afterwards, because, well, I'm fascinated by women who know their desires. Before she—anyway—she used that word, yeah. I'd like to feel complete. I would. You know, I never blamed—I totally get why people kill themselves. It's one of the most interesting things you could do, especially as an alcoholic. But I never felt the urge—it always seemed too easy, too satisfying. Too much closure has always made me uncomfortable. Ha—yeah, I see you squirming! Suzanne's probably recording this right now, honestly. Thinking I might say something incriminating. I don't care, I don't. Because that's her job in life, just as this is my job in life right now. You can't be offended by inevitabilities—it makes for a very slow life. I know people, veterans of this club—is it a club? What should I call it?—well, I know people get annoyed when newbies try to use this podium as a stage for their amateur stand-up comedy. Maybe I've done that just a bit, and for that I apologize. And I don't have to—I don't want—I don't think I need to say all the terrible things I did inebriated. I don't want to do that. You can pick up from context clues that yes, they were very bad. And I've already talked about them in depth with the people that matter. Today—here—right now is about talking about the things that I haven't gotten to talk about yet. That's all that's worth speaking on to me, that which has not been said just yet, and, okay, Suzanne is tapping her watch. This means I'm late for my community service—sorry guys, um, it was great talking to you, but I gotta go pick up shit off my old high school's lawn! Sorry, that was, um—thank you, really, for letting me talk so earnestly and for listening and, one second, Suz—seriously, this has been—it's been great, and I feel like a weight has been lifted—or is that corny to say?—and, anyway, you guys are wonderful and I hope you have a great day and—okay! I'm coming, I'm coming!"

Arguing With Maggots

This had taken place shortly after the Final War. I had always thought it smart that they called it the Final War, to ensure no war would ever happen again. My father was a lost little boy. My husband ceased to exist. No one had more ownership over me in that room than the man who kneeled before the guillotine. My mother, God bless her soul, could rise from the dead and blind me with the yellow rot of her cesarean scar, and I'd tell her to go to hell, for I was not alive until I met John, and only John could parent the pride of my life. Not even the baby brewing in my belly meant close to anything at all within those few seconds. Of course, it was only when I felt John's glass eyes on me that I knew I was with child.

It was snowing the day of his execution. I wore my nicest dress, shiniest shoes, and most vile perfume. My father's tweed coat, my husband's wool gloves. When I first met him, I was poor and I was ugly and I wanted to tell him, John, I know you don't like me, and trust me, I know how inconvenient that can be, but if you could try loving me, I promise that'll be easier, and much more satisfying than you would first believe. Once he loved me, I'd tell him things like, I can't relate to men because they are afraid of death. I am not afraid of death. I am afraid of not being loved. Men are fine with not being loved. But I can relate to you. I can relate to you, John. I didn't know why he was chosen, and I wasn't happy about it, not as you may expect. Shouldn't every mean man get everything he wants and more? Has that not always been the fruitful intention of the universe? Let's not waste time arguing with maggots.

The room opened like a hot tongue. The floors will never be fully clean. Walls stuck together with gray spit and bedrock. I didn't look up. I was far too afraid to see that the building still had a roof. God never meant for roofs. Matrons and other perverts hungry for their next fix. They've circled around him like a children's game. His skin frosted with sweat and sky, hair drenched in black blood, a smile wide and clean. The man clutching the rope didn't look like a man at all, or, if you rather, he looked like every man in the world combined. When my mother laid her head on the bosom of the oak lunette, I thought about my own death, as is only natural. But now I was thinking about the death of every person outside of me, of God himself, of the tender gore and the delicious silence, of the chance to finally be alone together. The last time I met him, John told me that love wasn't something he needed. I told him I know, and that I loved this about him. But then he told me love wasn't something he desired either, and that's when I stopped understanding. He fucked me until the windows sang. He had never fucked such a beautiful girl. I just needed something to hold on to.

I worked my way through the crowd, close enough to smell John's sweets: saliva like a can of paint thinner, soiled pants like a pot of steamed broccoli. He was smiling at the lady who wore pigtails every day. Doesn't he know that I, too, would wear pigtails every day if only I looked good in pigtails? How could he? I clicked my heels on the brown red of the ground below me and for a second, John's pupils sank well beyond mine. A pearly white pain raped my throat and then the rest of it. His face seized inward and he sneezed a brutal sneeze, a sneeze that shook his skull, causing the frame of the guillotine to jostle, and the blade to come bearing down preemptively.

His neck snapped, his head bounced off the platform and rolled toward me, scalene strings of blood slapping my shiny shoes like a whip, his eyes vaginal and coarse, his smile all the same. John never liked touching me in front of other people. John never liked when I talked for him. If someone doesn't want you, does that mean they don't want you forever? I used to ask this question every day, and every day I got it wrong. It was always changing while I had the courtesy to stay the same. I bent down to kiss its forehead and crushed the weight of my stomach. The lady with pigtails screamed in my ear. The rope fell limp and the man with it. I said bless you.

Everyone clutched their noses tight and bowed their heads in silence when I walked out. John always had his own ending. I hoped he could still find his way out, roof and all. I stood in the bright cloth of snowlight and thought how I should probably start a war of my own. Of course, they'd have to come up with a new name. But it was about time.

An Interview With Gordon Abel Mortim-er-Randell The Second

My name is Henry Fields. I am a reporter, a journalist, a husband, a father, and a novelist. I have traveled to actively war-torn countries to report on the inhumane horrors that took the lives of many of my colleagues. I have interviewed some of the most influential figures of our time, including, but not limited to, Elon Musk, Alexandria Ocasio-Cortez, Drew Weissman, and Sydney Sweeney. I have written three novels, the most recent of which has sold over 900,000 copies and earned me a Hugo Award. But what you are about to read, right here, right now, may be my magnum opus.

He is not comfortable in his own skin. He avoids eye contact like the plague and takes a moment trying to remember his own name. He has down-turned green eyes and sparse brows that maintain a furrowed position, as if everything he looks at dares to look back at him. His handshake is firm, long-lasting, sticky. He's tall, buff, much bigger than anticipated. His stance is wide and his gait heavy—the room feels like an arena with him in it, as if we are about to fight to the death, and I'm filling the role of his unworthy competitor. The man I'm talking about is the terribly elusive and frankly ingenious author of *To Bleed Quietly*, Gordon Abel Mortimer-Randell the Second. We meet in a hotel on East 77th. I bring my assistant, my equipment; he brings no one and nothing. Not even a phone. He says he can only travel if "untethered." After perfunctory niceties, he excuses himself to the bathroom. He stays in there for nearly forty-five minutes. We hear puking sounds—lots of gurgling, flushing, and some vague barking noises. My assistant, Harper Daly, checks on him several times throughout. I use this as an opportunity to jot down my thoughts on him so far, to look over my questions, to test my recorder. When he returns, his jeans carry a dark splotch over the crotch area. His right eyelid is twitching. He smells of malt vinegar and Febreze.

HF: Gordon. What a pleasure, an honor, to be here with you today. Truly. I've started recording—is that okay?

GAMRTS: Yes. Well—yes. Why is she here?

(Gordon points to Harper with a shaking pinky.)

HF: Oh, Harper? Just to take notes and whatnot.

(Gordon repeatedly slaps his face with both hands, possibly an attempt to wake himself up.)

HF: Are you comfortable? Is that chair fine?

GAMRTS: …

HF: Right, yes. I have to begin with the question that will, without a doubt, be on everyone's minds: Why are you here today? You are famously untraceable. You have rejected interviews and public appearances for decades now. You have nothing but contempt for the media—I mean, you've been arrested five times for physically assaulting paparazzi, some of whom weren't even photographing you, so why the change of heart? Why now? And, selfishly, I must ask: Why me?

(Gordon begins fingering his right ear with his left pointer finger.)

GAMRTS: Um—let's see. You're…good.

HF: I'm good?

GAMRTS: You're good. You're a good writer.

(Gordon grimaces and wheezes a high-pitched whistling sound, as if his finger is hurting his ear, yet he continues digging anyway.)

HF: Well…thank you.

GAMRTS: You've done very well for yourself. Very

successful, across multiple sectors of the literary world. You're a real…trailblazer. Many people love you. My son loved you.

HF: Oh, past tense, huh?

(Henry laughs. Gordon does not.)

HF: Um, but surely other successful writers have reached out to you, no?

(It is worth pointing out that Gordon's pointer is now knuckle-deep in his ear canal.)

GAMRTS: …

HF: S-Secondly, I want to emphasize once again how grateful I am to speak with you today. I'm sure many others are vying for this position, but I feel confident in claiming myself as your number one fan. Or at least one of your number one fans—ha. I read *To Bleed Quietly* at twenty-two years old, and it obliterated me in the best way. Completely changed my life, and that is no exaggeration. I mean, I even named the protagonist in my latest book after you—Gordon, I named him.

(Gordon sneezes into his hand. He wipes the snot on the chair's armrest.)

HF: Well…let's get on to the questions, why don't we?

GAMRTS: Yes, good idea.

HF: I'd be remiss if I didn't ask about the novel first. The people want to know—how much is fiction and how much is truth drawn from your own life? Do you relate to the character Troy? Is Troy's childhood loosely based on your own—your time being swapped around different foster homes?

(Gordon slaps his thighs. Then, he stands up and heads to the minibar. He chugs one shooter of vodka. Then a second, and then a third.)

GAMRTS: Hm. You didn't ask me about my upbringing.

HF: No, well, my team and I did a bit of research—
GAMRTS: You see how that's degrading in a way, don't you? If you had asked about my upbringing, I would have told you. But your knowledge carries… arrogance. A good interviewer assumes he knows very little.
(Gordon sits back down and belches. Spittle sprays onto Henry's face, which both men ignore.)
HF: Well, I wanted to be prepared and, I mean, there are public records available, a-and—
GAMRTS: I empathize with Troy a great deal. Existing devoid of parental love is a unique kind of terror. It makes you less of a person and more of a thing waiting to be killed. I see his dysfunctional relationship with sex as a search for a mother—search for warmth, for bodily validation. I see his homicidal tendencies as a search for a father—search for blood, for a mission, for legacy. But I'm sure you've already ascertained all of this.
HF: Wow. And just going back a bit, I'd like to extend my sincerest apologies. I would never want to offend you with misinformation or what you feel is an obstruction of privacy. I would like this to be a safe space that encourages open and honest communication.
(Gordon rolls his shirt sleeves up. Then, he cuffs his jeans. Then, he knocks three times on the roof of both of his shoes.)
HF: So, back to the book: much of the controversy surrounds the supposed stereotyping it instills of orphans growing up to become murderers. Some have found it an ugly stigma that perpetuates the idea that those without living parents are mentally ill or violent.
(Gordon makes a noise that sounds like a hiccup.)
GAMRTS: Yes. Where's the question?
HF: Well, how would you respond to that? Do you

agree that the book feeds into this…disparaging narrative?

GAMRTS: I'd respond by saying that those people are lacking, fundamentally, spiritually, in empathy. I think some of them are not even capable of empathy. They say they understand the trauma Troy goes through, but those are only words. If they truly understood, then there would be no confusion, no controversy. Each and every one of Troy's actions would make perfect sense.

HF: Right…interesting. But something can "make sense" per se and still be immoral, no? Still dangerous? Justification is a slippery slope.

(Gordon coughs up a substantial amount of phlegm, holds it in his mouth for a few seconds, then swallows it back.)

GAMRTS: There is no danger in truth. There is only danger in those who try to take that truth away. Let's move on.

HF: Yes, let's. Um, so, this book was written over four decades ago now, and there was a lot of vivid imagery of gay sex, that is, sex scenes between Troy and the male prostitutes.

GAMRTS: Yes.

HF: What was it like receiving the homophobic backlash at the time, especially as an eighteen-year-old? I mean, what was it like as an eighteen-year-old in general, writing what would turn out to be such an iconic cultural artifact and being constantly bombarded with so much…conflicting attention? You had grown adults theorizing about your love life, tracking your every movement, sending you death threats. I can't imagine—

GAMRTS: They were not empowering. The sex scenes were not empowering.

HF: Right, no—I never said they were—

GAMRTS: They were not empowering, nor were they nefarious. They were a product of a lonely man who didn't know how to like people—he was never taught. Homophobia seemed completely irrelevant. He liked having sex with men because he only knew of himself—no more than that. Nor were they even sexual. They involved bodily insertion and ejaculation, but an itch that is scratched does not carry sociopolitical connotations, so why should that?

HF: Right. Right. Well—

GAMRTS: I'm not trying to be vague. I'm answering the questions the only way I know how.

HF: No, it's great—you're doing great. And—

GAMRTS: As far as the attention goes, it's always been quite easy for me to tune out the voices of strangers. But I understand that's not the case for everyone. For some people, it can drive them to their demise.

HF: Yes, well, speaking of, I have to say: I loved the ending. Suicide can be such a cliché. Some writers employ this trope out of laziness—easy shock value, greedy symbolism, quick satisfaction. Yet Troy's death felt deeply original. It felt fated, as if what he went through was not a suicide at all. It felt like a different inevitable state of human condition: a third, nameless thing, sitting between life and death.

(Gordon scrunches his nose and looks into space for a moment, thinking.)

GAMRTS: No—it was just lazy. Fearful, really.

HF: Right. Um, well, so, here's something I'm dying to know: have you written anything over the last few decades? Should we expect a new book any time soon? I mean that is why you're meeting with me, correct? Publicity for your next project?

(Gordon slowly wipes his face with his hands. Henry begins to, possibly subconsciously, copy him. He then catches himself and stops. Gordon laughs.)

GAMRTS: I have written, yes. I wrote a great deal in my thirties when I first moved to Texas with my boyfriend. I also wrote a lot a couple of years ago, when I lost my son. I got quite into poetry. I'll publish some poems in literary magazines under different pseudonyms. That's about all I'm going to give you.

HF: Oh, I had no idea—I'm so—

GAMRTS: Tate was my boyfriend. Tate Pugliese. And my son, Gordon The Third, although most called him by his middle name, Milo. They're both gone now. I'm sure you know this.

HF: Um, no, I-I didn't actually—

GAMRTS: Oh, where did that cache of knowledge go? I thought you were prepared?

(Henry leans back in his chair. Gordon leans forward.)

HF: Um—I don't exactly get—

GAMRTS: Of course, I am even more disappointed, seeing as though Milo should be a name you remember as well. Ha! And I thought my memory was going.

HF: …

GAMRTS: But they're the only reason it's not. I only keep my mind sharp so I can hold onto those memories, really. Of Tate spelling words on my back with his finger as I'm trying to fall asleep. I was never able to guess what he was writing. But I remember the pressure of his touch. Light and calloused. Slow and shaky—especially near the end.

HF: …

GAMRTS: And, of course, Milo's laugh. Having a happy child is all I ever wished for, and it's exactly what I got. He'd get into these laughing fits as a kid, to the point of tears and wheezing, and all I did was imitate a fart noise with my mouth, o-or put a sock over my hand and talk. Sometimes, I caught glimpses of that laugh in his teens, in his early twenties, even. Of course, not near the end—no.

HF: …

GAMRTS: Creating a family—a world—out of two people, it's a beautiful thing. Especially when it's two people not given to you, but earned. Because it is all truth. But truth is delicate. Truth, remember, can be taken away.

(Henry rubs his hands together, anxiously, and repeatedly looks to Harper.)

HF: I'm sorry, Gordon, I don't—

GAMRTS: No, I'm sorry, I'm being vague again, aren't I? Cryptic? It's not easy for me to be clear, but let me try. You write about real things and fake things—you write about genocide, and you write about minotaurs. My boyfriend was interested in reading the former, my son in the latter. They were both big readers, of course—I could never surround myself with anything less. They both found you, loved you. In very different ways, for very different reasons. I found you just okay. None of us were all that interested in your interviews.

HF: Gordon, I don't—we may have to wrap up—

GAMRTS: So—let me finish, Henry, let me finish—so, they went to one of your events, the kind where you talk about yourself on a stage and hundreds of people pay to listen. There was one nearby, you were in Austin. They wanted to hear you speak, see your face in person—ugly that desire is. Perverse. The fascination they had with you reminded me of the way much of the public saw me when I was a teenager, so, naturally, I was disgusted by it. Disturbed. I never said this to them. I needed them to realize on their own just how harmful these kinds of relationships can be.

(Henry uncrosses his legs. Then he crosses them. Then he uncrosses them. He's now sweating profusely.)

HD: Oh, God, what did he do?

HF: Harper, stay the fuck out of this!

GAMRTS: Milo had always been a nervous boy with an uneasy stomach. But his excitement to meet you outweighed his anxiety. Of course, the anxiety was still there. While standing in line to ask you a question, he felt quite ill, but he didn't want to lose his place. So… my son shit his pants.

HF: Oh, um. Well, that doesn't—

GAMRTS: And someone had taken a video and posted it on Twitter.

(Henry and Harper gasp.)

GAMRTS: He only left once enough people started pointing and laughing. Within a week, the video of Milo running with soiled jeans and shit-stained footprints to the nearest bathroom got four million views. I'm just glad Tate was there for him when I couldn't be.

(Henry uncomfortably shifts in his chair. He covers his mouth, which is now holding back laughter.)

GAMRTS: "Shitmeister," they called him. The hashtag "MuddyMilo" was trending for months—people found out who he was, where he lived. He received death threats, worse than any kind I ever got. He couldn't go outside without a group of prepubescent boys berating him with insults and miming flatulence sound effects with their armpits. He killed himself because of the amount of bullying. He ingested crushed apple seeds—we found the pitted apples under his bed. It was the same way Gordon died in your book.

He idolized you to the end. He always felt like you were writing about him. As if writers in this day and age are even capable of such compassion.

(Henry's face twitches into an uncomfortable frown.)

GAMRTS: Of course, that didn't work—he had nowhere near enough seeds, so he immediately ran into oncoming traffic. My nosy neighbor told me this.

HF: Oh, my…my condol—

GAMRTS: That didn't work either—three people died, two were seriously injured, but Milo came away unscathed. No one knows exactly how he went, but the police found his body in a dumpster six miles away. Forensics couldn't figure it out. I don't even get the pleasure of knowing the answers.

HF: I'm really, truly—

GAMRTS: Things with Tate got messy. I was no longer a good partner. I didn't know how to be after losing everything that was mine. The breakup was long, tumultuous—painful. I remember—and I hate myself for it—creating a Twitter account months later to stalk him. I saw that he still followed you, still regularly engaged with your posts, even after everything that happened. That was a knife to the heart, it was.

(Henry habitually kneads a handful of thigh fat.)

GAMRTS: You seem curious as to why I reject the media, but it seems so painfully obvious. Because of this. If I let fame into my life, I would've likely turned into some diluted version of you. A version of a person that should never exist.

HF: Gordon, I am so sorry…but I also don't see how I can be blamed for this.

GAMRTS: You were laughing. In the background of the "viral" video, you were laughing into your microphone and pointing—pointing at my baby. This prompted more people to record. You were no doubt high on multiple substances; I did my research on you as well. You seem sober enough today, though, which is good. Yes, that's good.

HF: …

(Gordon stands up. His joints crack. His eye twitch returns.)

GAMRTS: Oh, and you retweeted the video with the caption "My work brings out the best in people, it seems" with a laughing-face emoji. And a praying-hands emoji. And the turd emoji.

(Henry stands up and backs away.)

GAMRTS: This is not revenge, by the way. This is fueled by logic, not emotion. I don't want you to think for a moment that you're going out based on a madman's whim.

(Gordon pulls a Swiss Army knife from his jeans pocket. His stomach grumbles. A thick, wet fart slips out.)

HF: Okay, Harper, grab him or something!

(Gordon runs and grabs Henry. He stabs him in the chest three times. Then twice in the stomach. Blood sprays like a rotating sprinkler. Henry's right fist clenches, but does not fight.)

HF: No! Stop! I—Grrrggeellgleg, grrgle, glugg, grr

(Gordon cleans off the blade with his sleeve and slashes his own throat, falling atop Henry. It all happens faster than eyes can acknowledge. Gordon belches blood into Henry's open mouth.)

GAMRTS: Blrbbr, bleerrrg, blurg, blurghh, bler

This concludes the interview. Harper Daly is the sole survivor and continues to tell her story today.[1]

---

[1] *Hello. My name is Harper Catherine Daly. I was Henry Fields' assistant, and I was present for his death. Henry wrote the first couple of paragraphs, and I transcribed the interview. Gordon didn't want to*

be filmed, which is why I was asked to take notes. I added details about Gordon's and Henry's idiosyncratic physical mannerisms, as you read — it felt significant since this interview turned into more of a recorded murder. I wanted to get this piece out there under Henry's name, since he did so much preparation, and was obviously very excited about meeting Gordon. Many are unhappy with me for not stepping in, but those people have never witnessed a murder themselves. They don't know the shock involved. The paralysis and the dissociation. The pure hope that what you're seeing is anything but reality. But, of course, I understand the desire to blame the last living thing.

Every time I checked on Gordon in the bathroom, he would be hunched over the toilet, cradling the seat, with this string of vomit hanging from his lower lip, and he'd say "Don't look, dear. Just don't look." I, of course, assumed he meant at that moment. I'm not exactly sure why Gordon didn't kill Henry from the get-go. Maybe there was a part of him that did want to do the interview. I think he did want to be seen, did want the fame. He just wanted it under the pretense of dignity.

Henry's wife and daughter deny knowing anything about the #MuddyMilo Twitter discourse and ask for privacy during this period of bereavement — they specifically request that people stop with the offensive memes about the deceased and refrain from commenting certain gleeful GIFs under their memorial posts on Instagram, such as Rachel and Phoebe from Friends happily jumping, or even the one of Shaquille O'Neal shimmying.

This interview will be loosely adapted into a limited series called *To Kill Loudly: An Author's Revenge; The Story of Gordon Abel Mortimer-Randell the Second, Told By Harper Daly,* set to stream exclusively on Netflix, premiering in July 2027, with me, Harper Daly, serving as executive producer, writer, and director.

My Angel Baby / Click Here For A Picture Of My Pussy

I can only tolerate faggots nowadays, forreal. For friends I mean. I'm really not tryna mess with anything with a dick, like a real one, y'know. They still tryna bang, with me looking like a whale and everything, it's crazy. Not one cent to their name neither, like. Girls fuckin' suck, too—they're jealous. They don't have my looks, or my money, or, like, my purpose, y'know? Like now I have purpose, you feel me, and they can't fuckin' stand it, God damn. Anyway I'm alternating a few fags. It's the butch half-fag I met at the strip club Eli and that dopehead fag I met at church Jeremy and then the really gay fag I'm talkin' to now. Punt. We walkin' out 7/11 now. He got the Bushmills, so the slurpees was on me. He got Coke, I got Minecraft flavor.

"Are you sure you're alright? To, like, drink?"

Minecraft flavor be tasting like, fuckin', dish soap and peanuts. I like it though. I nod at Punt lettin' him know to put more Bushmills in my cup.

"Look, at the end of the day, I'm not playin' 'round wit my baby, like, I'm not. But listen, my granddaddy told me how when I was a baby, he put whiskey on my gums to help me wit teething when my momma wasn't looking. And, fuckin', look at me now, wit all my mothafuckin' teeth."

I smile real big. Punt laughs.

"So it can't be that bad for, like, a not-born baby to have, like. Wanna stay 'way from LSD and vodka, though. Those are the main ones."

"Oh."

We walkin' t'wards the train tracks now. I showed it to him yesterday. Punt said he likes to watch trains go by, like a real fag. Sometimes, there're foxes and squirrels and I can throw sticks at 'em. Punt a real pansy-ass bitch. He's 'fraid of the squirrels, 'fraid of the sticks, he 'fraid of me, God damn! He's like seventeen or some shit. Only fag at his high school. We met, like, two days ago—he was cryin' to the Indian motel guy, sayin' he got no money, but he ran 'way from home, and he need a place to stay. I cuh tell he was a homo by the way he was standin', y'know what I mean, and I was just getting done with that day's trick so I told him to stay with me. Ever since I got pregnant, I been real kind, real gracious. That's what a baby do to you, it's lowkey beautiful.

"Your name so fuckin' retarded."

Punt trips over the tracks and almost eats shit—almost. I laugh.

"Oh—yeah, well, I don't know if you should, like, say that—"

"*Punt, Punt, Punt,*" I say in a real retarded voice.

He looks hurt. Poor Punt. I've let him stay with me the past coupl'a nights, cuh he real quiet, real nice guest. But he gotta start earnin', I tell him. I ain't no breadwinner. One day my looks gonna go, and the tricks will be done gone with 'em, like, I know this. He almost an adult, too. He needsta learn responsibility, like. I find a stick, throw it in the closest bush. I hear something kinda yelp—I laugh. Punt looks like he's laughing but also kinda like he needsa take a shit. I lay back on the grass. Punt still standin' to get a good look, real patient like. I like Punt, I do. I tol' him how I run away from home, too. We got that in common.

"Should be here soon…"

Punt lookin' at me all squeamish. Like I got a

nipple out. I check. All clear.

"What? You wanna ask me somethin'?"

He sits down, Indian style. He throwin' sticks at the tracks.

"I was just—I'm grateful for you putting me up, like, I'm gonna find a place soon, but I'm just curious. About the sex work."

I laugh 'cause he says nothin'. It's like this bitch needs permission to talk. My phone buzzes which catches his attention. Man, this bitch nosy as hell.

"Well, just, like—does it affect the baby? You're pretty big now and, I don't know, I was just curious."

I lay back. Ion need to look at his face—ion need pity. Ion need anyone's pity. The cloud above me kinda look like a dog with cat ears. Or like a cat with a dog tail. Or like a giant turd.

"Damn, bitch. It's like—well, I don't let anyone unprotected, you feel? And I let no one front door, like. Not a soul. I don't want nobody fucking up the path meant for My Angel Baby. So they go backdoor. Damn, it's like you—you really think I'm not…prepared and shit. Not responsible."

"Oh, no, I'm sorry. I didn't mean that, I swear."

Wind howling, grass itchin' my arms. Would be real cool if the train came right about now.

"So…backdoor? Doesn't that press on your belly?"

He even look gay sittin' down. All postured, straight up, and shit. Hands folded. Punt's black, too. Black homo. I be wondering if he got bullied a lot, I dunno. That's why he ran away. He's so young, he don't even know how hard life can get. Can't get too sweet on him now. Not good for 'im.

"Got special pillows."

Punt nods. My belly be lookin' beautiful from this angle. Wearin' my comfy trackpants that ride low, and my pink halter top, so my belly get a chance to breathe. It feels more like a part of me than anything else, like, if I was just this belly, that'd be alright with me.

"What are you gonna name…it?"

I think I hear an animal rustling or some shit, but there's nothin' here.

"Her."

"Oh, her—sorry."

My Angel Baby kicks. I see that little foot right near where my belly button used to be. She can hear me, she can.

"Well. I dunno. I just been calling her My Angel Baby. But that's gotta nice ring, right?"

Punt is alla sudden real quiet, but My Angel Baby still kickin'. My belly got these pink and brown stripes that turn white under the sun. They look real pretty under the sun, they do, like pearls, they do. I hear someone laugh—no, like, a buncha people laughin'. Some music, too. Sounds like it's coming from the woods, behind me.

"Hear that?"

"What? Hear what?"

Oh, Punt. Punt, Punt, Punt.

"It's people. Let's go."

It takes real effort for me to get up. Punt tries givin' me a hand, but ion need 'im. I start to walk into the woods, rubbin' my belly, lettin' her know I'm still here.

"Wait! But the train hasn't come yet!"

I laugh. The clouds part as if we was going that way.

"And it never will!"

2.

It's jussa buncha kids, smokin' dope and drinkin' and fuckin'. There's a keg and a speaker playin' Fetty Wap. Iss mostly guys—young guys. Few girls. Girls look at me with a real stank ass look, like they judgin' me. I tell you, this is why I don't fuck with girls, man. They're snickerin' and shit, like. Some guys be lookin' at me all excited, but some like little bitches. They 'fraid of a strong, independent woman, like.

"Yo! Who do we got here?"

Asian boy with a real small face says this. He smilin' and blinkin'—he look coked out as hell.

"What's good. I'm Lee, this my boy Punt."

He look me up and down, still smilin'. He don't look at Punt.

"Word, word…look guys—we got a pregnant bitch!"

Errybody roars and cheers and whatever—mostly the guys. Girls still laughin' and shit. Some white boys are moanin' like they're funny and shit—I just put my tongue through my fingers at 'em, ion give a fuck. White guy and black girl having sex on that tree over there, like no decency whatsoever, the fuck. She moanin' like it hurt, and he givin' a thumbs up to Asian boy while he cummin' inside her. Asian boy laughs.

"I'm gonna get some beer…"

Punt finished his drink so he makin' a beeline for the keg. I only drink beer when I'm hungover, plus my slurpee's still goin'. Brown boy with face tattoos comin' up to me. His jeans be basically 'round his ankles. He smells like rotten pussy and pork roll.

"Yo, so you like from around here or?"

"Do it matter, or…?"

"Nah, word, nah, I guess not."

He uses his shirt to wipe sweat off his face. His stomach real flat. He prolly feels real empty inside.

"Let me refill that for you."

He's pointing to my slurpee cup. His pupils are fuckin' huge, man, his eyes like wet and shit.

"Nah. I'm good."

He laugh and then say something in some fuckin' language ion know.

"Damn, bitch. Just tryna help."

"Okay, fine—fine. Whiskey."

He winks at me and takes my cup. I've always been lucky with men, ion feel bad about it. I got big tits and soft hair and a real big mouth. They love that shit. I could be fuckin' knocked up and actin' like a bitch, and they still want more. I go by Punt. He's talkin' to the black girl who was getting her pussy pounded a second ago.

"Yeah, we all go to high school together. Silver Oak?"

The black girl says this. She be soundin' real quiet, real shy for a girl havin' sex on a tree.

"Oh, yeah. I've heard of it. I'm actually not from around here, I'm—"

"He's wit me."

Punt don't know shit, obviously. He gon' be telling these strangers all our goddamn business. The black girl looks awkward, like. I look 'round. Lotta people are dancin' now. One kid throwing up purple into a bush.

"Oh. Cool. So, um, how old are you guys?"

"Fifteen."

Damn, dude. Poor Punt.

"Oh, okay. I'm seventeen."

They both lookin' at me, like.

"Yeah. Same 'ere."

We getta dancin' for a lil' bit. All I can really do is shake ass with my belly like this, but whatever. Black girl is dancin' real sexy, all the guys are eyein' her. I hope she ain't no homie hopper or nothin'. Hope she's careful. Punt dancin' kinda weird. Voguein' and shit, ion e'en know. It's kinda funny, actually. But some girls are laughing at 'im and some guys whisperin', like. Alla sudden, errybody passin' 'round a phone, laughin' and shit. Some people stop dancin', stop drinkin', just lookin' at the phone. And they lookin' at me. Lookin' at me and Punt. They got a picture of me or sum'in? And why they laughin'—what's so fuckin' funny? I feel like I hear my name. I didn't even tell those motherfuckers my real name. I take the phone from a skinny ass white boy—ion give a fuck. But it ain't me, it ain't. It's a website. It's porn. For a girl named Moody Sinclair. She's got her big ass tits out, and her big ass ass out. Big, fat white girl with a real pretty face. Tiny mouth, but still real pretty. I scroll— white boy is trying to take the phone like he got no manners or shit. There's a button. **CLICK HERE FOR A PICTURE OF MY PUSSSY**. I click. I click the next button to pay the charge—goes straight through white boy's phone. He's screaming at me now, calling me fat, calling me a cunt. Who raised this boy? And who's got this kinda pussy? Pink and tight and shiny. It's entrancing and shit. Like a third eye. I ain't gay or nothin', but this shit is beautiful. Like it's not even sexual, it's somethin' else. It's somethin' else.

"What the fuck, dude?"

"I ain't no dude, bitch."

He rip his phone from my hand, and he don't care no more after looking at the fuckin' screen. He showing all his friends, and they're all laughin' again. A different laugh from the first laugh. A kinda shocked kinda laugh. A kinda horny laugh. It's all so gross, highkey, like. See—this is why I stick with fags. Get no fuckin' respect, you heard.

"C'mon. Let's go, Punt."

'Cept I don't where Punt is. He's refilling his cup. Now his hand on his hip and shit. One of the skinny white boys call him a faggot, and some others, too. The one with the fucked up teeth says it real loud, though. He's cornerin' Punt, askin' him to suck his dick, tryna be funny and shit. Punt don't look scared but he don't look happy neither. He just look still like a statue. White boy still hollerin', talkin' shit. I go up to him and punch him square in the fuckin' mouth. Knock one of those fuckin' fucked up teeth out.

"What the fuck?!"

He fall back onto the keg, slammin' hard, like it sound like it hurt, like his back cracked like a stick, I'm tellin' you. He crying on the ground, rolling around and shit. His mouth's all red. Some of his homeboys are laughin, others are screamin' at me, some are eye-in' Punt.

"Run."

And I swear, we both look at each other, and we run like fuckin' lightning, bitch. I've never run while with My Angel Baby. It's like double-gravity. Like weights at my ankles, you heard, like I'm goin' backwards. The grass is real muddy like, and it's hot as all hell, but I love it, I do. My Angel Baby still kickin'—she wants to run, too.

"Are they still comin'?"

I'm so outta breath, like. And running in flip-flops ain't easy neither. Punt looks behind and stops. He shakes his head, holds his chest. I turn. Such pussies. Some ran only a few yards, just for looks. Tryna look macho and shit. Little boys they are, really.

"Don' worry about 'em. They're fuckin' retards."

Punt kinda laugh. His face all wet. I can't tell if it's sweat or tears neither.

"Yeah…they're retards."

3.

We walkin' back to the motel now—needa put my feet up, needa get ready for tonight's trick. Punt be sleepin' on the floor, but I give him pillows and shit. I need the bed myself, I am pregnant after all, like. My phone won't stop buzzin' and shit—it's annoying the hell outta Punt. I look at him before he gets the chance to ask a question.

"I know the number. It just ain't someone I'm tryna mess wit right now, thasall. Don't worry about it."

He nods like he understands. Sun almost settin' now. The sky is blue but clouds are pink. Smells like dog shit and French fries.

"Thanks for doing that…by the way. Thanks."

Punt smilin', his face still wet. We pass a Mc-Donald's. Homeless guy be shakin' and shit. Dressed in a winter coat despite it being hot as all hell. I get the loose change from my pocket and put it in his shaky cup.

"Don't worry 'bout it."

When we finally get back to the motel, my trick is there waiting for me, like. Twenty minutes early. He's not like my other clients, like, he a real clean-looking guy. Suit and tie, like. Prolly got a job doing with money, like banker. He prolly a banker. His smile real creepy, too. Real big. Ion like when guys have big mouths. He got gray hair, all done up nice, though, like. Real *Pretty Woman* situation goin' on 'ere. I tell Punt to wait in the lobby and he nods.

"Well, hello, there, Ms. Lee."

"Hey. Come in."

All I be knowin' about him is his "name" is Joseph and he likes anal. All he be knowin' 'bout me is my name Lee and I only supply anal. I usually find these fuckers in real life, they're usually beggin' me to hit or sum'in. But sometimes, when demand is low, I use this lowkey sketchy-ass site. Since I've been pregnant, I've, like, mainly used the site.

"Lovely place you got here."

He lyin'. The ceiling's got water damage and shit, the bathroom walls sound like there's a family of rats. Whole place smells like milk. But I know he just talkin' to talk, so, whatever.

"Yeah, word."

He seem like a normal n'uff guy, besides the mouth. And he's short, but I like the shorties. Less to them means less chance they'll be able to kill or rape me, you heard. Always got a knife in my bedside table, too. Never be too careful. I always make sure we do the deed in a spot where I can grab the knife pretty easily, like. He actually look kinda nervous, just walkin' 'round the room like that, rubbin' his hands together. His fingers shakin', his breath all weird and spiky. Men are usually nervous at first, then get comfortable. He's goin' backwards.

"So, h-how's your day, sweetheart?"

I go up to him, I kiss him real hard, tongue and everything. His tongue shy at first, but after a minute he gets into it. He grabs my ass, tries touchin' my belly but I just move his hand to my left tit. I set up my special pillows, I grab the lube next to the knife, and we do the mothafuckin' deed, like, that's all there is to it.

"Fucking hell. That was good. Thanks, sweetheart."

He slaps my ass real fuckin' hard and throws a few hundreds at my feet. That never changes, the fuckin' cockiness they feel af'twards. Gross, highkey.

"Yup."

I grab the cash, pull up my underwear. He smilin' that big-ass Jack Nicholson kinda smile, like. He wash his hands in the bathroom, and then leaves without sayin' nothin' more. I get dressed, go down to grab Punt. He drinkin' the Bushmill's with the Indian motel guy. They laughin' and shit.

"Punt. We good, so."

They both look at me like I just slapped they momma. Feel like I'm interruptin' somethin' and shit.

"Oh, cool, cool. We were just talking about—"

"You can't do that here, you know."

Indian motel guy alla sudden got a voice.

"Do what?" I ask.

"I don't give a fuck. But they're replacing me with a real corporate guy—replacing alotta people that work here. They won't let you, so. Just get prepared."

How the fuck does this bitch know what I do? He just assumin', like? It's fucked. It's offensive, man, I mean. He dunno shit. He don't. I been staying here for the past coupl'a years, mindin' my mothafuckin' business, like. Can't start, like, not even gonna go there. I just wave on Punt and we walk back to our room. That's why I like Punt, he loyal like a dog.

"He dunno shit."

Punt nods like he agrees. I open the door, can't tell if it's me or the room, but someth'n smells like a infected toenail, like. Like dick cheese.

"Ima shower."

Punt nod and lay on my special pillows. I turn the faucet, let the water get hot. Listen to the rats talkin' to each other. Take off my clothes. My body look real fuckin' weird naked, like. All lumpy and stretchy. And my face looks tired, man. I'm gettin' forehead wrinkles, like, I can tell. My eyes all tired, saggin' like my tits. I pull my skin back, tryna see what I could look like. Could be smooth, tight, shiny. Nah—it don't matter, it don't. Priorities, like. Gonna have to look for jobs for Punt, tomorrow. He gettin' a lil' too comfortable, I can tell. The rats real active tonight, damn, like—wait, no. I hear voices. Like, people talkin'. Punt got somebody over? Where his fuckin' manners? I turn off the shower and run out with my towel on and errything. I see him talkin' to someone on my phone, like.

"What the fuck?!"

"Yes, she's here, and she's safe. She's right here, actua—"

"Hang the fuck up! Now!"

He hang up. I see the number that was callin' and then I get even madder.

"I'm sorry, I-I read the texts, so I decided to answer when she called—I was just trying to help you like you—"

"I don't need your mothafuckin' help, you hear me? You hear me, Punt?"

He look so sad. He look like a lil' puppy. Like he 'bout to cry. He ain't ready for the world, he truly ain't. He don't even know. And he still sittin' on my special pillows.

"Yes. Yes, Lee, I—I'm so sorry."

I take my phone. Ain't in the mood to shower now, like. I take the Bushmills and drink the last sips. He get off my bed, sit on his pillow on the floor.

"It was—"

"I know who it was. Drop it, Punt."

I climb into bed. I turn my phone like way off. Punt fiddlin' with someth'n in his pocket. I look at him, like what now.

"Zahir gave me some of his leftover ecstasy."

He holds up a baggie of white shit and kinda smiles.

"Who the fuck Zear?"

"Zahir. The clerk. We were just talking to."

I nod. He got no survival instincts, like. Makin' friends with the most useless people, shit, man. Someone gon' take advantage of him one day, and I won't be there to protect him, you hear. The rats talkin' comes back.

"So do you wanna?"

My back all fucked from the runnin'—I put a special pillow underneath it.

"Nah."

He be lookin' like a lil' puppy again. Goddammnit, Punt.

"I ain't your fuckin' momma. Do what you want."

He snort some white shit and I rub my big belly. She sleepin' right now, I can tell. She real still, real heavy, My Angel Baby. I go on my phone, look up that Moody Sinclair bitch. I know it's weird, but I just like staring at her pussy, I do, like. Her clit kinda be lookin' like that dangly thing in your mouth, her vagina hole so dark like that shit go on for miles. I bet men love to eat that bitch out, with a pretty pussy like that. I take a screenshot, like.

"Our day—our life is almost like TV. Like, have you seen *Gummo*? It's like the movies."

I laugh. His nose is all white, his pupils big and wet. He s'pposed to be home right now. With a real bed and everything. S'pposed to be in school. Prolly has someone lookin' for 'im somewhere. Prolly.

"Yeah, Punt. Sure is."

4.

I wake up, both my tits out, back sore as hell. Check my phone. The other guys, Eli and Jeremy, they been ditchin' me, like. Ain't answer my texts or nothin'. Haven't seen 'em in weeks. Last time I saw Eli, he was shootin' up as he was gettin' a lap dance at the club. And Jeremy was talkin' to a homeless guy about Jesus and shit. I really don't got much in common with 'em, now that I think 'bout it. Neither of 'em have really found themselves, like. Or maybe they have, and that's just who they are, ion know.

"You believe in karma, Punt?"

'Cept Punt ain't here, his pillow all empty, like. Hear a knock at the door. Maybe Punt got coffee.

Still naked so I put on my striped maternity dress that make me look like a beach ball. I open the door. 'Cept it ain't Punt. It's her. It's Chelsea. Motherfucker.

"Oh my god. Oh my god, Kay. You're huge—you're pregnant!"

She still look the same. Still tall with that real Jewish nose. Still her dark, frizzy hair and her red lipstick. She try huggin' me, but it's real awkward like with my big belly in the way. My Angel Baby, protectin' me.

"The fuck are you doing here?"

She laughin' like I'm kiddin'. She try lookin' at the room behind me, so I close the door a bit, like.

"Ya'know what, I ain't wanna know. I want you to get out. Leave, like."

She sighs. She don't move an inch.

"You know I can't do that, Kay—I don't want to do that. Look, can we talk? Please?"

She look fat, kinda—just her stomach, it's all bulging. She pregnant?

"Fine, then *I'll* mothafuckin' leave."

I grab my cigarettes, close the door behind me. I starta walk downstairs but she just follow me, like. She real fast, too.

"We're worried about you, seriously. We just want you to come back home. Your parents haven't seen you in five—"

"Shut da fuck up."

The Indian motel guy ain't here today, issa different guy. Some bald, fat dude. He starin' at me like a real bitch, like I done somethin'. I can't—not now. I walk out the lobby, ain't holdin' the door open for Chelsea—ion give a fuck.

"I'm confused…is this a joke? Why are you

talking like—"

I light my mothafuckin' cigarette.

"What the fuck?! Put that out!"

She try taking the fag from my hand, but I just swat it away and put my fist up, like.

"Don' try an' mess wit hood, bitch."

She laughin'. It's so early, like, the sky still orange and shit. Birds squawkin'. I ain't in no fucking mood for her laughin'.

"Kayleigh, you are literally from Upper Montclair."

"Shut da fuck up, bitch."

I blow the smoke right into her fuckin' ugly squirmin' face. She on the edge of crying, lowkey.

"Why—what are you doing? You know what your parents say? Tim calls his brother almost every week, crying. Just in absolute tears."

Once again, like, women really be prayin' on my downfall, like. Can't trust bitches forreal. She keeps goin' as if I haven't stopped listenin', like.

"I don't know…how you got like this. Maybe all that *16 and Pregnant,* it made you adopt this persona. Were things just too good for you? I don't know if it was because of—"

"Punt!"

Fucking Punt, my Punt, my poor Punt. He layin' on the sidewalk only a few yards from me, his body all limp, his face in the concrete, like. I run up to him, toss the fag, hold his head. His face like a violet color, his lips chalky, he be lookin' ill—sick. Real sick.

"Wake the fuck up, Punt!"

He start laughin', this motherfucker. He cough a bit then laugh some more.

"Lee!"

His breath be smellin' like piss and tequila. His eyelids all lazy, he ain't lookin' at me, his eyes can't find me, like.

"What the fuck goin' on Punt?"

People watchin' and ain't helpin', like the motel guy who still has that bitch ass look on his bitch ass face. Chelsea still behind me, tryna talk or someth'n. Birds screamin' and the sun bleedin' into my eyes and my knees really be hurting when they on the gravel like this. Punt gets to standin' up, his neck all swinging, his limbs good as dead. Takin' care of three people with this body, ain't so easy, you feel me.

"Oh, well, after you fell asleep, I went out with Zear—Zahir. We got drinks I think. Still a little drunk, actually. Ha."

"Yeah, no shit! What the fuck, Punt? You don't even know 'im!"

For a skinny motherfucker, he real heavy. My Angel Baby kicks. She's tryna run. Me too, girl, me too.

"You didn't know me either and you still, still let me sit on your special pillows."

Chelsea look real scared, as if he's 'bout to beat up her ass. As if he ain't a drunk, skinny fag. She don't know nothin', truly.

"Yes—this was who I talked to last night. He told me you were here."

She lookin' all proud of herself, puttin' the pieces together. My brain ain't able to process what she said because if it do, Punt would be on the ground, and I ain't lettin' that happen, not right now. My back sore, my knees raw, my feet achin'. My Angel Baby kickin' and my cigarette wasted. I'm done, I'm fuckin' done, I swear.

"Look, Chelsea, okay, I'm sorry—I'm sorry for you and my uncle and my parents, I'm sorry. I gotta go."

She block my path.

"Could you just give me a reason why? Why did you choose this? One reason."

I look at Punt. His eyes closed, mouth wide open. He ain't here, he ain't. I hope she knows this is all she's getting.

"It makes me young forever. Everything I'm doing makes me young forever. You feel me."

She finally looks at me like a person, looks at my belly like she not tryna kill it. Looks at me as if I tol' her somethin' she ain't already know. She takes another big ass sigh.

"It's not like you're a teenager, Kayleigh. You're twenty-four. You have a nice home and a-a loving family. You're choosing this. It's offensive, honestly. It's probably very offensive to your friend here—Punt, was it?"

"Why would it be offensive to me?"

Punt alla sudden awake. Only one eye able to open though. My Punt.

"Because…I mean, I-I'm assuming this is how people talk, you know…where you live."

"I'm from Saddle River."

"Okay, look—I just—Kayleigh, please? Just come with me, just come home, babe. We'll figure this out."

She look real desperate if you want the truth. Real desperate. Her face is all old and wrinkled, her forehead all stripy. I'll tell ya, when I was a lil' girl, I thought she was beautiful. The most beautiful woman. She was the cool aunt, you heard. She was always sneaking me her makeup. She taught me how to take a shot and told me what to say to a guy in bed. She was there for all of it. Until she wasn't, of course.

"I got weapons, you hear. Don't think I don't, like. Come here again, fuck with us again, and I'll fuckin' kill ya."

She actually cryin' now, real silent, just tears rollin'. She come near me, I put up my fist, and she still come near me anyway. All she do is she kiss me on the cheek with her gooey lipstick and she walk away like nothin' happened. And nothin' did.

"You believe in karma, Punt?"

Punt pouts then pukes purple on my bare feet. I take him back to the room and run him a nice, warm bath.

5.

Tonight's trick is the same dude from last night. I tell him to say he's my boyfriend to the motel guy. He ain't dressed in a suit and tie today. He in khaki shorts and like a football Jersey. His breath smell like Hot Cheetos. I tol' Punt to stay in the bathroom while I'm working. He listenin' to Lady Gaga with his headphones and paintin' his toenails.

"How was your day, gorgeous?"

Joseph's real cocky today, his hand like grabbing my ass right as I let 'im in. Still got that big ass smile, and his dick already growin' like.

"Whole lot better now," I lie.

He's grippin' my throat and squeezin' my left nipple. You give these men pussy once and they think they're God or sum'thn. He spin my body, throw me on the bed, don't give me time to set up the special pillows or nothin'. He hike up my dress and he put it in—no lube, no condom, you hear. Like nails on a chalkboard is what it feels like. He's fuckin' lovin' it, I tell you. He's makin' noises that I never heard no man make before in my goddamn life. He hollerin', he callin' me Mommy Girl. White boys are such perverts man, highkey. At first it be hurtin' the good hurt, but now it's kinda hurtin' the bad hurt. Almost like I can feel it in my pussy, my stomach, too. I feel like an animal is inside me, like. He got my arms pinned behind my back, his nails diggin' into my thigh. All I can see, all I can think about is that knife sittin' in my bedside table. Seems so far away. Seems not right that it ain't in my hand. I dunno if I wanna use it right now, but he ain't even givin' me the option, like, rude as hell. I feel like I must be shittin' right now. It feels like he's scraping stuff outta me, you feel. Like something is comin' outta me, like, someth'n has to be comin' outta me. Is this what sex s'pposed to feel like? Is this good? And that's when it happens, I tell ya, that's when my motherfucking water breaks, like. He's still yellin' and moanin'—he ain't even notice. I can still smell his Cheeto breath, and now I can smell his dick cheese, too. I let him get a coupl'a more pumps in—I know that My Angel Baby is patient. But then I feel almost like a rippin' feelin in my stomach, like period cramps but so much fuckin' worse, you feel. I start moanin'. Joseph be thinkin' I'm cummin' until he notices the puddle of water on the carpet and he's all screamin' like the pussy he is. Punt runs outta the bathroom, like what the fuck now. Someone bangin' on the door as my body is splittin' in half—they're screamin' now to open up. I grab my special pillows, lay back on 'em, on my lil' puddle. Breathe, breathe.

"Oh, fuck, no—no, no, no, fuck this, I'm going."

"Hold my hand, Punt."

Punt do as he told. He look real scared. Fat bald motel guy opens up the door, his head all red and throbbin'. Joseph run out with his dick out, lookin' even scareder than Punt. Motel guy got his motherfuckin' finger pointed in my direction. Breathe. Breathe.

"Hey! I know what you're doing! You can't do this, you gotta get—"

"Give me some motherfucking help here, retard!"

My Angel Baby turned out beautiful, she did. I think Punt became a man that day, for real, guiding My Angel Baby out her path. That cunt of a motel manager had to cut the umbilical cord with my rape knife, but all turned out good and shit, like. She was all pink and slimy at first, her face real pruny and wrinkly, like—real scary lowkey. A lil' alien motherfucker. But she's a beauty now forreal. My Angel Baby. Real pretty. Although, I can't call her My Angel Baby no more 'cause now she gotta name. Moody. She's with Punt now. I taught 'im how to hold the head and everything. He gotta job as a maid at the motel. I tol' the motel guy that I'd stop turnin' tricks if he let my boy cop a job. Plus, I said, I'd tell the police he raped me if he didn't. So Punt a workin' man now, you feel. I'm layin' in bed now, my belly still big, but this time empty. I go on my phone to spread the news you hear, and that pretty fat bitch's page pops up. I tap on the link for her pussy—give her the ten dollars. Refresh the page, tap again—another ten. Then again. Then again. I do this until I get a notification from my bank saying shit ain't lookin' so good.

The Throat Goat

Gardenia. Named, appropriately, after the vibrant flower. And she was a flower. She only opened up to you if you fed her daily, typically with affirmations and fun facts about aquatic mammals. The Internet's name for her was not at all as apt nor as beautiful. Rather obscene, really. The Throat Goat is what they called her. Because, apparently, she also opened up physically. I had to look it up, but "Throat Goat" is a title given to those who are phenomenally talented when it comes to oral sex—goat being an acronym for "Greatest Of All Time." No gag reflex is what MattTheRapist69 commented. He said, "I bet this bitch got no gag reflex Fr." Unlike MattTheRapist69, I am not interested in casting such lewd assumptions.

Gardenia was smart. Smarter than I was at her age. She had a strong understanding of what was happening in the Middle East. She had a favorite Rohmer series. She knew not to be afraid of spiders because it is clear that they are far more afraid of us. She was twenty-one years old when I first happened upon her Twitter. She had a large following due to her unabashed and unfiltered portrayal of her wild sex life. "This dude just spelled my initials with jizz on my stomach," accompanied by a purple heart emoji, was the first tweet I read of hers. She was funny, all right. But most of her stories centered around her success when it came to blowjobs. This is what landed her the aforementioned sobriquet, which I was never actually sure if she minded or not. Her bio provided a link to her Instagram, which I found far more tame.

Pictures of her covered up at the beach, pictures of her laughing with friends, pictures of her college graduation from an Ivy League school. Caramel-skinned, brown-eyed. Sweet, sweet smile. Her

Instagram bio provided her email, which I utilized pretty much immediately.

Gardenia,

My darling. Smart, funny, beautiful. It's difficult to imagine you're real outside of my screen! I'd love to take you out. Coffee, tea, a real stiff drink—pick your poison! All I want is the chance to know more about you. Get back to me, sweetheart.

With love,

August

xxx

Nineteen minutes later, I was notified with a reply.

Dear August,

It's great to make your acquaintance! I'm not often hit on in such a polite way. Thank you for that. Of course, I cannot go on a date with you. Not without first learning some things.

- Gardenia

We emailed all night. I told her whatever she wanted to hear—I'm an open book! I told her that I was a sixty-one-year-old man living in the Southwest. I told her that I was a physical therapist. I told her that I enjoyed murder mystery books. I remember her calling me "basic" for that. Almost every time I asked a question of my own, she found a way to evade answering. I didn't entirely mind because some people need to tell you things on their own time—questions can be more of a deterrent than an incentive, and I understood that. Still, we talked. Talked about politics and culture and religion and art. God, the breadth of her knowledge! I found myself, at many times, the conversational weak link. Especially when we spoke of her work. That was one part of her life she was more than happy to share with me.

She was a lab technician. She made medical implants out of cow collagen, specifically used for brain tumors. She compared the work to arts and crafts, saying the collagen looked and felt like wet Play-Doh. She was saving lives and comparing it to a children's toy. I almost fell in love with her right then.

I began to email her every day, and she'd always email back, although she was never the one to initiate a conversation. I was able to break down her walls over time. I'd call her beautiful, and she'd feel inclined to tell me a new fact about herself—almost like Pavlovian conditioning now that I think about it. Of course, that's not why I'd call her beautiful; it was simply a happy bonus. She told me she was an only child. She told me she wanted to marry a tall man with an odd face. She told me she didn't have much luck with dating, and she used Twitter as a means of catharsis, as crude as it may have seemed—her word, not mine. There seemed to be one man in particular who made her life a living hell. She called him "Nick" in her tweets, although I'm not sure if that was his real name. Tuesday morning, 8:57 a.m., she tweeted, "Nick cancelled on me last night. I waste my everything showers on the worst people bruh." I didn't know

what that meant, but I could tell it had negative connotations. The next day, 3:36 p.m., she tweeted, "Nick
texted me a dick pic, then said 'wrong person sorry
lol.' AND IT WASN'T A JOKE." What a scumbag. Unworthy to have her number, definitely unworthy to be
making her feel this way. I emailed her after I saw she
tweeted a link to the song "Yellow" by Coldplay.

My Gardenia,

(If you'll allow me to call you that)

*Why, oh why, must you choose such horrible men?
I don't know if I'll ever wrap my head around it.
Please leave Nick. Not even so I could have you, but
so YOU could have you. You deserve better than
this, my angel, my beauty. My Gardenia!*

As always, with love,

August

xxxx

Minutes passed, then hours, then days—no response.
I thought I had ruined it, I thought I had gone too far,
I thought she would never talk to me again. But she
did stop tweeting about Nick, so evidently, I had one
positive effect. But also, she simply wasn't tweeting
at all. Three days and eleven hours later, I received an
email from Gardenia. Thank the heavens.

Dear August,

I'm sorry for not responding. I had an issue at work. I accidentally sneezed and ruined a forty-thou sand-dollar lot of product. So the jury was out on whether or not they were keeping me for a bit. It's fine now, they let me stay. Thank god.

Hope all is well.

- Gardenia

Jesus! The stress that job put her under, all for a measly sneeze? Can no one see what I see? Has the world gone completely mad, completely blind? In response, I emailed her a picture of me smiling. Then, she emailed me a picture of her smiling with a peace sign. The sweetest doll face you ever did see! Her big, button eyes. Bright, porcelain cheeks. Long, silky hair I wanted to comb until my hand gave out. That started a chain of picture-sending, specifically pictures of faces. I did ask to see her body, but she was never interested in that, and I knew not to push it. We just sent "selfies," as the kids call them. To be completely transparent, I did masturbate to those photos. I think the fact that we were speaking meant this was acceptable; I wasn't some stranger. Plus, I am human after all. Once, she sent a selfie of the lower half of her face and her cleavage—that was the closest I ever got. Her tongue was sticking out, her breasts were plump, bouncy, shining, perfectly symmetrical. They looked soft. I responded right away.

Sweet Gardenia,

I know you won't let me see your body, but you

Months went by of emailing her, every day, at least
five times a day. Some of the best months of my life,
truly. Every time my phone buzzed, I'd grow an erec-
tion just from pure excitement. I'd go to bed smiling,
thinking of her words, and wake up smiling, thinking
of her smile. We never did go on a date, but that didn't
deter me from talking to her. There was always some
new excuse. Friend's birthday party, family emergency, overwhelmed with work. One time, she said that
her childhood hairbrush broke in half, and she didn't
feel emotionally equipped to meet any new people for
a few weeks. Whether or not any of them held any
truth—I'll never know. She was shy, and that was
okay. She needed time—and that's okay. But I always
had to make myself available. I had to make it known
to her that *I* was ready.

About eight months in, we had grown comfortable with one another, but not as comfortable as
I had wanted. So, I felt the urge to tell her, to sanctify
our bond. Tell her my story, tell her why I stumbled
upon her Twitter in the first place. I told her that my
daughter died. My daughter died when she was fourteen years old from leukemia, which was two years

ago. I told her that's when I knew our connection was special, me and Gardenia's. She was a healer of cancer, my daughter suffered from cancer—it was kismet. I told her that my daughter loved social media, but social media did not love her back. She was brave enough to post herself online during her sickness, and because everything is possible on the Internet, of course, she got hate. Hate about her appearance. People can be so cruel—a cruelty that I still have a hard time believing. That's not what killed her, no, but it did hurt her, and I could've killed someone for that—nearly killed myself for that. I was an angry mess for about a year. But then I learned to stop fighting the feelings, to try to see what she had seen. So I made a few social media accounts. I found girls similar to my daughter: bright, beautiful, funny, optimistic. And I saw the kind of undeserved hate they got from men with faceless profile pictures. So, I'd comment nice things under their posts. Sometimes, I'd send them money. This was the only thing I found to relieve my grief. To help other girls, the way I failed to help my daughter.

Gardenia waited forty-seven minutes before she responded to that one.

Dear August,

I can't begin to imagine that kind of loss. I am so sorry. Although, like I said, my work is more so aiding the process of removing brain tumors, not so much treating leukemia, but I understand and appreciate the sentiment. I'm sure she was a great girl. I have something I'd like to tell you, too, if that's alright.

- Gardenia

Of course, I said of course. I waited patiently by my laptop, refreshing my inbox every eight minutes. I knew she had something important to say, and I wanted to be there for her during that process as much as I could be, as much as she'd let me. Four and a half hours later, she emailed me a link to a two-page document. In the document, she explained that everything was a lie. Everything she said on Twitter about her sex life was a lie. She said she had actually only slept with two guys in her whole life. And that she'd never given a blowjob, and never really wanted to. She said she wasn't all that interested in sex. I emailed back and asked her why—why lie then? She emailed back promptly, saying she didn't know. She said maybe to acquire an audience. Maybe to convince herself she was a sexual person, since that's so sought-after in this day and age. But I still think there's a different reason. I think it was to meet someone like me, who would prove he'd love her just the same, either way.

The next month was total bliss—we had been totally honest with each other. Complete vulnerability. I knew this was just one step closer to meeting her in person. I knew this was a necessary catharsis, and we no longer had to pretend to be everything we weren't. It was like losing your virginity, and the girl opposite you smiles upon seeing your naked body instead of dry-heaving. It reminded me that bad things could lead to good people. I was better with my schedule, going to bed on time, and waking up earlier. I made healthier meals, and I moved my body more. I was more present at work, more graceful with my patients. She had made me better. She had.

I couldn't help what I did next. I saw how gratifying vulnerability could be, and I abused that. I was greedy—it was my hamartia. I emailed a picture of my penis and balls and taint to Gardenia at 5:25 p.m. on a Wednesday. She didn't respond that night. It wasn't the most flattering picture—the lighting was poor, and the subject wasn't as erect as maybe she would've liked. But it wasn't about sex; it was about being honest with her. Show her who I was, so that she could love me. Or at least feel close enough to meet me.

The next morning, I awoke to the most horrible news. Gardenia posted a string of volatile tweets, all castigating a man named August. Me—she was castigating me. I don't remember most of the sentences verbatim, but she used words like "creep" and "pervert" and "old man." She was talking about me on the Internet. And she was angry, she was hurt. The one tweet I remember with crystal clarity was "He's dangerous. He's threatening to hurt me. Be careful on the internet, girls." Dangerous? All I had ever wanted to do was make her feel safe, and I seemingly had failed. I felt a tooth-twisting, gut-emptying pain, the likes of which I hadn't felt since my daughter died. I didn't know this kind of pain was even possible twice in one lifetime. I emailed her immediately.

My love,

Why, oh, why would you do this? Did I really scare you, darling? I believed we had something. Tell me I can make it right. Tell me what I did and I'll never do it again. Just talk to me. Talk to me, for God's

She never did respond. I took the next week off from work. I did nothing but lie in bed, stare at the ceiling, and mentally punish myself. I deserved it. For making such an angel, a doll of a girl, feel anything less than perfect and loved. But then months went by. Months went by, and I grew angry. Was this just another lie? It's not like that was exactly out of her wheelhouse, to lie on the Internet for attention. Was this all a publicity stunt? Was I just her toy? Was I her pawn? Cunt. I couldn't stop thinking that word, and I think of myself as a polite, even-tempered guy. I'm a feminist, for God's sake! But that girl was a cunt—she just was. To use me like that. If anything, my line of thinking was more feminist. I was worried for the actual girls and women in danger of online predators, and there she was, casting false claims, giving actual victims a horrible reputation. A couple more months went by, and I felt brave enough to check her Twitter. Her latest post read "God, I need to stop talking to men on the internet just because I'm bored," and that's when I finally realized. I realized what I should have known from the beginning: she was a girl. I thought I had found myself a woman, but she had been just a girl all along. Weak, emotional, fragmentary. Over time, that line of thinking faded as well, because I simply chose to focus on the good memories. I didn't need to let one terrible incident define everything we had. And I did—I had something with Gardenia. And what a beauty she was, folks.

I'm retired now. I have a girlfriend who lives with me. She's Mexican and has fake breasts. We like to go to the aquarium together—she's a marine biologist. She likes to tell me which animals are deadly and which ones are just pretty, and I like to listen. I don't use social media as often as I used to. But today, I'm scrolling through a Reddit thread titled: **Anyone remember the Throat Goat? Lol**, reminiscing on fond memories of Gardenia through other people. MattTheRapist69 has plenty to say, of course, but there are a plethora of kind voices as well. *Yes I remember her she was so fucking funny lmao*, says AlbinoRhinoGyno3. *My husband went to high school with her haha. Said she was very smart and much more shy than her online persona lets on*, says Woman_With_The_Most. *I lovedddddd her ! She made me feel good about letting guys go backdoor on the first date!*, says User6117825714. God, Gardenia did so much. Imparted such a positive impact on such a wide range of people. It doesn't matter that her words were lies—what matters is the result. And what a result. All those lives she saved, and all of it was a joke to her, simply a means of passing time.

Gardenia and I ultimately lost contact, or more accurately, she lost contact. I can't give up on beauty—it simply goes against my principles. But I did some digging on her friend's social media, and I've found some information. She's thirty-five now, which, I suppose, I could've worked out on my own. She's a project manager at the same biotechnology company she started at. She's married to a woman, a doctor woman, and she has two daughters, both with her caramel skin and brown eyes. Her Twitter has been deactivated for seven years, her Instagram for five. Her last email to me is dated thirteen years, two months, and sixteen days ago. My last email to her was yesterday morning, congratulating her on her eldest daughter's communion.

Transcribed Message Of A Mourning Man Talking To His Dear Friend Caught On Nothing Whatsoever

"His negligence with me feels violent, his lack of response feels violent. After all, any calculation is a form of violence—just as my calling his violence violence is violence, but self-defense begs to be judged by an entirely different standard. I correlate pain with patience, and it's the reason why I talk of him to you all these years later. A pathetic part of me believes that you must wait for the wound to grow deep red in hue before you can scream. Enough perfect gunshots, and you'll make yourself a chorus, my friend! I know you don't like when I get this way, but I cannot take that into account right now. And I am happy for you and your beloved—I am. That is no question. On your wedding day, don't forget to get married, if you get what I mean. On my birthday, I forgot to be born. I only remembered a few decades later and by that point, everything already happened. He was not included in everything, no—if only! If only I could forget him to the point of unknowing! His problem was—you know what his problem was?—his problem was that he saw my companionship through an academic lens. Love is objectively the simplest thing in the world and anything as animalistic, as intuitive, as that has a right to be feared. He had a penchant for the pedantic and when faced with something that refuses to be over-intellectualized—well, his sense of self nearly collapsed! The kind of person that makes things difficult because that means, at the very least, they've made something. As if fruit is necessary when the roots are enough to keep you upright! I'm just going to lie down on the floor here—is that okay? No, don't worry, look, I won't be long. And before you give me that look, I say this as a knowing hypocrite because all I do is for thought, and, although this is dreadful to admit, everything else is secondary. Eating, social-izing, reading, their exact purpose is as fuel to think more—enjoyment and health, they're precisely su-perfluous. But I still resent—I still resent that compul-sive need, as guilty as I—you know, I could not hold a candle to the theoretical when under his eye. Not even necessarily archetypal, but theoretical. He loved anything vague, sweeping, man-made. Anything that could be spit out in one breath. Symbolism, but not the symbol itself—let alone the manifest representation of the symbol! No, no, I would not characterize this line of thinking as paralyzing. Yes, well, it is cold down here, but it's nice. Did you mop recently? Almost no dust to be found—spit-clean. And, so, when you love a narcissist, you love their games, the most prolific one of all being silence. It's a ghastly torture for everyone who has to listen to what they're not saying. I know this has not been the case for—yes, well, you have worked much harder at finding peace than I have—you and your fiancée will have plenty of well-earned happy days, let's agree on that. Do not take what I say into account, it is a bore, but I must say it all the same. He, like all of us, believed introspection was cheap, overrated, but in order to keep that itch scratched, he breathed his questions into me. I was a composite of all his neuroses, I was an operatic tic—I was a second him. God, don't say his name! Of course, I don't miss him, not how you're implying anyway. How can you miss someone whose scent you don't even remem-ber? It's ludicrous, it's out of the question. He was a titan—love was more of a gift than a mechanism, and I accepted that, I accepted it the moment I laid eyes on him, it seems you're the only one struggling to accept that. I apologize—that was—I'm getting to the meat of it now, though. Impersonal introspection—that was his forte, that was his craft, and I let him. Getting to know himself by destroying me. More invasive than a bone marrow transplant, more perverse than having sex with your sister. I couldn't have refused—you see how that would be just another move in the chess game, right? You do see that? Yes, as I can see you're getting ready to go, but this floor really feels quite nice on my face, I must admit. Cooling, yes. Of course, being given a gust of soft wind in the shape of a hand's silhouette after being slapped until you're red in the face—well, it's not—it feels like death, there's no other word for it. That's what he gave me—he gave me death, he gives me death every day. That's my reward. A repeated death is a horrid thing because there is no time for reflection, no space for nirvana. No person available to play God, you see? It's all chemical, physical. That's what it was—he had to have the theoretical, so I was left with the physical. And don't mention dialectics, that had no voice in our dynamic—despite his Achilles' heel being reason, it—well, I lived outside of that. That's not what I was. And what was I? I was next to him, that's what I was. I was the person standing next to him. And I believe, no, I know that—What? Ah, I see. No, you go ahead— love is calling after all! Answer before the bell runs dry! I'm going to lie here a bit longer, if that's quite alright. I think my leg has fallen asleep and I'm going to let the rest of me follow suit. But before you go, I would like to say, can I say just one more thing? I would like to say I just remembered what he smelled of—oak and marmalade. He did. He smelled of oak and peach marmalade."

Sadly, Allen

Let me tell you about him. His name is, sadly, Allen. An old man's name. The same name as my gay sixth-grade teacher who told me I was advanced for my age. I asked if that meant I was going to skip a grade, and he looked me up and down and said, "No, I'm sorry, I meant your breasts, dear." My Allen wasn't nearly as interested in my breasts. He just respectfully acknowledged them as if they were work colleagues. There's a new breed of men respectfully acknowledging breasts as if this makes them more "feminist," as if women care about their social values while being penetrated. Word to the wise: don't be afraid to grope your girlfriend. Anyways. Allen was probably the love of my life, but honestly, could just as easily be someone I forget about in two years. Maybe the two aren't mutually exclusive. But I hope they are.

Allen looked five-foot-nine but was actually six-foot. And I know what you're thinking. *He's just lying about his height*, as men often do. But, no. On our second date, we smoked a blunt in a Target parking lot and then walked around the store. We mostly bought snacks—he was the type to get hungry when high, instead of horny, like me, which should have been the first red flag—but I casually diverted our path towards the household items section, like leading a horse to water. I then, randomly and casually, happened upon a measuring tape and proposed we measure ourselves "just for fun." Obviously, he made a dick joke. And, obviously, it didn't land. But believe it or not—the proof before my own eyes—that man stood at six feet tall. Maybe he looked short because he was thicker, wider. Wide in a buff sense. He was a fitness junkie; he chronically drank protein shakes, sanctified nutrition labels, and engaged in cardio three times a day, and, *apparently*, "sex doesn't count." Which is bullshit.

I only liked Allen's fitness obsession because it meant that he would take sex very seriously, make a sweat out of it, and this sweat would plaster his shaggy bangs to his giant canvas of a forehead. Allen's big forehead was my least favorite part about his appearance, but luckily, I didn't have to worry about zoning in on it while fucking. Besides that, he was an extremely conventionally attractive man. Clear skin, strong calves, no missing teeth. That's an inside joke between him and me—you wouldn't get it. We originally met through my friend, Lauren. Lauren is part of a book club, despite being a youthful thirty-one-year-old, and some matronly spinster in said book club offered her son on a plate like a rotting slab of meat. *Would you want to date my Al? He's the cutest thing, c'mon, hon'*, were her exact words, according to Lauren, accompanied by a pixelated photo of Allen holding a football over his crotch on an iPhone 6. If I were part of that menopausal cult and heard those words and saw that photo of Allen awkwardly covering up a boner, I'd probably recommend that she look into late-term abortion. Then I'd take a shit in the middle of the room and walk out because, why not?

Lauren actually went on a date with Allen before telling me about him, and yes, they did have sex. But I don't mind, as long as Lauren isn't ridden with syphilis, and neither does she, as long as Allen doesn't tell his mother that Lauren is a boy-sharing slut. She said he wasn't well-endowed enough for her, but we all know that Lauren has an interminable void of a vagina, so this isn't saying much. I said I'd be happy to take him off her hands, like any good friend would, and I don't think Allen minded this swap either. When

Lauren gave me his number, he was away in some European country, visiting some friends. That meant that we would have to text for two weeks before meeting in person, which was less than ideal. Physical and sexual intimacy is integral to finding out if you like someone even a little bit. *Why don't you just not contact him while he's away?* Well, I couldn't do that under the assumption that he would change his mind about seeing me after two weeks or, worse, forget about me entirely. So, we texted. Lots of witty banter, mostly on my part, a healthy exchange of nudes, and, at my demand, hundreds of selfies from him. Allen had this terrible ineptness when it came to selfie-taking; he always posed teeth-first, if you can imagine that, as if he were sending a picture to his dentist. I loved it *so* much. I never told him I found them funny, but it's okay because I masturbated to them too. I didn't tell him about that either.

We were both able to survive the two weeks and spent his first day back getting insanely drunk at an Irish pub near my house. I still remember the rickety bar chairs, the perpetually filled glasses of Guinness, the fifty-year-old bartender flirting with me, and me flirting back to get a reaction out of Allen. Allen gave him a lousy tip out of contempt, and then we consummated the date by doing hand stuff in the bathroom. He tried and failed at getting me off, and then I tried and succeeded at getting him off. Almost immediately after he jizzed in my hand, I puked, decorating the bathroom stall in a mahogany bile. I puked several times, actually, which was weird for me. I'm not the puking type; I pride myself on my tolerance for alcohol consumption. I told Allen this too, reassuring him that this was not an accurate representation of who I am.

"It's okay, no need to apologize. Breathe through it, babe," he consoled me, a fist of my hair within his grasp.

I usually hated when people called me "babe," but hearing this through fits of dry heaving was oddly comforting. I like to imagine what we looked like from a third-person point of view: me frequently gagging and wiping hair from my face with a sticky semen-coated hand and Allen crouching in my barf with his soft dick hanging out of his pants like a sad Christmas ornament. The rest of the night escapes my memory, but he told me that he ordered me a car home and made sure I got safely into bed, like a gentleman. I woke up with dried vomit staining my chin and an unavoidable feeling of déjà vu.

We spent the next month in total bliss. Yeah, I missed my exes, and yes, I fucked some Tinder guys when he was too busy for me, but, thus far in my life, it had been my healthiest relationship. Allen was a new archetype of man I hadn't yet discovered: kind *and* good in bed. He was the first guy to ever make me orgasm, and when I told him that, he surprisingly didn't get a big head. Plus, he would visit me at work. He'd do this bit where he pretended not to know me and read my name tag and pronounce my name wrong and complain about my lack of customer service. It got old very quickly, but it was cute. I'd always make him his favorite: espresso macchiato. Then, I'd spit in it. I guess I thought it was sexy and funny, but I never even told him that I did this, so it was kind of pointless. Our first fight actually took place during one of these seemingly innocuous workplace rendezvous.

"One caramel frappuccino for an *Eileen*? Am I

pronouncing that right?" I joked.

He smiled, with fewer teeth than I wanted, but enough to make me smile back.

"Ugh, yes, thank you, Dorf."

"Please stop calling me that, sir, or I'll have to forcibly remove you from our premises."

I'm sure everyone within earshot hated us, but who the fuck cares? He took a sip and made a sour face.

"It's not actually a caramel frappuccino," I re-assured, slightly annoyed.

"No, God, it's just this song. I hate Christmas music."

Wizzard's "I Wish It Could Be Christmas Everyday" was crackling through our shitty speaker system, despite it being early November. He rubbed his right jowl and opened his mouth, probably eager to change the subject.

"You can't hate Christmas music." I was half-joking for Christ's sake.

"What?" he spat out through chortles.

"It's just, like—people who say they don't like Christmas music are usually just saying that to seem edgy. It's not a thing that you can 'choose' to dislike. You like it, deal with it."

He didn't laugh. He just shrugged, kissed me on the cheek, and left. I called in sick to work for the next three days.

Allen wasn't very funny or interesting, but he did have a few cool talents. For example, he was an exceptional artist and was always sketching something. One time, he drew me, without my consent, mind you, and I knew it was good because I started hyperventilating upon seeing it. I looked fat, and my nose looked big. I still partially think he was trying to hurt my feelings when he showed me that. He also had a really discernible stutter that would only manifest during the worst moments. It was hilarious, but since the humor wasn't intentional, I never gave him any credit for it. That's not necessarily a talent, but it did make him more unique, more human, so it feels like an accomplishment of some sort. A lot of the time, he felt like a larger-than-life entity, and I think I resented him for that. I still do.

One evening, about three months into seeing each other, Allen showed up at my doorstep, bangs glued to his forehead with a thick film of sweat. He probably had just gotten back from the gym. I absolutely hated it when people showed up unannounced. I had only answered the door because I assumed it was my DoorDasher misinterpreting the concept of "no contact delivery."

"Hey, what's up? We weren't supposed to hang out tonight, were we?"

He made a beeline for my room and sat on the edge of my bed, head in his hands. As I followed him, I accidentally—or maybe purposely—caught my reflection in my vanity mirror. I remember staying there for a moment, not entirely displeased with how I looked but a bit anxious because Allen had never seen me without makeup before. I could hear him trying to mitigate his sobs with his hands. I raised my eyebrows to myself in the mirror to make sure this was real life and my senses weren't failing me. I felt extremely awkward. I'd never seen a man cry before. I wanted to kick him out. Instead, I sat down next to him and set a tentative hand on his shoulder.

"Allen?"

He looked up at me with bloodshot eyes. It reminded me of when we got high at Target, and I desperately wanted to bring that up to change the subject, but I refrained.

"Fuck. I don't know what I'm doing. I thought they liked me there, I-I thought they were going to promote me, but, God. I'm so stupid. Sorry—I just got fired. It was…h-h-h-humiliating. They used that fake corporate j-j-jargon I've used with clients. It's—ugh."
I felt second-hand embarrassment that he was so depressed over leaving a job. It seemed like a blessing in disguise. Not even in disguise, just a blessing. I hoped my McDonald's would arrive and forcibly disrupt this moment.

"Well, then they're fucking stupid. They can't see what I see."

I made sure to choose my words carefully, but my mouth felt abnormally dry, cutting my response short. He placed a hand on my thigh. His fingers were trembling. We naturally had sex, and coincidentally, it was the best sex of my life. He was extremely dominant and agile—I suppose eager to channel his rage. And he had a really plaintive look on his face the whole time, like he was solving a Rubik's cube or just saw a lone balloon floating in the sky. It was hot. Afterward, he asked me to be his girlfriend. He whispered it to himself, really. I pretended to be asleep. He was still emotionally overwhelmed, and I couldn't take advantage of him and answer a question like that when he clearly wasn't thinking straight. My Door-Dasher never did come that night.

The next day, Allen woke up to three missed calls from his mother. His grandfather died. Rough week for Allen, evidently. He spent the next two weeks in total isolation, very rarely contacting me. I missed him at first, but after the first week, the separation actually felt like a healthy interim in our relationship. And at some point, it just seemed that whatever we had was over. And again, I was definitely sad at first. I drunk-called him a few times to no avail and sent a few "I miss you" texts with concomitant nudes, but I got nothing in return. I know he was grieving, but would it kill him to send a heart-eyes emoji? Anything at all? Even if he told me to fuck off, I would've treasured that. It was like he knew silence would be the most effective punishment.

Of course, after two weeks, Allen reached out to me. I played it cool, I proposed we hang out, so I could see how he was doing. He came over to my place, and he didn't talk about his grandfather, and I didn't talk about our short-term estrangement. We just watched a movie on my laptop, had sex, and fell asleep. The next morning, I woke up to Allen stroking strands of my hair in an excessively sentimental way. Once he saw my eyes open, he started speaking.

"I'd like to be your boyfriend, babe."

I felt shocked, not by the request, but by the phrasing. He said it as if he asked for breakfast in bed, or maybe like a request I'd actually fulfill, like giving him a wet willy. But that's the thing, he didn't even ask. He said it with a definitive tone, too; it was almost derisive. "I'd like to be your boyfriend, babe." As if he had the unalienable right to be my boyfriend. But, then again, if he asked, I would've thought that he was a pussy. Why are you asking like an orphan begging for a modicum of gruel? Am I your mother? Do you really know that little about me that you have to ask instead of declaring? I guess there is no good way to propose a monogamous relationship. I laughed.

"Is this because I said 'I love you' that night at Dave and Buster's? Because we talked about that, I was drunk, so, I mean, it was a joke, obviously—"

He sighed and pinched the bridge of his nose, an ostentation of his I never was able to overlook. I felt bad. He made me feel bad. Like I disappointed him.

"What d-do you want, Mia?"

I don't remember what I said. I don't even remember a general outline of how I responded. Maybe just use your imagination. Eventually, he left. We had broken up, obviously. I remember hugging him goodbye and him gripping my waist as we parted. I thought it was manly and hot, and I missed him for a second. He was standing in front of me, and I missed him.

I actually got a lot done once Allen was out of my life. I learned how to play backgammon, I reached out to a high school teacher I used to have a crush on, and I really put myself into my work, which was easy to do with the newbie to distract me. There was a new guy at my workplace, and I was training him. He was six years younger and a complete idiot: I was infatuated. This new crush consumed my time for the next few weeks, making the transition post-Allen an easy one. His name was Bear, and he liked Zen philosophy and YouTube compilations of people shitting their pants in public. He had a Neutral Milk Hotel tattoo and called everyone "man." We had sex once, but his dick was too small, so I had to call it off after that. This is what Lauren must feel like, I thought.

The next week, I actually found out that Lauren and Allen found their way back to one another. Those lovebirds. Lauren posted an Instagram story of her nails stroking a man's head in her lap, with a decorated Christmas tree in the background, despite it being January 7th. It was obviously a ploy to show off her new acrylics. I swiped up, asking who the mystery man was. Next thing I know, Lauren's calling me, and I'm trying to decipher what she's saying through pitchy whimpers. At some point, I made out the word "Allen," and I immediately hung up. I wasn't even angry, I just didn't want to deal with that conversation. But a few days passed, and then I got angry. Really angry. I found Allen's mother's Instagram and direct-messaged her, saying *Your son's new girlfriend is a slut. And she has a giant vagina. BTW*. I was sober when I did that. You don't even want to know what I did when I was on substances. Lauren was never a very close friend, but now she was nothing at all.

I remember the last conversation Allen and I had with crystal clarity. It was three days after I sent him a picture of the fifty-year-old bartender's dick next to me posing with a duck face. I bumped into him at the local strip mall—Allen, I mean. I was walking out of the liquor store, and he was walking toward the gym, a metaphor so perfect that I wish it weren't true. It was really bound to happen, I guess. Sometimes, I play back the conversation in my head when I'm plucking my chin hairs and try to come up with a different response. A clearer, more eloquent response. Something that would shock him. Something that would hurt him. I fail every time.

"Hey," I half-yelled.

I awkwardly changed my path to walk closer to him, already regretting it.

"Oh, hi," he said as if he didn't see me at first, even though he clearly did.

"How are you?" I asked.

He smiled and shrugged.

"How's Lauren?"

He fucking pinched the fucking bridge of his fucking nose.

"Really? I—Look. I am sorry about this, Mia. I know you don't really care, but she's good, we're doing really well, actually—"

"I miss you, Allen."

I had, and have, no idea why I said that. It just came out, but it felt right. He swiped his bangs up so they plastered on top of his head instead of to his forehead. I grimaced. He changed his posture so that one leg was sticking out, with a hand on his hip. It was girlish.

"You didn't want to be with me, Mia. You can't change your mind."

"People change their minds all the time. Literally all the time."

I stopped fumbling with my keys, which I hadn't been aware that I was doing until then. I wanted to come off as steadfast and impenetrable. Allen took a deep breath and scrunched up his face as if he just tasted something sour. He looked like a child.

"You don't have goals or values or any…real interests. I want someone with those things. Lauren is a veterinarian. She loves reading, and she runs a poetry blog. I mean, she's family-oriented—I don't mean to compare, it's just—fuck, Mia, do you even want this? Do you really even want this? Or do you just want to win?"

I hadn't been expecting any criticism. I laughed, accidentally producing a really unflattering snort noise. I laughed again, this time snort-free, as if I got a do-over.

"I-I don't want to…win. I don't want to win, that's not—I have goals. Is this because I work at Starbucks? Because that's fucked up—"

"No—look, okay, I'm sorry. That was uncalled for, what I said."

My left knee was itchy, but I didn't want to bend down to scratch it and make it seem like a charade to show off my cleavage. Not that he'd care anyway. He was never one for my breasts. I let the itch writhe and smiled, sarcastically.

"Yeah. It was."

He took a step closer as if he was going to touch me.

"I'm sorry, Mia, but I have to take hold of my life, and this is what I want."

Everything went a little blurry. Like I just stared into the sun and couldn't get my vision back to normal. I suddenly remembered I had a few loose Twizzlers in my pocket. I grabbed them and ate them, probably quite obscenely, but I didn't care—I felt that my blood pressure was dropping, and fainting in front of Allen would be far too embarrassing. Allen eyed the Twizzlers.

"Those are very low in nutritional value, by the way," he said in his partly serious, partly joking way.

I smiled. Everything was clear for a moment again.

"Yeah, maybe my teeth'll fall out," I joked, mouth half-full.

He gave a perfunctory half-smile and started to walk away. He then turned around, as if I willed it myself.

"And, uh, please stop texting me, or…I'll have to block you."

His left quad was habitually flexing as if he was trying to get his reps in, even now. I shrugged.

"Bye, babe," he said before turning back around.

I cringed before walking away too. I got in my car, chugged a bottle of Smirnoff Ice, and texted Allen *So…that was weird, right?*

The Twins

And that's the funny part, they're twins—the two nurses. Antipode is their name—no, that can't be right. Sonata—yes. Sonata because their faces are like a song. Both have sharp noses and blonde bangs and curly ears. It's strange, though. To go into the same field as your sibling. I think it even stranger to be assigned to the same hospital. Of course, they could have asked nicely to be assigned to the same hospital, but when has asking nicely ever really worked? I want to ask them about it nicely, but words are a foreign concept at this point. Plus, how would one respectfully introduce what seems to be their everyday reality into conversation? "You have a twin. Which is already strange. You wear the same hairstyle. Not what I'd do if I had a twin. And you have the same job in the same place. Ahhh! Please explain this to me!" It seems oppressively normal the longer they exist. My mother doesn't say anything, my father looks at both of their asses, unbiased, and my doctor hardly acknowledges their presence. As if I'm the insane one for thinking about it—for even noticing. You can see why I wouldn't want to shed light on my insanity. They're gorgeous, so I don't entirely mind there being two of them to look at. That's actually the word that introduces language back to my cognizance—gorgeous. Their beauty is so strong that it returns some much-needed structure to my world. Tropism is another word, I think. Or is it? Yes, it is. A good word, that is. I start remembering more words, because thinking is nothing if not a domino effect, which is how I eventually earn the confidence to ask them a question, to ask them their names. I open my mouth and out comes a miasma of wriggling shapes, but anyone with a functioning brain could understand the implications. And anyone with a trusted heart could offer me the sympathy of wanting to understand. And anyone with gum could offer me a piece—remind me, why does my breath smell so putrid again? But they laugh at me—the both of them. Wrinkly and shrill and buoyant. It seems like it lasts ages. Laughter is not right—this is serious. I don't remember why everything feels serious, but reasoning doesn't always have to matter. This undoes everything, though, words are once again hidden, choking behind my tonsils. I mimic their laugh back, as this is the only way a human can respond. The doctor is telepathically sending messages to my parents as his mouth seizes with the movements of mastication. My parents' heads bob up and down like they're trying to get their eyeballs to roll backwards. The nurses are putting a glass cylinder in my inner forearm—the glass bubbles red as a response. I think it strange that they need to help each other do this. Maybe one is less experienced than the other. I don't mind a twin-nurse shadowing—as long as they don't laugh at me again. But then how would they communicate? This confuses me until the bright, dry pain of my arm replaces the confusion with a taste: brine. Possibly a lemon-zested chicken. Still, the antipode of my elbow bends toward them, a natural tropism. Yes, tropism, that's right. They are the sun, and I am hungry. Actually—I *am* hungry. The twins look at my lap. A tray. Green beans. Breaded chicken, the inside rotting with sweaty pink. I stuff the chicken in my mouth and nod until the food turns to sludge. I swallow and a soft breeze like honey plummets through my ribs. When I look back at the twins, there's only one. The other one has fled? No, God, no. There was only ever one. My vision—it faltered. Twitching hour—no, not yet. My vision can't be

trusted until I eat, remember this. I clench my teeth
and laugh, as if I knew this all along. Trop—no, we
already did that—troglodyte is what they must think
of me. My face is swelling with a wet heat and my
right eyelid feels especially idle. Not a pleasant sight.
They can hear me think. I know this because in response they say "He's such a handsome, young man,"
perfectly in sync. I look to the tan man and the fat
woman to my right—they do the head-bobbing thing
again, as if their necks are bound to their chairs but an
enticing well of apples hangs just inches from their
face. It's good that I'm handsome, and it's good that I
ate. I can't tell if I'm thinking these things or if the
twins are saying them. And there was something I
was supposed to remember, but I can't be bothered as
the doctor's mustache is far too proud for me to pay
attention to anything else. Maybe he's poking fun—I
could never grow a mustache of that density. It probably says so in the charts he's looking at now. I hear
someone crying and I really wish they'd have the decency to be quieter. Patience is the real antipode— no,
anti*dote*. The mustached-doctor says this. And what
does he mean by real? Probably what everyone else
means if I had to guess. He says I look like Glenn
Close—he says I've got more morose—he says I overdosed. Overdosed on Sonata. Overdosed on a song?
Likely on the gorgeous girl before me. Well, who
wouldn't breathe her in until their nostrils wept? Is
she my wife? Perhaps a concubine? Oy, look at this
guy, thinking he's worthy of a concubine! I've never
done drugs. Of course, that's not true, but you must
remember to say that when they ask. Why would they
ask? It's my mother—she's the fat woman and the person who's crying. How can she be both? My father

hiccups, then burps, and the nurse covers her mouth, laughing. That's right—because laughter is how you communicate. Remember when I thought there were two of her? God, what was I like? Words are back, of course, they're back, but we are faced with a much larger problem—my mouth refuses to move. My tongue is rusted like chalk, my gums like virgin pavement. This would be fine if I had nothing to say, but, of course, I want to say that my mouth is dry. Maybe the chicken resorbed all my saliva until nothing was left. I see a plastic cup of water and a straw on the table beside me—just out of my reach. I must ask nicely. Ask for what again? For the water, yes. The twins rattle their heads, like they're trying to shake a molar loose— I'm ascertaining negative condemnations from this. But my father is drinking a Diet Coke, see he's chugging it right now! That's not fair. "That's not fair! That's not fair!" Do you hear yourself? Like a little kid. I remember when I was a kid and everything was loud and crumpled, just like this. I was class president, giving a speech about the importance of recycling to my grade. I was six, maybe ten. I stuttered through the whole thing, hands shaking, Molly Lyndon laughing at me. I'm not sure my point entirely came across since the classroom's recycling bin was thereafter still mainly reserved for Anthony Hartman's loogies and Beth Ventura's toenail clippings. That was the first and last public speech I ever gave without a little powdered courage. My doctor says that the young man should try society. He says that financial amounts of liquor can expedite a Glenn Close. I've never fancied the actor very much—Sonata is much prettier. And why is he speaking of money? Does he know we have very little? Your parents are paying for something serious.

Or is it that your parents are paying, is that the serious part? I'm here for a serious reason and my parents are seriously paying for it. I know this because I feel guilt, and guilt will fight through any force on Earth to reach you. An earthquake, yes—an earthquake. What an inconvenient time for my world to move. Everyone stares at me like I caused this—and maybe they're right, maybe I did. But can I be blamed for it if I don't remember? Twitching hour, the nurse says. But that's not how the phrase goes, is it? She punctuates the statement with a spiky laugh, that of a crone. My mother holds my hand and it feels like cement, not in texture but in movement. It's perfectly still, and that's how I realize that I'm the one shaking, not the Earth, not this time. She coughs—always looking for pity. She looks different. She says it's been five days since I was transmitted—committed—*ad*mitted here. Five days? She was always one for hyperbole. I tell her that it's only been fifteen minutes since I sat down to have this nice chat with everyone, but instead of laughing, she cries. My father comforts her with his non-soda-holding arm—now he's sitting beside me as well. She must not know that crying is an inadequate response, but I will not be the one to break this news to her. She says I have to fight. She feeds me water, tells me to drink, clutches my rattling fingers. Why couldn't I drink a few minutes ago? This entire room is devoid of reason. I ask my dad for a sip from his as well, but the Diet Coke is gone, or was it ever here? Now, my father's soda hand combs through my hair. I can't feel it, but I can see it and I think that matters. He smiles a kind of smile you give your diseased dog before you put him down, which makes me laugh. Something laughs with me—it's the new doctor. He's effeminate and young and—oh, no, it's the same man, but the mustache is gone. He was obviously discomfited by my envy. Beside him is a black woman with a binder. A laminated badge hangs around her neck. She's not wearing scrubs, which seems important, but somehow not important enough for me to figure out, like climate change or that one character actor's name. Glenn Close! We're close to getting ahead—a bed. That's what she says, that they're close to getting a bed for me. What am I lying on now, then? Suicide is very serious, she says. Oh, so that's what's serious—been serious this whole time. I'm glad we finally figured that out. I must keep telling myself that suicide is serious, lest we forget. Everything is repeated, and if it doesn't repeat, it means it never happened, right? A sprightly blonde girl saunters into the room holding a needle like a birthday cake. Oh, it's the twins! They're back! Purple scrubs, and all. Bangs pinned back this time, with foreheads like magic. What's the word for them again? Gorgeous—that's it.

The Extra

Okay, so, yeah. Let's get into it! Well, so, I first met Ted Brightly on a Wednesday in October of 2004, and I was—or, God, was it a Thursday? Jeez, come to think of it, it may have even been a Friday! How could I not know this? Wait, *what* is going on right now? No, no— it was *definitely* a Wednesday. A Wednesday evening. I apologize for the miscommunication, oh my—yes, because Wednesdays are trash night, and I remember hurrying to take the trash out so I could catch the ten p.m. viewing of the pilot of Ted Brightly's show *Jock- strap*. I hurried so much that I caught the trash bag on a corner of my patio's staircase, resulting in a tear in the bottom of the bag and trash juice soaking my left foot. I watched the entire episode with maple syrup and tuna juice marinating in between my toes—yes, I remember that, because how could I leave and wash myself and possibly miss the first episode of *Jockstrap*? Only everybody was talking about it. I'm sure you've heard of it, of course, but maybe just for the audience, I'll give a recap. Okay, so, *Jockstrap* chronicled the life of Eddy Earnheart, a seventeen-year-old boy who was born without male genitalia, and well, this was nev- er scientifically explained, but it's not something you think about because, you know, the show is just that good. Anyway, Eddy begins to really feel the brunt of his castration around puberty. Boys start noticing that he uses the stalls, not the urinals, they notice his lack of penis-related jokes and general lack of horniness. And things really take a turn for the worse when he joins the football team in high school. He had no idea that locker room culture meant being naked in front of other men, swinging your dicks around. He wears a stuffed jockstrap at all times, even showering, which the other boys take notice of, and this is how the show starts. So, and, we aren't sure if Eddy has a vagina—I always pictured Eddy's genitals as a smooth surface, honestly, like a Ken doll. Again, this is not something you really think about. But, really, I always thought it was such a shame Ted wasn't cast as the lead role, especially seeing as how similar their first names were.

Anyway, the show is about the obstacles Eddy faces as a penis-less teen trying to fit in. There's an episode where he scores a date with the head cheerleader, Brittany De Bastiani, so he ties a cucumber around his waist with plastic wrap, just for the visual illusion, you know, except Brittany ends up actually stroking his penis outside of his pants and this causes the cucumber to break in half and Brittany screaming and driving Eddy to the ER, which got a good laugh out of me, I'll be honest. It's also about the friends he makes who love him despite his deformity and the moral lessons school-sanctioned American football has to offer. And, of course, my Ted. Ted Brightly plays the main bully of the show, a character named Keith Wilson, which, let's be honest, bears no resemblance to Ted's name whatsoever. Keith suspects that Eddy is penis-less and is dead-set on showing the world, or at least their high school, that he has nothing in his pants. He never achieves this, of course, but it does make for some pretty wacky scenarios, like Ted hiding cameras in the boys' bathroom stalls, only to catch Brittany De Bastiani hooking up with the harelipped physics teacher! Jeez, that got me—that was a real laugh. Anyway, the show only lasted one season.

I'd watch every Wednesday night at ten p.m. for that autumn. I'd make my hot cocoa, put my comfy socks on, and close all my blinds. I was always excited when it was an episode featuring Keith; I'd take them very seriously, of course. I always learned something when watching Ted. I'd study his facial expressions, make them as he was making them—sometimes before! I was always jealous of that famous Ted Brightly dimple. For ninety seconds every day for three years, I'd push the soft end of a safety pin in my cheek just so I could match—and look!—you see it? Yep, that's my home-grown dimple, right there! If only it was that easy to replicate those delicious abs of his—ha! And—you'll find this funny, Letterman—for the first few months, I was saying his catchphrase in my sleep. *The ding-dong's got no schlong! The ding-dong's got no schlong!* I know this because of a complaint from a neighbor who's likely so unhappy with their life that they have to take out their anger on others. So, yeah, anyway, I guess you could say that I was smitten. It was like my whole life was leading up to that one trash night. Love at first sight, David!

Of course, once Ted came into my life, things had to change. I had no other choice but to work from home. This transition may seem drastic, but it honestly saved me thousands on gas, and I didn't much care for my coworkers anyway. I thought about telling my boss the truth, but I didn't want to exploit Ted as this kind of scapegoat. I didn't want repercussions coming back to him—this was *my* choice. So, instead, I said that I developed this horrible disease, one where I'm allergic to outside air and also other people. Much more dignified in my opinion. My boss acquiesced, and since then I've been pretty much glued to my couch! Not literally, of course. I'm kidding, of course. But in another way, I'm not really kidding, because, you see, I wanted to be available to Ted, television before me, remote at the ready. I also cut off some friends, told some family I'd be traveling, little things. He didn't ask me for this—God, Ted would never! But I wanted to, it was of my own volition. Ted always liked how autonomous I was.

I'll be honest here, Letterman, I will. Ted did not book much after *Jockstrap*. Culture got "woke," as the kids say, and Ted Brightly was seemingly forever burned into people's minds as the something-phobic bully. This image only worsened when the sexual allegations came out, which I don't even want to speak on, frankly, because any friend of Ted's knows that this is absolute blasphemy. I don't even want to speak on that—I will not—but, listen, there are no small parts, only small actors, and come to think of it, Ted might've been the one to coin that phrase. Yes, well, I'll have to look it up later, but I'm pretty sure that's right, I think it was Ted who said it, it would only make sense. He mainly played what I guess you'd categorize as minor roles, background characters, extras. A waiter without lines or a postman without lines or a person standing without lines. God, this sounds embarrassing—like he never had any lines! But, no, he did, of course, he did. I actually took note of every line he said in a film, show, or commercial between 2005 and 2012. And they went as follows:

Wazzup!

No chance, bud. We do this together or not at all.

**Hiccups* — I'm counting this as a line, because it was also a bit of a burp.*

The tests came back positive. You have six weeks

The last one sounds more promising than it was. Ted was in a medical drama. They introduced him and killed him off within the same episode. An air conditioning unit fell on his head, poor thing.

But, yeah, so I'd check his IMDb page pretty religiously, making sure I was up to date on his newest projects—the least I could do, really. Ted was just incredible. Always brought something new to each character, yet you could still sense Ted was in there somewhere—his warmth, his courage, his innate humor lingering. He was never shy to let a piece of himself stick around in each role. Really magnificent. And I'm not obtuse enough to think that he wasn't popular with the ladies because of this charm, this fame. No, no—I *know* he was popular with the ladies.

I found an online forum of women who were "crushing" on Ted—that was the word they used! Crushing! Such children, as if Ted would ever go for someone prone to that kind of vocabulary. Of course, after spending some time stalking this forum, I found out that they actually *were* children. Girls between the ages of twelve and fifteen, to be exact. I felt sad for them. A twelve-year-old girl must have better things to do with her time than to "e-chat" with these people she doesn't even know. And it's not that I was jealous, it wasn't that. But a girl of that age doesn't even know who she is, let alone the kind of people she should choose to invest her time in. I understoo—I understand the allure of Ted Brightly, of course, but you must be practical with your interest. They were using it as a bonding agent—offensive if you ask me. But I did find out some fun facts from this forum, I can't lie. Like Ted had a birthmark in the shape of Idaho on his lower back. Ted had two beagles, Beevis and Butthead. Ted liked Eminem songs and PB and J sandwiches. In that way, it was useful.

And, so, fast forward, I thought spring of 2013 was going to be spectacular—I thought it was going to be his big break! Finally! He was re-posting promotions for the forthcoming indie drama *Liz!* that winter prior. He was being very subtle about it, which I admired. I was so terribly excited when the film was finally offered on one of my streaming services. Did the cocoa, the socks, the blinds—even shaved my legs, just in case. Ted was in the movie for nine and a half seconds. He was performing cunnilingus on the protagonist, who was on her period, to a Wilco song. I had to convince myself that the blood was smeared grape jelly to withstand looking at his beautiful face being violated like that. I fell asleep that night mentally cursing his agent, wishing ill fate on the slutty, bleeding actress. He was a pearl in a sea of shit—if only the industry could have seen this.

And I don't want to make it seem like our life was all dandy, no, because things in our relationship actually took a bitter turn when I found out about the affair. It's not—I don't know if I should call it that— things between Ted and me weren't exactly serious or official, but there was, of course, a mutual understanding that we weren't seeing other people. So you can imagine how hurt I felt seeing paparazzi photos of him leaving a Manhattan nightclub with English rose Eliza White. Her first name being incredibly similar to that horrible movie's title—I'm sure this was a challenge for him to overlook. Eliza was this waifish twenty-two-year-old actress from Birmingham. She was one of those actresses technically terrible at her craft but young and beautiful enough to keep booking roles. White first gained widespread recognition at nine years old, playing a supernatural being in the HBO sci-fi series *Sandpaper*. I can't remember if her supernatural abilities had to do with sand or paper—I don't know, I never bothered to watch the show. But, so, when you get famous at such a young age, you're going to be at least slightly famous for the rest of your life, which worked in favor of her lack of talent. If Ted had to cheat, it was less than satisfactory for the subject to be such a brainless hack who only seemed interesting due to her overplayed accent and obvious eating disorder, which she conveniently labeled as Lyme disease when the media grew suspicious. Switching the name of one disease for another—it was a great metaphor for Hollywood, maybe for life itself. Let's not get into that—this is a family show! Keep it light! But, anyway, at this point, unfortunately, Ted had established a serious problem with alcohol, so I could not leave him now. Not while he was this vulnerable.

When I speak of Ted Brightly, people think I have this fragile handle on reality. They think that I think what I'm watching on my television is real. It's so condescending, David! Of course I don't think that, of course! But I do know that Ted and I had something. So when Ted got with another woman, in real life, mind you, I couldn't help but draw offense. I didn't think he was doing it to hurt me, per se, I believe it was a symptom of his childhood trauma. His parents died when he was young. He never told me this, he never felt comfortable, but I found the obituaries online in hopes of helping him as any good friend

would. From this, I gathered he had an anxious attach-
ment style, a fear of abandonment, and a weakness
for hotheaded women. And these hotheaded women
were taking advantage of that. Of his handsome face,
his needy tendencies. These women were using him.
It was sickening, truly.

Ted had a procession of flings throughout my
years of knowing him, but none made quite the impact as Eliza did. He had the folk singer girlfriend
who cheated on him with Josh Radnor and the indie
director girlfriend who forced him to be in her shitty Vimeo short films and that year he tried getting
into alternative stand-up comedy, which was a cruel
mistress all on its own. And yes, of course, those four
nothing-women spreading false claims to gain vic-
tim-based notoriety. But, really, Eliza may have been
the worst of the worst, I have to say. She was a real
party girl, an industry-born euphemism for self-hat-
ing drug addict. She abused Ted—emotionally and
spiritually. She led him astray from his values, from
his career, from me! She was too young for him, not
even in body but in mind; honestly, Ted probably
would've been better off with one of those e-chatting
thirteen-year-olds, or actually—I didn't say that. Let's
cut that—can we cut that? I'm just saying how she
was immature, a poor influence on Ted, a key impetus
for his battle with alcoholism. The two dated on and
off from September of 2010 to May of 2018. In May
of 2018, Eliza died of a heroin overdose. Ted quickly released a statement, expressing his grief, saying
he lost the "love of his life." That was not pleasant to
hear, I will admit that. But I could not bear to judge the
words of a sick man.

Ted checked himself into rehab two months

later. I like to think this was because of us, his friends, who were urging him to make a change, to turn his life around, to leave the bottle alone, to ignore the young doxies. I know it was the reason he wasn't booking—he could have been a star! But let's not go there. Ted stayed at the facility for a little less than a year. And when I lie on my deathbed, I will think of this as the worst year of my life. There was no word from him. No statements, no pictures, no updates. He was giving me the silent treatment, and God, did it hurt. I know people need space when they're healing, but I would have appreciated the comfort of knowing he was, at the very least, alive! People don't talk much about the emotional strain alcoholism can have on friends of the afflicted, but to anyone watching: I see you, I hear you. You matter, and I know you're hurting right now, and it will get worse before it gets better. Sorry—forgive me—I'm, I'm tearing up here. It's one hell of a disease, David. I had nothing to watch, nothing to look forward to, for eleven and a half months. I was facing a deprivation similar to my Teddy, and at least there was that companionship—the companionship of suffering. I tried '90s sitcoms, some Leonardo DiCaprio movies, but nothing satiated me the way Ted did. It was crazy of me to even attempt filling what was clearly a Ted-Brightly-shaped hole! But we all eventually find our ways to cope. I re-watched *Jockstrap* twenty-three times that year. I grew such empathy for Keith. It's now difficult for me to understand how anyone could see him as a bully. He was a normal guy who had a clear grasp on reality, and he was scrutinized for it! He just wanted to expose the truth! Eddy was lying to the world about his genitals, and Keith was the bad guy? As if! I was grateful for that year, I suppose, because I noticed details from *Jockstrap* I never noticed before. Like, in episode seven, when Keith said purple was a gay color to wear, but then in episode nine, Keith is seen wearing purple-laced sneakers. Excuse my French, but what the hell? How could the producers have missed that? And just an insane overlook on my part—I'll take accountability. Anyway, after many grueling months, I got word that Ted was getting out on June 11th, 2019. So I did my best to prepare. Made a clean house, put on my most expensive dress. Getty Images had Ted leaving the facility looking fatigued and disheveled. He had gained a significant amount of weight and there was a balding patch settling on his crown. He had new wrinkles around his eyes, he was dressed in tattered sweats, but he was alive, and that's what mattered. He obviously had a long way to go, but at least the hard part was over. We had made it through—God willing.

It was three years later that Ted finally booked again. And this time, a recurring role! Thank the heavens! For a show titled *What Men Do*. I would occasionally hear updates about the plot, about the cast, the characters, but I learned the dark truth when I sat down to watch the pilot on October 9th, 2022—socks, cocoa, blinds.

It was a horror series about a male-exclusive cult surviving on a deserted island. At the end of season one, we find out that the entire environment was constructed by radical feminists as a way to torture men with rape allegations who never went to prison. The women captured them, drugged them, brainwashed them into believing that they were now living inside this sort of *Lord of the Flies* scenario, and sat back and watched from the comfort of their homes as the men turned on each other (via their carefully placed CCTV). All so woke, trendy—*blegh*. And I saw the twist coming from a mile away. Anyway, the men created this sort of hierarchy, and Ted played the role of the master's primary slave. His character was despicable, depraved, and always submitted to doing whatever the master asked. It was episode four that truly horrified me, made me swear off Hollywood *forever*. The men were growing bored, so the master requested a talent show of sorts. Some danced, some sang, but the master was not happy with any of it. He told Ted's character, Gorm—that was the kind of names the feminists gave the men, *Gorm*—so, he told Gorm that he must fuck one of the island's animals. The master was sure that this would be funny and also invigorating for the men who felt they were lacking certain visual stimulation. So Gorm did as told, and the men loved it. Listen, Letterman, listen to me—these idiots had *the* Ted Brightly repeatedly inserting himself into a wild pig on national television for one minute and fourteen seconds. A public death like no other—this was the lowest of the low. Forgive me, I can't think about—I-I just have no words—forgive me. I couldn't stand the thought of not watching anything Ted was in, but this was crossing a line. This obliterated the very concept of a line! I had no other choice but to boycott the series! I found the social media of all of the crew—producers, directors, makeup artists, PAs—and I messaged them individually, messaged them all to go to hell, excuse my French, but I just couldn't have lived with myself if I had done nothing. Sometimes, you have to take a stand for the people you love, David, you just do. I wrote and sent them an essay arguing in favor of Ted's greatest qualities, all of which they were neglecting to highlight on their show. It was sixteen pages long and, honestly, a masterpiece, I still re-read it sometimes—I can send it to you after we're done here, actually. None of them emailed me back, too afraid to reckon with their own degeneracy, it seemed. How this show got four seasons and not *Jockstrap*, I'll never know.

I do wish my story didn't have to end on such a sour note a-and I'm going to try to talk about this as gracefully as I can manage. This past year, my dear, sweet Ted Brightly died, and a part of me with him. And of course it had to be on my half-birthday. I'm not one prone to sentiment, but, yes, I cried. I cried and I cried for my dear, sweet Teddy. Oh, Letterman, you know me too well. I know it's only my third time on this show, but this studio—well, it truly feels like a second home. I like to think he was thinking of us during his final moments. I know that's selfish, but what grief isn't? It's hard for me to talk about his filmography because I now abstain from watching television, movies. I rebuke Hollywood as an entity. And I would like to mention his side gig, because Ted was so much more than just an actor. No, when Ted wasn't acting, he was teaching. He was a beloved drama professor at a community college. He did this out of the kindness of his heart, his love for the youths, for imparting wisdom on the less fortunate. We always wanted kids of our own, David—you know that. We never got the chance. Sometimes, life gets in the way, it just does. But at least he had this outlet, thank God. I tried going to the school, to see his students, mourn with them, speak on my memories of Ted, perhaps equipped with a microphone and a podium, but security labeled me a "consistent threat," and I was court-ordered to stay at least one hundred yards away from the premises at all times. Everyone expects grief to be pretty. News flash—it's not! It's just not, people! That's why I'm so grateful for this platform, I really am. So if you could get the camera in close here, I'd like to—I want to give a message to my Ted, to my Theodore Leon Brightly, who may be watching from up above. Yes, I'd like to think he is. Ted Brightly: Taurus sun, Cancer moon, INFP Myers-Briggs, Type Eight Wing Nine Enneagram, and one hell of a pickle-ball player! Oh, you were full of multitudes, weren't you? Ted, I like to think back on our *Jockstrap* days— God, remember how young we were? How innocent? *The ding-dong's got no schlong!* Do you remember that, Teddy? Oh, Teddy. When I heard the news that you killed yourself—by slitting your wrists with a pizza slicer at your niece's fourth birthday party, no less!—I had forgotten how to see, how to breathe, how to move. Living wasn't even on my radar. And—which camera do I look at? Oh, I see—and, but, so, I forgive you, Ted, I do, for all of it: for the women, for the drinking, for no goodbye! I threw my television out, out of principle, of course, but I still see you in my dreams, Ted. We're drinking hot cocoa, you're giving me a foot massage, and I'm reading a bedtime story to our daughter. That's the life we wanted, and that's enough for me—that's practically just as good as hav-ing it. And I quit my job, Teddy, don't be mad, please. It's only so I have more time to think about you, to reminisce. They're taking away my house next month, but it's all good, really, it is, because you gave me the best. You gave me the whole world, and to expect any-more—well, it would be a sin. Oh, Ted, how we used to laugh. I like to think you're up above, laughing at a teen boy's smooth private parts while you think about me. Yes, you are, aren't you? And, so, before I go, I want to say thank you to Ted, to Letterman, to this amazing audience! Give it up for yourself, guys! You are the reason we do it! And, oh my, you see that? You hear that, Teddy? They're chanting your name, Teddy! Ted! Ted! Ted? Ted, are my blinds closed, Ted? Which camera do I look at, Ted? Ted, is that you? Oh, come here, my—Sorry, for a moment I thought I saw Teddy in the audience, my Davey. Oh boy, my mind is going, I can't let—Anyway, a recurring role! Fast forward— and keep it light! Let's get into it! God willing! God willing.

What's In Your Eye Dear

These comments never get to me because the fact is: everyone is ugly. I'm just allowing the floodgates of criticism to open. Most don't do this. Or if they do, they deal with it in such dramatic, unnecessary ways, as if it's even something *to* be dealt with. I wasn't going to cut up my body like my friend Martha or abuse prescription pills like my friend Martha or sleep with narcissistic men with clinically small penises like my friend Martha. Upon further thought, I should probably check up on Martha, see how that dumb bitch is doing. But, no. No games, no tricks, not for me. I am brave enough, old enough, wise enough to know that none of these things would help. They wouldn't necessarily "hurt" either—they were zero net value, so why bother? It's hard to keep up with the comments while I'm performing anyway.

I decloak my satin robe, toss it on the floor. I climb onto my freshly cleaned, pink-clothed bed on all fours, back arched. I stand on my knees in front of the camera, breasts bare and swinging, thighs stretched open. Someone enters the chat and sends me thirty dollars. Another enters and buys one of my wish-list items: a cast-iron skillet.

I type. I only have seventy-two viewers right now. A bit of a slow day, but I'm just warming up. I lie back,

prop myself on my elbows, and open my legs even
wider.

I pant even harder, just to ensure that this user stays. I
massage my breasts, pinch my nipples.

I crawl on my stomach and lift myself on my arms into
a cobra pose, just so the audience can really see the
length of my breasts: the swimming stretch marks, the
sad puppy-dog eyes of areolas. I turn so my back is on
the bed, keeping my eyes on the camera. My fingers
trail south, pulling my underwear off, and tossing it
with calculated indifference. I won't subject you to the
rest of my routine: not unless you're willing to pay ten
dollars an hour like these fuckers, that is.

By the end of the hour, I have amassed one
hundred and ninety-eight followers, so not too shab-
by. I slide my panties back on, poke my arms through
the robe. My lips kiss the camera.

I end the livestream, and Martha texts me as soon as I
finish. She says my orgasms aren't realistic and I need
to work on that. And it's true, I very rarely cum, with
myself or anyone else. So I never really masturbate,
not with pleasure, at least—zero net value, and all. I
used to have sex when I really liked a person, as a reward for making me like them. But I haven't been in
that situation for many years. But, anyway, the men

believe it, so I don't see the issue. It's not like everyone watching is a world-renowned whore like Martha, who can somehow not only cum every time she records but also *squirt*. The elusive squirter. It just isn't fair, really—her biological advantage. She begins her stream, I click. I do this purely for research purposes, to see what new moves are hot and trending. She's also the only other slut on here who is over fifty years in age and over a size fourteen in dresses so I unfortunately do feel some semblance of camaraderie. I don't mind being an outlier when it comes to sex work. Honestly, I prefer it. Too many thin, tan twenty-year-olds; men will find one who's good enough and ignore all others. Now, I *am* "the one," and just being myself has proven good enough for some of these freaks. Supply, demand, my friends.

Who wants to see my tiny, pink flower?

Her seductive voice needs some work: it should be an intonational mix between an eight-year-old girl and an eighty-year-old smoker. Hers is all little girl, no smoker. And referring to her vagina as a flower? Really? So cliché. What's next? *Who wants to see my widdle nipples? What about my no-no area?* Please. But, then again, maybe it works for her target audience: likely men who want a menopausal body with a baby's soul. She twirls the silver, crispy ends of her dry bob. It's like a plastic wig. She bites her bottom lip and furrows her brows, and her fingers slide under her striped panties. I can see her husband—and occasional screen partner—hiding in the corner behind a houseplant, clad in tighty-whities and a ball gag, waiting for his cue. I get a notification and exit her stream. It's from Brian.

He's a Korean, forty-two-year-old cardiothoracic surgeon. Or, at least, that's what his profile says. I give
him specially catered live videos, ones where he's the
only audience member. He requested them after seeing me stick a glass cube in my asshole for four hundred and sixty-three people, my most popular stream
yet. Plus, he paid five hundred dollars per video, no
matter how long it was or what I was doing—to an
extent—so it would be stupid not to do it.

Once nine p.m. rolls around, I am completely
ready for Brian. He likes my hairy legs, my round belly, ashy knees, gray roots, wrinkles—all of it. But there
are a couple of things he likes me to change about my
appearance. He likes me to paint my nails black, wear
red strap-on heels, and draw a mole on my right cheek.
He says I look eerily similar to his middle school the-
ater teacher, and this costuming apparently helps
the charade. It's sweet thinking that he buys porn to
reminisce about a real woman. But then I remember
him telling me that he was married with a kid, so, less
sweet. I leave his last message unanswered, but I call
first—a level playing field. He answers on the third
ring.

Hi, Brian.

Hi, Big Eyes.

He asks me to do a series of tasks:

1: Suck on my left big toe for six minutes.
Difficult position, but I get it done.

2: Finger myself with whatever is closest to
me—it's a stick of nail polish, and it's
surprisingly unproblematic.

3: Rub my big belly, pretend that I'm pregnant,
talk to my unborn and unreal baby. I take
pause at this one.

What?

I type.

You heard me. Do it.

Brian likes weird stuff, but I didn't peg him as a guy
with a pregnancy kink. This is only our fourth session,
though, so I suppose I don't know him too well. I do it
as best as I can: I rub, I make "shushing" sounds.

Are you serious?

I can't see his face, but he sounds angry. Not fake-
sexy-angry but real-angry.

*This isn't a joke to me, and it shouldn't be to
you, seeing as though it's your livelihood.
What the fuck do you—*

I hang up before he can finish. I've never done this on
a stream, and I definitely have never done it to Brian, but I don't even feel the urge to call him back. I

message him two hours later, saying I had connection issues. He messages back, apologizing for his tone, along with a link to a package tracker for something being sent to my house today.

I click on the link within the link. I'm taken to a sex toy shop page. What pops up is a bright pink piece of thin rubber. I click on the arrow: a different angle of the product showing that the rubber can grow in width to produce a sort of funnel. I click on the arrow: a video of a naked dark-skinned girl with long labia and puffy nipples. She fondles the rubber funnel, pulling it in and out like an accordion, sensually fingering its opening as if it's sentient. She then fills it with murky Brita water and clicks the cap on. She lies on the ground, opens her legs, and inserts the toy in like a tampon until it disappears entirely. She clenches her abdomen and water squirts out of her vagina, ostensibly from the funnel. It's called, aptly, *The Squirter*. Squirting is *very* in right now; that's why Martha has twice as many subscribers as I do. I always wonder why men are so turned on by squirting—it seems a little gay, wanting liquid ejected from genitals. But no judgment here, as long as it doesn't give me a UTI. My doorbell rings.

The next time I see him, the next night, I vow to do better. So I prepare myself: I use my new skillet and heat up three cans of beans. I consume that and four beers—for the bloating. I double my dose of Estradiol, hoping the extra burst of hormones will enlarge my breasts. Must. Look. Pregnant. But first, I have to do my daily livestream. I decide to try out my new contraption. I insert the water gun before I start streaming.

I think she ate someone since we saw her last

Please find God. It's not too late.

Kys

I don't care what they think. Their criticisms feed me—literally, that is. I flick my nipples, I play with the skin of my stomach, I do practically everything that doesn't involve actual penetration—can't interfere with the toy.

Can't imagine what her kids think Lol

In all honesty, sometimes I do daydream about a relative popping up, maybe a horny nephew or a curious cousin or my mother. That would be the only thing that could truly embarrass me, traumatize me, and finally force me to find a different channel for income. I don't necessarily hate my job, but I definitely don't want to keep doing it in my old age. I don't know what I want in my old age. I haven't found a good motivator to pursue that question just yet. I see Martha is watching, and I let my silky hair fall over my face like water, just to piss her off. I squeeze my eyes shut, grab onto the pink cloth of my bed, and clench. Nothing. I clench again. Nothing again. I know I don't have the abs of the skinny black girl, but this should be user-friendly for all body types. I simply make the noises and "cum" for them. I kiss the camera goodbye. Done.

I buckle my heels, re-paint the chipped corners of my nails, and place a dot of eyeliner south of my right nostril. I call him.

Oh, baby. You look especially beautiful today.

He wants a relatively normal performance. Dildo-blowjob, anal beads, and clitoral stimulation. The toy has to work this time. It has to.

Cum for me, baby.

I can hear his grunts grow more rapid, more breathy. He's close, and he likes to "cum" together. It's showtime.

Those beautiful brown eyes. I'd like to cum into those eyes. I'd like to blind you with my cum.

I clench and clench and clench. I clench with the force of trying to push a big-headed baby out. No water, no squirting. All that slips out is a fart. It was the beans and beer. He laughs.

Oh, my baby. That's okay.

His moans stop, and his voice is no longer airy, but concrete. He has stopped jacking off. I ruined it. He doesn't sound too angry, though—surprisingly.

Listen, can I talk to you?

I nod my head. I try not to talk on the video chats—only when absolutely necessary. It feels like my voice is the only thing I have left; better to hold onto that as long as I can, to increase its value.

> *What do you do? Or what did you do before this? Were you always a cam girl?*

"Cam girl." Wow, I haven't heard that in a while. I decide to tell the truth. All truths are some version of lies, anyway—they live in the same universe. I type, squeezing my elbows together as I do so, just so he can have something to look at while he waits.

> *Well, I was an elementary school teacher for twenty years. But I fucking hated it. I hate children, sadly. I wish I could've realized that earlier, but. Is what it is.*

He clears his throat.

> *So, I'm guessing no kids of your own.*

I shake my head.

> *I want you, like, really want you, baby.*

I smile and bat my lashes.

> *No, like, actually want you. I want to fuck you.*

I accidentally let my face fall from interested to disconcerted. I try smiling, but I look like I'm in pain. My left eye twitches.

> *I'll pay ten times what I pay per video. I'll pay*

half of it now, wait.

I can hear him type on his phone. I play with my breasts as he types, just in case this is a test. I get a notification. There it is in my account: twenty-five hundred dollars.

> *Tomorrow. Before your stream. I want you*
> *before the rest of them.*

He's watching me process this all. I feel vulnerable. I've never been a prostitute. I'm not against it morally, but I feel much more confident in my solo performances. The camera makes me seem like a star. Reality, not so much. I nod my head and hang up. He didn't even ask for pregnancy stuff today, what a waste.

The next day, I clean my sheets, clean my room, clean my house. I shave my entire body, apply moisturizer, blush. I just feel like I have to do something out of the ordinary. I use permanent marker for the mole and for my nails. I need my appearance to be as convincing as possible—no opportunity for smudging. I brush my hair, click on my heels. The doorbell rings.

He's Indian. Odd for him to choose Korean as his preferred ethnicity, but whatever. Lie, truth, whatever. And he's young, definitely younger than forty-two. I've dated younger men before, but this is the first time I'm feeling weird about it. I decide to leave that to psychoanalyze later. He only lives an hour away and says he took the bus—odd for a doctor. He's short but has sharp bone structure, so it's fine. We make small talk—him about his dying wife and his mentally disabled child, and me apologizing for my failures with *The Squirter*. He says he likes my voice, describes it as "clerical." I'm unsure what that means, but I nod like it's a compliment. He says he likes my smooth legs, my red shoes. He kisses me first, and I put my hand down his pants—level playing field. I won't reveal to you what happened exactly. Not because you aren't paying, but because it wasn't my proudest show.

He leaves, and I get ready for my daily livestream. I insert Brian's toy, and I click. I run my hands over my body, I wave to the camera. My left eye stings with him. My hair is crunchy with him. It looks like Martha's: dry, crinkly, brittle. Maybe now I know why it looks like that. My attention turns back to my eye—it goes from uncomfortable to burning. I look at myself on my computer screen: it's all swollen and red. People are watching. Five hundred and sixty-eight. My most yet. I get a notification. Brian sends a text saying he will pay the rest of the money when he gets his paycheck next week, punctuated with a fire emoji. So many new people are joining, all asking for the same thing: pregnancy play. I rub my belly, and I talk.

I love you.

I say, out loud, to the imaginary child.

I love you.

I say again. One hundred more subscribers join. I continue like this, rubbing, talking. I've definitely gotten better. I coo, I tell the baby that I will be a great mother. I tell the baby that its father is simply on the other side of that screen. The people love this. They're sending me money and gifts and nice comments like "hot" and "keep going." I start crying. Simply from the semen in my eye—it's a surreal kind of pain now, but I believe the suffering adds to it all. My eye is red from inflammation, my face is red from the blush, and my stomach is now red from the contact burn. I look hot: a hot red thing of a woman.

What's in your eye dear

One of the new subscribers says this. I look at his profile picture. A young man. Mid-twenties, maybe. Prematurely balding. Big eyes. Rosy cheeks, yellow teeth, bubbles of spit soaking his smile. He looks autistic—he has that unrestrained, autistic smile. I think about the fact that someone has probably told him that he has an ugly smile. He doesn't, though. He has a beautiful smile, and how dare you insult such a shameless expression of relief? But why would he even ask me that? Is it not obvious what it is? Is this not all obvious? If that's the case, why is he here? This place should only be for people who know what's obvious and what's not. I continue crying, sobbing, really, so hard that my blurry eyes can't analyze his appearance any further. In my tears, his smile looks more similar to a rotten, open wound. I stuff my face in my pillow like a mouth to a napkin, then look back at my screen. The picture is gone. Everything is gone. All black. My computer died.

Martha texts me. She tells me that clips from my private videos with Brian have been posted to the Internet. He apparently runs a meme account with one hundred and forty thousand followers. I look it up. My nephew follows it. My cousin follows it. My mother is probably Brian in an Indian-man-mask and a strap-on, that sadistic cunt. I want to sue him, I will sue him. But the thing is—the damage is done, it's done. Now, no one will have any need to buy my stuff.

I put on my robe, I lie back, and I exhale, which feels more like work than reflex. I rub my belly, missing the patch of hair that trailed its circumference. Trace the rings of my areolas. *The Squirter* is still inside me. I yank it out, dryly, painfully, and the water spills out onto my bed, the pink turning the dirty magenta of my nipples. My stomach still throbs with yesterday's gas; I let the burps and bubbles of my guts play like a symphony. My hand creeps downwards—I touch myself, just to see if anything has changed. Nope. I still feel nothing, worse than nothing, I feel as if I were raping my own body. It feels perverted with no one watching. My body provides no real use to anybody anymore. What a pity. I imagine a camera hanging over my head like a guillotine. I touch my belly.

I love you.

I say.

And the crowd goes crazy.

Transcribed Message Of A Father Talking To His Child Caught On A Forever 21's Dressing Room CCTV

"Alex, listen, put that down for a second and listen: I know I have not been a good father. No, look, listen, I'm talking serious now—serious talk, got it? I was not a good man, in any sense. But, you know, my father was an even worse man. Now, that's not an excuse, but it is a reason, and isn't a reason better than nothing? Maybe not, I don't know, maybe not. I suppose that's only something you can answer. I love to justify, don't I? That's why your mother divorced me, you know—she said I was too defensive. Not angry, but *defensive*. She said it was all the cons of being married to a lawyer without the pros of wealth and status. Well, I might as well tell you all of it now, right? Why hide? What? Am I scared? No, no, I'm not scared. It's hard—it's—some things are still hard to explain to you. You haven't quite reached the age where I can properly—you're only eleven for Christ's sake—basically, I'm sick. I'm very sick, and sometimes a person can get so sick and live in so much pain that the only humane thing to do is let them rest in peace, let them die. You understand? Well. You will one day, it's okay. It will all be okay. Anyway, I'm trying to say that I know I was not a great father—I wasn't. And maybe that's why you turned out so...confused. No, look, I support you, son, I do—you know that. But it's hard...hard for me to swallow, to understand. You know, the dresses, and the makeup. Even if you were a girl, born a girl, I wouldn't let you wear makeup at this age, but of course, your mother feels very strongly about you being able to express your—anyway. What, what do you—? No, no, I'm not being mean. Don't you know how lucky you have it? Jesus! If I did some of the things you did as a kid, my father would beat me to a fucking pulp, I mean—Sorry. I'm sorry. I'm sorry about that. Yes, quarter in the swear jar, ha. I'll never get a chance to settle that tab, will I? Look, I'm just—I'm trying to say—yes, hello? Someone's in here. Yes, hi, hi—listen, I'm trying to have a conversation with my son here—oh. Well, yes, that's good to know. Thirty percent off all bathing suits, okay. That's good to know—got it. Thank you, thanks. Thirty percent off, huh? Probably only because it's the middle of winter, right, son? Ha. Really acting like they're giving us a bargain. Anyway. What was I saying? I was saying, I could've been kinder, more receptive to your feelings. That's why I'm here right now, right? I wanted our last day to be a good one for you. The arcade, McDonald's, now this…place. Seems a bit horrific if you ask me, but, you know, I want you to know that I can be good. That I can do good things. And I just need to tell you these things before I go, things I never got around to telling you. Alex, please? Can you put the mini-skirt down? I'm trying to talk to you. Yes, I'm sure it will look fabulous, but just one second, please? Right— Alexa, right. I'm sorry. God, this place is creepy. The glaring lights and the needy employees, and every-thing looks so cheap. And it smells like pastrami in here—anyway. I never had a stable job, or, really, a sta-ble anything. I was easily distracted, you see. I don't want you to be the same as me, I want you to—Alex, hold off on the ascot, please. Thank you. I'm saying I want you to figure out what you want early. That's the hardest part of life. When you realize what you want, you just need to get it, but I never did find out what I wanted. Largely because I was so deeply unhappy with myself, with my circumstances. That clouds your desire for desire, you see. I'm not sure if I've ever had a "good day"—not once. Well, of course, except the day you were born. Of course, except that—tremendous day. Tremendous. But life has been very…painful for me, son, and with time, it's only gotten worse—I've only gotten sicker. I don't want the same fate for you. I have no idea if you were cursed with the same burden I've been given—I don't know. But all I know is my father never gave me one of these talks, and my life would've probably been a hell of a lot better if he had. Or maybe not, I'll never know. Maybe I'm putting too much pressure on fathers, maybe what they say really doesn't matter all that much. Is that right, son? Or—no, don't answer that. Either way, I'm going to give it to you straight: we all want to be special and interesting and rich and loved and the best. We do. But please listen to me when I say, take what you can get. I competed for seemingly better jobs, better women, and I ended up losing all of them—the ones I had in the first place, the ones I thought I was above. If you can—Jesus Christ, Alex! Would you listen?! I—oh, yeah, actually that skirt does look really good. Really accentuates your calves, yeah. I want you to feel free, son, I do—but not too free. Too much freedom can leave you with nothing at all. You want something. You always want to have, at least, something and—damn, this place is shady. Those lights, and it smells like dog shit now, you smell that? Swear jar, I know, I know. Are you sure this place isn't a cover for a money laundering operation? Ha. Ah, nevermind. In many ways, I'm proud, though. My disgu—or, my…worrying may be a disguise for my pride. Because I could never do what you do. Show up to school in lipstick, face the bullying. In some ways, that makes you a better man than me—or—well, yeah, you get it. But know its limits, know your limits. I didn't. I sure as hell didn't.

I thought I was invincible and now look at me. Now, look where I am. I'm still in love with your mother, you know that? She'll say I'm not, she'll say all sorts of things about me. They're only half-true, you know. But none of that matters now—no, it doesn't. Let's focus on—well—what I'm trying to say, what I'm really trying to tell you here, son, is—wait, is there a fucking camera in here?!"

My Boyfriend

I oil my split ends with pizza grease, shave my stray eyebrow hairs with my dad's old razor, it only makes sense after all, I mean, I've used his cum as eyedrops— my boyfriend's, not my dad's. My boyfriend likes me disgusting is what I'm trying to say. He referenced that letter Napoleon sent to Josephine: *Will be home in three days. Don't wash.* I don't know if I find it funny. It might be, who knows. It's not ideal for my entire body to smell like tuna and blue cheese all day, but it's better. Better than my last lover, who needed to shower before and after sex. He broke up with me mid-fingering because he was unhappy with my "vagina's surplus of discharge." I told his frat brothers that he liked a finger up the butt to get back at him.

College guys are freaky, and my boyfriend is no exception. Since September, I've had three hookups. My Introduction to Sexuality and the Mind professor, the shower-guy, and my boyfriend (my boyfriend likes how I'm basically a virgin). My professor wanted me to spank him while he wore a maid's outfit, the shower-guy actually *did* like a finger up the butt, and my boyfriend loves disgusting women. Women who smell like methane, with skin like gravel. Vagina like an oil spill, mouth like a rabbit's anus. Maybe I'm being dramatic. Maybe I'm being ungrateful. At least he's not a cuck or gay, which, apparently, is asking for a lot.

I only have one class today, but I'm dreading it. It's not exactly fair. Now I have to look at him as if I haven't seen him naked, bent over my twin-sized bed, feather duster in hand. As I swish my mouth with pickle juice, I instinctively go to wipe off an eye booger. I stop myself—I don't want to disappoint my boyfriend tonight.

Today, we're speaking about sexual infantilism and other dysfunctions. I raise my hand, curious about the difference between neurosis and hysteria, but he pretends like he doesn't see me. Probably for the best anyway. Don't want the other students to think anything is up. I poke at the sleeve of the big-nosed girl next to me. She pretends like she doesn't feel it. She just scrunches her big nose and continues looking at Mr. Huxley. College feels like an experiment in not being a person. Mastering the art of being invisible. No one talks to you, and worse yet, no one is obligated to talk to you. Not even the professor needs to know your name. It's kind of like being dead. That's why I feel so lucky to have my boyfriend.

Huxley ends the class by giving everyone a condom. He does this at the end of every class. I wonder if he buys them in bulk, if he has a discount, if he uses them himself. He doesn't look me in the eye as he hands me mine—our fingertips brush, though. He's so obvious about it. Sad, really.

I go to the store. The cashier is pretty but has a neck tattoo. She hands me back the incorrect amount of cash and I say thank you. I get home to make dinner before I go to my boyfriend's. My main food groups are salt and cucumbers. I'm not anorexic or anything, it's just all I can afford. Sprinkle kosher salt on a cucumber: a perfect meal. My dad gives me two hundred dollars a month, and I have to save most of that for school supplies and meals for my boyfriend. A girl with big breasts and pigeon toes walks into me. I apologize. The crossing guard doesn't see me despite my being in the middle of the street. I say it's okay. My front door is open. I walk in to find my boyfriend on my bed, clipping his toenails. He seems unconcerned with the directions in which the nails are flying.

"Hi."

"Oh, hey, babe."

I drop my stuff, close the door. I think about whether this makes sense—if he's supposed to be here. If I'm supposed to be here. I knock on the wall three times as if the density will give me the answer. It sounds hollow, as if there were another room on the other side. A groan echoes. I look back to see a nail flying into my boyfriend's face. He laughs.

"Um…"

"Oh, yeah, sorry, babe. I just wanted to check your place out. It's…nice. Well, actually, no, it's not good. Not good at all. But in a cool way."

I nod. I feel relieved now knowing that this is definitely my house.

"How'd you get in?"

He stands up and sweeps the nails under my bed with his foot.

"Door was unlocked."

"Oh. Right."

I feel anxious about him seeing me eat my cucumbers with salt. I guess I can skip dinner tonight.

"Who's this?"

He's pointing to a framed picture of my dad smoking a cigar hanging over my bed.

"My dad."

He makes a face like a smolder.

"Huh. You look nothing alike."

I don't know the appropriate response to this, so I laugh. He steps closer to me and grimaces as he does so, as if his body wants me, but his face doesn't. I hope his body wins in the end.

"Jesus, you smell like fucking shit."

I click my tongue in a sexual manner.

"Yeah, well, I'm disgusting. Just for you, baby."

I put my hands on his chest and breathe in his body: hot and sour and rotten. Wait—that's just me.

"What?"

He takes hold of my hands, carefully, fearfully, as if they were guns and I was going to use them.

"You like me disgusting, remember?"

He laughs and looks back at the picture of my dad. It's still there, don't worry.

"Liz, that was a joke—well, mostly. I just liked how sweaty you were that day. I didn't want you to shower. But, you know, you should, like, shower sometimes."

I made the all-too-common mistake of believing a man's word as undeniable truth. Shit.

"Well, uh, c'mon. Let's just go."

He drives us to his place. He wants me to meet his roommates tonight. It's a big deal—I've never met the friends of a boyfriend before. I hope they're nice, but not in a way that makes me fall in love with them. Equally, I hope I'm not too much of a siren for them. That would be problematic. His house smells worse than me: like fish and feet and sweating dogs. Wait—again, that's just me.

"That's Derrick. That's Derek. And that's Ferdinand."

Two Asian guys and one Middle Eastern guy in a living room, soaked with bongs and beer bottles and dirty socks. Exactly as I expected—too much so. I wonder if they choreographed this setting just to fulfill my expectations. That would've been nice. I smile, making sure to look at all of them for an equal amount of time, but they're focused on a video game. The screen has cartoon prostitutes and cartoon rifles and cartoon dying children.

"Cool. Two Dereks."

The tall Asian one groans and stabs a stripper as she's giving him a blowjob.

"Yeah. But we spell it differently. And I can tell by the way you pronounced it that you think it's spelled D-E-R-E-K. But mine is spelled D-E-R-R-I-C-K. So."

The short Asian one stifles a laugh and blows up a hospital with seven grenades.

"Oh, sorry. How do you pronounce it then?"

The tall Asian groans again and jizzes on the stripper's open wound.

"Like Derek, but, I don't know, I could just tell you were spelling it wrong in your head—whatever."

The Middle Eastern guy runs over the tall Asian guy in an ice cream truck three times. The tall Asian guy calls him a racial slur. They laugh.

"Oh. Okay."

The tall Asian looks at me and scratches his armpit. The short Asian asks my name. My boyfriend's hand is suddenly on my back: I love it when he gets jealous.

"What the fuck is this stain, Liz?"

I try to look at the back of my shirt—it feels oily and smells like ketchup. Likely a tomato stain from yesterday's pizza. Well, really, three-weeks-ago pizza. I'm planning to ration out the pie to last me a whole month.

"Liz, oh, Liz. Oh, Liz."

The short Asian one is humping the air and moaning sexually while saying my name. Obviously, making fun of my boyfriend. It could be funny—I don't know. All four men laugh.

"Shut the fuck up, bitch. C'mon, let's go, babe."

I don't mind his bedroom. Pictures of busty anime ladies taped to the wall. Half-smoked cigarettes lining the windowsill. Uncased pillows packed with mold. It's sexy. He makes it sexy—cool, even. I kiss him, hard. His mouth tastes like hand sanitizer. I put my hand down his pants and stroke. His dick feels like a worm.

"Sorry, I—"

Ugh, I hate it when this happens. We learned about performance failure the other day. Huxley emphasized the importance of relieving the guy of any shame, any guilt.

"No, it's okay, baby—"

He laughs.

"No, Liz, like, you smell terrible."

Projection. An only natural response.

"I'm sorry, I'm not trying to be mean, I'm not. But, like, I actually cannot fuck you right now."

I sigh and sit down on his bed. It's cold and wet. I'm anxious that it's coming from my vagina. An overflow of discharge, just as shower-guy suspected. And now that my boyfriend wants me clean, he won't find this sexy. I sink into it, let it permeate my jeans, my underwear. No, no—I'm likely sitting on a semi-recent cum stain. Thank God.

"It's okay when you're in a relationship... these things can happen. Just because the lust is fading doesn't mean the love is."

I'm echoing more words I've heard Huxley use in lectures—they sound better when I say them, though.

"What?"

The cum stain feels warm now. My body was the heater it needed for reanimation. That's a great metaphor for me and my boyfriend.

"It's just that, being a boyfriend is a lot of pressure—"

"I am not your boyfriend."

His face contorts into something ambiguous, more ill-intentioned—a frown, possibly.

"Oh."

I get up and walk over to the anime picture. I want to say "Who's this?" as a sort of call-back to earlier. I'm not sure if he'd find that funny, though.

"I thought I was going to visit your family for Christmas."

He laughs and meets the object of my gaze. Maybe he's laughing at the flagrance of her breasts. Yes, it is funny now that I think about it.

"What the fuck? Where'd you get that idea? I'm not even visiting my family—I'm going to Morocco with the boys."

"Oh."

He sits on the cum stain. He seems unperturbed by its warm and wet nature.

"Don't you want to be a therapist?"

"Yeah."

He fiddles in his bedside table drawer. I see the same brand of condoms that Huxley gives us at the end of class. He fishes out a loose cigarette and lights it without even opening the window. The smoke wanders in my direction but dissipates before it can touch me.

"You need to get better at understanding people, then."

We take a shower together, at his request. It's

hot: he soaps up my breasts, my armpits, my vagina. He takes it all very seriously. My boyfriend loves to take care of me. Somehow, in the shower full of steam and lavender and dandruff shampoo, I can still smell the cigarette smoke. When they're soaked in water, I see just how yellow his fingers are from the filters. He sticks a yellow finger inside me. I make the noises men like to hear. I try to give him head, but he shuts off the shower, as if one finger-pump in my vagina was the natural conclusion.

We dry off. I dress back in my stained clothes. I ask to borrow a shirt from him, but he says he doesn't have any that would fit me. Fair. Plus, too many women wear their boyfriend's clothes—it looks homely, tacky. I sniff the pizza stain. Now it smells of mustard and firewood.

"Could you order us a pizza, babe?"

He wants pepperoni and sausage. I let him eat the whole pie. He puts on the show with the busty anime girl. She's fucking a squid. The squid first eats her out, and then she rides one of the tentacles as if it's a dick. I don't understand the logistics of a squid being able to breathe and fuck above water, let alone the tentacle-as-a-dick-anatomy, but I won't question it. Now that I'm clean, I get a more accurate read on the scent of his room. The now-dried cum stain smells of pennies, the pillows of decaying flesh, and my boyfriend of hollandaise sauce. I see a boner prickling in his pants, growing behind the laptop screen. I try one more time, I tiptoe my fingers along his neck, striding across his jaw, pulling down his bottom lip slicked with pizza grease. He belches, and a shred of regurgitated meat shoots out of his throat and onto the laptop screen. It conveniently lands on the anime girl's bare vagina.

"Damn, I'm beat. You can walk back to your place, right, babe?"

When I get home, I eat half a cucumber and a teaspoon of salt. Instead of sprinkling a little and then biting a chunk and repeating, I fit the entire cucumber half in my mouth, along with the teaspoon of salt, and force my throat to swallow. That doesn't suffice, so I eat the pizza as well—the remaining slice and a half. The texture has turned to cardboard, so first I have to microwave the pizza and then I have to blend the pizza. Then, I drink the pizza. I pretend it's soup, which, technically, it is. I stare at the picture of my dad. The lit tip of the cigar is cut off so it almost looks like he's sucking this disembodied dick. Only if you squint your eyes, though. Huxley would say this is all Freudian, call it a symptom of sexual repression. A knock on my door bounces off the thin walls. I wipe liquid bread off my mouth. The picture speaks.

"Did you pick up the prescription?"

I nod. The picture grumbles.

"Good. Good. What about my cigarettes?"

"On the table."

The picture coughs a dry cough. I say you're welcome. I finish my homework assignment on sadomasochism and email it to Huxley. He'd better not give me a bad grade just because of our history. And it is his favorite topic after all.

The next day is Saturday. No class. I go to the campus park to study like I do every Saturday. I sit in one of the wooden lounge chairs, usually surrounded by bright flowers and vibrant shrubbery. Although most of the shrubbery seems to be dying, and the flowers are just seeds, so my surroundings are really just mud and yellow ferns. I see single people walking and I feel bad that they don't have a boyfriend to walk with. I see couples walking and I feel bad that their relationship sucks so much that they have to show it off in public to feel good. And I see shower-guy. He's walking up to me. He's wearing a backwards cap and a "D.A.R.E." tee-shirt—ironic, I'm guessing. His eyes are hollowed and his stubble needs a shave. He probably had a late night sexually assaulting underage girls and force-feeding a freshman his own vomit. I'm glad I left him—too much toxicity.

"Hey. You're in Huxley's class, right? What's your name?"

"Lizzy," I say with a laugh. Brave of him to initiate contact, but he's still so mad that he's pretending not to know me. Cheap shot.

"I wasn't there yesterday—do you think you could give me the notes I missed, Izzy?"

I scoff. I shrug. I sigh and hand him my notebook.

"How're the brothers?"

He drops the notebook into the vacant garden before him and picks it back up without wiping off the mud.

"Um. Uh, well—my brother is good. He's good. Don't talk to him much, but—"

"No," I laugh. God, he's such an idiot. "No, I mean the frat brothers."

He's silent for a moment.

"I...don't...know. I'm not in a frat."

He looks at me as if I were the stupid one. Men and their psychological games. He takes a picture of each page, laughing, and hands the notebook back to me. Our fingertips don't brush, but I know he was thinking about what would happen if they did. He walks away and clenches his butt as he does so, probably missing the feeling of my pointer deep inside of him. A blonde man in a tweed suit catches my attention. He's walking with purpose. He's walking as if he must. He walks toward me: it's Mr. Huxley. Jesus! What's with these men just "casually" bumping into me today? Are they stalking me? Should I tell my boyfriend? No, I don't want him to get so jealous that he does something he'll regret. I'm not blind to the laws of the universe: I'm a young, pretty, vulnerable woman, and men can't help but find themselves drawn to that. But I'm a person, too. I am not this idea nor accessory. I have needs and boundaries. My dad did tell me I'd be a heartbreaker when I was younger, but this is getting out of hand. Mr. Huxley sits in the lounge chair next to me, pink-faced, out of breath. His hands are shaking. A green vein pulsates in his left temple. He's probably embarrassed.

"Thought you'd be here. Listen. Elizabeth. You gotta stop emailing me those inappropriate things, okay? I am your professor. Please don't make me go to the Dean. Please."

Playing hard to get. I'm familiar with this one. Seeing him stressed and hunched over in a lounge chair feels wrong. I want to tell him to lie back, mostly to see the indents of his crotch.

"My name is Lizzy. It's not short for anything, it's just Lizzy."

"Did you hear what I just said?"

His voice oscillates between having an edge and the cadence of a crying toddler. He's pulling out all the stops. I prefer the edge.

"But what about the first day?"

"What about the first day?"

His forehead is glazed in sweat. Reminds me of various sexual positions I've seen in him. He's a real sex-sweater. He never got me off either. That's unrelated but feels important.

"You showed me a dick pic."

He laughs, and his face burns a bright red, as if I pricked his arm right now, all that would seep out is air because all the blood is stuffed in his head.

"Lizzy. We were going over penile anatomy. That was a diagram on the board—you do realize that that wasn't my actual penis? Right? You do realize that?"

I nod. I know people like to rewrite history out of shame, out of guilt. But he should, of all people, know that denial is an unhealthy coping mechanism. I try to think of the diagram, but all I see is his horse-cock hanging from the curtain of his maid's skirt.

"What about the maid's costume?"

"What? What maid's costume?"

I shake my head, casually, as if I misspoke. Or as if he misunderstood me. As if someone mis-something-ed and it's actually no big deal. He's about to pat my knee, but stops himself. I stroke his trembling thigh since, apparently, I'm the only one with any courage around here. He sighs and walks away, temple still throbbing, and slips on a mud patch. He doesn't fall, just a rolled ankle, I believe. I pretend like I don't see it, for his sake. I open my muddy notebook to study for our next test on the Electra complex, but all I find are doodles of Mr. Huxley's genitals.

My phone buzzes on my walk back home in the evening. It's my boyfriend. He's breaking up with me. He's angry. Angry that I'm telling people that I'm his girlfriend. It's not like I really told anyone—just the big-nosed girl in class and the cashier with the neck tattoo. The big-breasted, pigeon-toed girl, the crossing guard, Mr. Huxley. But that's basically nobody. Self-sabotage, that's what this is, that's what he's doing. I think the real issue is I was too clean for him—it rubbed him the wrong way. He was a dirty man with a dirty room, and I simply could not condone that. It's punishment, is what it is. It's difficult dating a sexual pervert, I know that now. I try sending him a hotline number for pedophiles—hoping that they would be equipped to handle this as well—but it seems like he's not ready to face his demons yet, as he responds with even more anger. I tried. It's fine, I'll start a relationship with Derrick, that's what I'll do. He sent me a video of him jacking off his horse-cock while repeating my name, which means he wants me. So obvious, really. Or was it Derek? Well, anyway—you get it.

Ms. Kraut-kremer's Class

"And even after the liposuction and the eating disorders, I still didn't feel small enough—still don't. I'd, well—I do this thing where I hunch my shoulders and suck in my breath, and it makes my frame seem tiny and it, and my breasts appear larger. I've been doing that every time Todd and I have sex, and I did it really, like a lot, the last time we had sex. It was really mostly a show for him. He's depressed, and his medications make it so—well, he can't always get it up. I tried to get him to stop taking Prozac, but he refused. That's honestly reason number one why I'm leaving him: he chooses pills over love. So, but, I make a real thought-out performance, you know, to help with his disability. Arch my back and tweeze my nipples every ten seconds, and do the thing I just said. He loves it. Or, at least, I think he does. Come to think of it, I don't know if he even came the last time. That asshole."

The Indian girl with the septum piercing says this—Angela. I can tell she thinks her ability to over-share is brave and endearing when it's really neither of those things. She most definitely constructs her personality around her complicated relationship with her father. She's wearing a sweatshirt three times her size, which insecure girls do to look small, but it really just makes them look poor.

"Good, Angela, *goooood*. Anyone else care to share a vulnerability?"

"My dad's dying of cancer!" someone yells. "My glucose allergy has prevented me from living the life I want!" another adds. Ms. Krautkremer slow-claps and lowers her head.

"Very well done. These are making for some fabulous icebreakers, guys."

She walks to the back of the classroom and then back to the front, slow and pensive. Her brows furrow, her tongue clicks, her palms rub against each other like a comic book villain.

"Now, I want everyone to...stand up and shake. Yes, good idea—let's stretch. C'mon now, guys, don't be shy!"

I look around to see everyone standing up and flinging their limbs about. I've already got them all figured out. The white girl with dreadlocks sitting next to me is undeclared with a black Buddhist boyfriend. Her name is something feminine that she purposefully shortens to something masculine, like Danielle or Alexandra. She likes kratom and ketamine and writes autofiction about losing her virginity at fourteen. I crack my neck, then my fingers. Clara. The Latina with the hourglass figure and B-cups in all black behind me—she's a dancer. She likes Joan Didion and tattoos of bows and sororities in theory, but not in practice. She's taking this class because her boyfriend is taking the class. Peter. The one with the steel-framed glasses and eyebrow piercing, carrying around his annotated copy of *Infinite Jest* like it's an award. He's Clara's boyfriend, and he's here to overuse the word "ostensibly" and find new avenues for pussy. I shake out my left leg, then my right. And, of course, Ms. Krautkremer. A self-proclaimed "kooky" teacher. One with unbrushed white hair and bulging blue eyes. Saggy tits covered in handmade sweaters. Flat ass, prognathic jaw, a neck like wrinkled labia. Turquoise rings, worn-out clogs, and a need to dramatize every word she says. You have sex dreams about her, and you're unsure if you should feel ashamed of those sex dreams. I sit down.

"Good? Good. Now, let me get into what this class is really about—what The Odyssey of Writing is all about, why don't I?"

She smiles. Her teeth are straight, but they're entirely gray, like dead skin. Her lips are painted in fuchsia and her eyelids in lime green.

"It's about you. It's all about you. You have to start thinking as if you're writing in your head. Change your mindset so that you automatically think in sentences worthy of writing down."

I agree with her. And I like her. And I like that I agree with her.

"And I'll give you a real cheat code because no one wants to tell you this, they want you to think that all stories are interesting, but some stories are just more interesting than others. They just are."

She clears her throat before continuing, meaning the next sentence is going to be groundbreaking. Or at least intended to be so.

"Self-mutilation, rape, and seeing your parents naked."

I look around to see my classmates fervently nodding. I wait to nod before more is said.

"Those are the three most universally interesting topics one could write about. So that is your first assignment in this class. Write something, any form, any length, that has to do with one or even all of those themes. The more you can get in, the better. Due tonight."

She gives us the rest of the classtime to brainstorm ideas. I decide to write a poem. Poetry has always been difficult for me. The abstractness gives me headaches or makes me feel stupid, but that's good:

I want a physical and mental challenge. I make my character, my subject, an old asexual Indian man. It's the least I can do to make my story stand apart from my classmates' other cutting, rape-victim protagonists. But I give him my name. The plot goes as such: the man, Michael, leads a happy life, never having sex, not even feeling the urge, because he had a good upbringing, a good family life, a good childhood, and we all know sexuality is simply a trauma response from bad parents. He lives in a God-forsaken—name undisclosed—town, one riddled with crime and debauchery and general disorder. But it's okay because his parents are kind people: his father kisses his cheek, and his mother reads him bedtime stories even when she's tired. His lack of sexuality represents his inner peace.

He was born and bred as a spiritual person, a person who believes that energies can be transferred from one human to another, both through thought and touch, so naturally, he becomes a master of energy work. He makes a living doing this and finds it very fulfilling—people travel far and wide for his contact healing. However, his most masterful and transcendent work comes from the pain he inflicts on himself for other people, but only a select few request and receive this. At times, he has cut himself open and bled on clients to heal their minds. Once, he created a gash from his sternum to his belly button which he pressed into the back of a patient for a full hour. This patient went on to win the lottery and cure cancer.

Besides this, Michael lives an ordinary life. He lives in a hut in his hometown, all alone. He likes pineapple and brisket and the occasional glass of Scotch. He likes writers like F. Scott Fitzgerald, but not writers like William Faulkner. He likes making tea when he feels ill and freestyle dancing when he feels happy. He likes succulents and over-watering. He is a simple man.

Upon his seventieth year, he is old, he is tired, and both of his parents have recently passed, peacefully, in their sleep, hand-in-hand. He knows he has little time, but he wants to spend the rest of it dedicated to his craft. He feels he hasn't reached his peak—he hasn't performed his magnum opus of energy work yet. As he's desperately searching for his next muse, a new trend of misconduct plagues the town: "corpse banging" is what the streets call it. Gangs go out during the night, dig up freshly deceased corpses from their graves, then rape them. This tragedy rages on for weeks, and the wrongdoers go unfound and unpunished. Every day, a different cadaver's face is plastered on Michael's daily newspaper, a different dead-eyed victim. One day, upon drinking his tea and tending to his final living succulent, he scans the paper and feels his entire body calcify: his father's face comprises half of the front page.

Michael does the only thing he can do in this situation: he goes to the police station to verify his father is the victim, carefully saws off his father's penis when the cops aren't looking, and fucks himself with it when he's back in the safe solitude of his hut. In this way, the energy is transferred: Michael is now the one who has been raped, not his father, and now only he alone must bear the trauma. It is his greatest, most profound work to date. After what he feels is a sufficient amount of time, he stops and smiles, proud to have taken that burden off of his parents and shifted it onto himself, his final "thank you" to those who made him.

Later that night, Michael dies of natural causes in bed, holding his own hand.

But as a poem, the story reads:

A boy—a man, with a groin, but no grain,
Mother and father, speak kindly to blame
Yet fire and fallacy and fear reign on,
This war could hardly count as won

With and without a touch, he heals,
He pries himself open for all,
And in worship, you'll keel

The gods have died and the terror only grows,
Man sinks old and his followers blow cold
The one above—his reputation was tarnished
Only one can make it right
By taking his manhood, he must harness it

The saint, the master, the son—he saves
People from heartbreak or failure, even graves

I finish and turn it in before class ends. I look over to see dreadlocks girls scribbling. *But I don't like being the one in control of my fate. That's why I never leave a fortune cookie unopened or uneaten* her paper reads. So surface-level. And where are the necessary themes? It's like she's not even trying. It's honestly exactly how I'd expect a college girl to write, and that's the worst crime of it all: the predictability of her soul. Ms. Krautkremer dismisses us before I can read any more. As my classmates leave, each one finds an arm loitering outside the door to hang onto—boyfriends and girl-friends and regular friends just patiently waiting for the class to end. College kids these days are so lonely and underdeveloped. The only kind of love they know is infatuation and chronic companionship. They need a chaperone just to go to the post office—just to walk home, evidently. Angela open-eyes-kisses whom I'm assuming is Todd, a white guy who looks anemic and underfed, just as I suspected. Dreadlocks girl finds her black boyfriend wearing Mala beads and a patchwork fleece. Clara latches onto one of her dancer friends and purposefully ignores Peter; she's mad because he was making eyes at Angela for the whole class. I walk home alone. I reread my poem three more times, each from Ms. Krautkremer's point of view. God, I'm good.

THURSDAY / 11:30 a.m.

I enter the classroom as if walking on air, as if some other sweet force is pushing me in, as if my legs don't need to function—I'm well past that. Unmoored, like a rising hot air balloon. I feel high, above everyone else, knowing I wrote something they could never imag-ine in their worst nightmares. The fluorescent lamps don't feel as oppressive or futile today; they're more like hungry spotlights. I change seats. Dreadlocks girl smelled of body odor and sandalwood—I don't need her scent abating my creative flow. I sit down next to a young man. He's not much better—he smells of hal-itosis and cigarette smoke. He has a light grazing of a beard. Hazel eyes, greasy ginger hair. Flannel, jeans. I can't exactly categorize him yet.

"What's your name?" I ask.

He scoffs.

"Michael."

I laugh.

"Oh, me too."

He nods, raises his eyebrows in sarcastic shock, and gives me a fake smile. I suppose the category of dick will have to suffice. I really can't take jealousy to heart. Ms. Krautkremer clears her throat and slaps her hands together. The rings clink like a butter knife to a wine glass.

"Hello, class, *helloooo*. I'm going to be honest with you guys because honesty is important, is it not? I am no great reader or writer. I do not have any kind of degree in literature. But you know what I do have a degree in?"

Ms. Krautkremer lets her jutting jaw hang open. Clara sneezes. Someone hiccups.

"*Life.*"

Michael writes something down in his notebook. What could he have possibly written down?

"I have *lived*. I've experienced so many things, more than the average person. Which honestly makes me the most qualified person to teach this class."

She's a sister of the dean's—that's how she got this job. Or she's fucking the dean. One of the two. Her eyelids are mint green today. Lips still fuchsia.

"I've read everyone's submissions for the last piece. There were some good ideas, but I've been largely…disappointed."

She looked at me when she said, "Some good ideas." Or maybe she was looking at the other Michael.

"I need you guys to dig deep. If you haven't

suffered enough, then you need to work on that."

I nod and look around, hoping to join in on her disapproving attitude, hoping to come off as one of her instead of one of them. She walks to the back of the classroom, then back to the front, continuing to chastise the students. I stealthily zone in on Michael's notebook. I see the beginnings of a poem.

THERE IS NO TRUTH
Some may like it, but don't find that as diagnosis
For a man with a soul like his Has nowhere to go but

Wow, this is even worse than predictability—it's just plain bad. It's trying to outwit itself; it's trying to say everything by saying nothing. Pure laziness. How easy it is to call yourself a poet nowadays. Michael scoffs and noisily shuts his notebook. Ms. Krautkremer clears her throat.

"But don't look so forlorn, guys. I have an exercise we'll try today that I think should produce epic results."

Ms. Krautkremer huddles us into a circle, and orders us to hold hands and close our eyes. She asks us to scream our greatest fears, and in this way, it will stay anonymous, which is obviously flawed logic because we all sort of know each other's voices—plus, it's not like our eyelids are sewn shut. I hear some quiet grumblings and shoes squeaking. There's silence for a long time. So long that I stop counting the seconds because I just assume it's been an eternity. At a certain point, I believe no one is ever going to say anything until I hear "Sex!" sung by a clearly gay male voice. I open my eyes. Everyone else's eyes are closed. Really? Do they all trust each other that much? Some

laugh, but a laugh of comfort and gratitude, because
then people begin to scream, really scream, completely over each other, with relief and volume.

"The Hat Man!"

"Dying alone!"

"Western propaganda!"

"Myself!" Angela bellows. She's standing opposite me. Her lower lip is quaking.

I'm not sure if I find this lame or beautiful or
both. What does any of this have to do with writing?
I don't need a faux sense of community, I need technical advice. Something concrete—I already have the
spiritual down. And suddenly something floods me,
a murky, shaking breath of vulnerability. Then that
flushes out of my system like a sneeze, and a profound
power takes its place—knowing I'm the only one with
sight. I find myself lifting my head and momentarily
closing my eyes.

"Not having anything to say," I state, loudly,
not exactly screaming. They have to scream to excrete
their truth—I've never submitted to such ostentation.

I open my eyes. I see a few students half-smil-
ing, but most are looking comatose. There's silence for
a while. Somehow, even longer than the first silence.
A silence that makes my ears ring and my vision go
fuzzy. I bet some are regretting their screams after hearing mine. Some more shoes squeaking. Peter coughs.
Then: "Black people!" cried by, of course, dreadlocks
girl. Ms. Krautkremer's bug eyes pop wide open.

"Okay, okay! That's it for today. Yes, well, I
think I'll cut class a little early, why don't I? Give you
a head start on that short story due next week."

Everyone shuffles back to their seats, grabs
their bags. Dreadlocks girl's face is entirely flushed.

"And class? Remember, you have a required reading—I've sent you all a link. It's a book called The *Odyssey of Writing*. Written by…yours truly."

She does a little curtsey. Peter coughs again.

"Well, um, yes, so, make sure you buy the book and have it for the next class."

Clara leaves and holds hands with her dancer friend, who was waiting just outside the door. The two women kiss on the lips. That can't be right, I could've sworn she was dating Peter. And Peter now has his arm over Angela's shoulder as they walk out together—at least I was right about one thing.

"Michael W.? Can I speak to you in private?"

Ms. Krautkremer asks this. Some students stifle laughter as if this is primary school and I'm about to get scolded. I loiter by her desk. There are Hello Kitty stickers and multi-colored gel pens and smiley faces on papers where scores should be. Maybe this *is* primary school. She waits until the last student leaves, then holds up my poem, printed, for me to see, as if I hadn't written it myself. There's no smiley face, just a big bubble-lettered question mark.

"Well, I mean, I…I just don't get it."

I smile. I like that I've confused her—isn't that the whole point of poetry? I tell her the entire intended plot anyway, wanting points awarded both for its intention and its obfuscation. At first, her stoic jaw clenches, her nostrils flare, and her eyes half-close as if she is about to sneeze, or maybe orgasm. But then she laughs, a steady laugh of pride and delight, and nods her head softly, subtly, letting a smirk grow at the corner of her mouth.

"Magnificent, wow. That's good, Michael. That's *veryyy* good."

She performatively slow-claps for me—just the motion, not making any real sound. I kind of want her to make the sound.

"I shouldn't say this, but you're already becoming my favorite. I can tell you're a *bright thinker*," she whispers, then winks. I wink back for some reason.

I walk home. The stakes are high, and my next story has to be perfect. But my mind is completely empty. I feel as if I had given everything to my poem. I spend the following weekend reading Ms. Krautkremer's book, the whole thing, front to back. It's mostly her talking about her love affairs with younger men and a manic episode she had in Peru—very little writing advice to be found, which I should've expected, really. Still, my mind is empty. I go people-watching; I go to the zoo, the park, a bar. But everyone becomes caricatures of themselves, no one feels real enough to write about. I always thought "writer's block" was a cheap, lazy excuse, but how wrong I was! It is catastrophic, disabling. It feels like I've never had an idea before in my life. What was it to think? How do people fix this? Why do people take writing classes? All they do is make you aware of your thoughts, which is ostensibly the worst thing a writer could do for themselves. The number one killer of creativity is someone asking you to be creative.

TUESDAY / 11:30 a.m.

I am trying to think of something, anything. A sequel where Michael's estranged son is a gay anemic with a weakness for large doses of NyQuil? God, no—sequels are for posers. Everything feels like it's already been done before; everything feels fake and trite. Maybe I'm not cut out to be a writer. Look at these kids—they're just kids! They know nothing, and neither does the teacher. What am I doing here? Actually, how did I get here? I don't even remember walking here. I hardly remember waking up this morning. This class is making my memories hazy. It's turning me into the walking dead. Everyone's looking at me now. Can they hear my thoughts? Ms. Krautkremer looks angry—puckered purple lips like a shedding snake.

"What?" I ask the air.

Ms. Krautkremer laughs an embarrassed, passive-aggressive laugh and slaps a clogged foot on the floor.

"Michael, I asked: What's your short story about so far?"

I had nothing—I have nothing. I look around, and everyone's still watching me. Clara looks at me with fear. Dreadlocks girl is giving me an amphetamine kind of smile. Angela stares through me like she's imagining my head on a stick. The lights feel like a lamp in an interrogation room. My classmates, like callous jurors. Ms. Krautkremer, a disappointed mother.

"It's about…a…girl."

Ms Krautkremer forces a smile out of her snake-lips and dead teeth.

"And…she tries to make herself…smaller. Smaller whenever in sight of her boyfriend. Her boyfriend has these prescriptions that—they make him unable to perform at times, which she takes as a…personal offense. She wants to leave him, but she'll never summon the courage. She sees his impotence as a challenge, and because of this, she starves herself, gets plastic surgery, contorts her body, all this stuff, and, so, she neglects to focus on his pleasure, so much so that one day, she goes as far as raping her boyfriend. It's not exactly purposeful: she's staring in the mirror behind him as she rides him and gets lost in the alluring, fabricated beauty of her body, so much so that she doesn't hear his protests."

Ms. Krautkremer's mouth is agape, silent. She looks both confused and disinterested.

"And…she also cuts herself with nail clippers and walks into the bathroom to find her mother masturbating," I quickly add.

Ms. Krautkremer smirks and finger-snaps—I guess snapping is her thing now.

"Wow."

Some other students join in and begin snapping as well. Only a few, though. I hear a strained wheeze and then a maniacal laugh.

"That's my story. I told that story on the first day of class—he stole my story! And I never raped Todd, you asshole!"

I turn to see Angela's eyes welling up, her teeth gritting. Why is she here? She should be in an acting class. Or therapy.

"It wasn't a story. It was a series of unnecessary facts you shared. Anyway, don't diminish my work like this. You had nothing to do with it, and to claim otherwise is—"

"Okay, stop! Stop."

Ms. Krautkremer walks toward Angela, placing a cautious hand on her shoulder. I stifle a laugh.

"Angela, does this sound similar to a story

you've written?"

Angela scoffs and looks around, begging for sympathy, which no one will provide—callous jurors defending my honor.

"No, it sounds similar to my fucking life! To my fucking reality!"

Ms. Krautkremer sighs and sways her pointer finger in the air.

"Oh, dear Angela, reality means nothing, don't you know that? Have I taught you nothing?"

They both look at me. Everyone is looking at me. Still.

"I find that plot tremendously interesting, Michael. Well done."

I smile and do a little bow in my seat. We spend the rest of the class silently reading Ms. Krautkremer's book. Not much teaching in this class, huh? I spend my time working on the short story. I find new avenues of my protagonist's personality. She's ethnically ambiguous and has abandonment issues. She cheats on her boyfriend, tending to go for the sensitive, intellectual types. She likes fortune cookies and mint-flavored vapes. She likes writers like Mary Shelley, but not writers like Jane Austen. She puts her fingers down her throat when she feels sad and tells strangers to kill themselves online when she feels angry. I sense another masterpiece on the way. Just as I'm figuring out the ending—protagonist's boyfriend killing her and her lover—Ms. Krautkremer dismisses us. Angela walks up to me, slowly, hands shaking, eyes watering, her body swimming in a box of a dress.

"Um."

I give her the time to think. She obviously needs it.

"I-I know your life sucks ass seeing as though you're this lonely middle-aged man taking a shitty college class, but maybe try doing something interesting with your life, so that way, you don't have to steal mine."

Her voice cracks on the last word. I never got a good look at her body before. She's definitely skinny, just unfortunate bone structure—broad chest, square hips. She smells of cinnamon gum and sulfur burps. I clear my throat.

"You weren't going to write about that anyway. It paints you too terribly. You're much too insecure for that."

Her eyes flutter, her lips part. She lets snot slide off her piercing and into her quivering mouth.

"I really hope that I—that I never know what it's like to be you."

Angela walks away and buries her head into Peter's chest, who gives me a disapproving head shake, as if his opinion of me means anything, *Infinite Jest* still in hand like it's an accessory—no, like an extra extremity. All so melodramatic. I turn my attention to Ms. Krautkremer. She's talking to Michael—they're both smiling. He runs his fingers through his greasy bangs, inciting Ms. Krautkremer to push a knot of white hair behind her ear. It's unattractive for a woman to act coquettish past a certain age. I can hear her saying the words "bright thinker," unnecessarily elongating the guttural sounds. Her speech is this whole affectation. A tonal hybrid of Transatlantic-accented, Quaalude-popping housewife and Russian warlord with half a lung. She's snapping now. I leave, begin to walk home, past the racist druggie and the curvy lesbian, past Peter and Angela. Her whole being is ostensibly ostentation—Ms. Krautkremer's, I mean. She's probably having an affair with Michael. They'll fall in love, a turbulent kind of love, the one that exists between a boring asshole of a man and an old kook of a woman. Michael will find out that she's still sleeping with her lover and/or brother, the dean. Michael will end things by writing about her, painting her horribly and accurately, and he will turn it in for his short story assignment. Ms. Krautkremer will be heartbroken. She will consider failing him or suspending him. But she won't. She'll ask to see him after class. And she will say, "God, I pray to never know what it's like to be you." Then, she'll try to slap him in the face, but she'll miss, and he'll hold her in his arms, crying, and he'll cry, too, two broken people holding each other in an attempt to make one whole person. And Michael will reveal he's fallen in love with another woman, a classmate, the ethnically ambiguous protagonist! Yes! Yes, that's good. That's good, Michael. That's very good.

It Feels So Good To Be A Victim

He stands at six feet and eight inches tall, with a dick like a dead earthworm drying in the July sun. He likes slapping me, but is strictly against choking me. He dreams of marrying a black woman and raising her biracial babies from a previous marriage—one boy, one girl. And I'm trying to explain this to him, to Jeffrey, that sex between two people is actually just rape. One person always has more power, more access, and that person is the rapist, the other person, the rapee. He's not understanding me, but it's more like he just doesn't want to understand me.

"Oh, really? So I just raped you, right then? That was rape, then?"

He's propped on his elbows now, a defensive pose—feminine, even. But you can be as gay as you want when you're as tall as he is.

"You're making it out like I'm saying it's bad."

He's laughing now.

"Um, yeah! It is bad! I'd say rape is bad, yeah. And you can quote me on that."

I'm laughing now. He's so scared I'm going to cancel him and his three-inch penis. It's cute.

"Yeah, but you know what I mean. I mean, there are, like, two versions of rape. The vicious rape you're imagining in your head, and then the more vague, structural rape. I'm talking about the second one. The one where, like, I don't know if I actually wanted it or not, and you really wanted it."

He lies back down. His Juul lies comfortably, coolly, in the divot of his cobbler's chest. I hit it and set it back down in its natural pocket.

"You…didn't want it?"

Is he mocking me now? No, no. His eyebrows are squirming, bending towards each other. I rub his hairy beer belly. I love lanky guys with protruding bellies—like pregnant anorexic women. It's a weirdly comforting anomaly. Makes too little sense to require any real thought. That's the sweet spot.

"No—it's not like that. It's more like…do I ever want it? Am I even a sexual person, or do I just feel the need to please you? And, like, I don't know. I don't. Probably won't…ever."

He takes a nice, long inhale of the Juul. His stomach makes a guttural gurgling sound. He coughs the smoke into my face. It tastes like saffron.

"Well. That's convenient for you."

I leave shortly after that. Tell him I have to get to work, even though my shift doesn't start for a few hours. I really head home to have sex since real sex can only happen in solitude. You imagine what you did—the thigh touches, the French kissing, the dick-sucking, the inevitable pain. All that sexy stuff. You imagine it all as your plastic dick seizes against your swollen clit. And then you cum, and then it's sex. Most people don't understand this, and by extension, don't understand me. I'm not saying my view of the world is right or wrong. It just is. Anyone who denies it is lying. My vibrator dies mid-climax, and it's a strange feeling—akin to constipation, or dry-heaving. That feeling when nothing meets something. I could see where Jeffrey was coming from, of course. The convenience of seeing sex as rape, of being able to label every hook-up as a rapist. And I've thought about that, about publicly admonishing my bodies as rapists. For the attention, fame, etc. But people would catch on, call bullshit on my dramatics. I take a cold shower, shoot down two shots of espresso, and head to work.

I work as a production assistant for a late-night talk show. The host is this overweight gay man, Mr. Cherith, whose whole schtick is sexually harassing the guests and self-deprecating humor about how fat and gay he is. I work closely with two other production assistants, Brayden and Brandon. They both want to fuck me. I know this because they told the audio guy, Shaun, that there's a running bet over who will be able to fuck me first. Shaun is like a father figure to me, so, of course, he told me. He asked me if he wanted me to report them for sexual harassment, and then I said only if we can do the same for Mr. Cherith, and then we had a nice laugh about it all. Shaun is the first person I see in the studio today after I swipe my badge in, just like every shift.

"Hi there, little lady."

He's a relatively short guy. Gray hair, crooked nose, close-set green eyes. He has a strong stare. The kind of stare where you always know when he's looking at you and, more importantly, when he isn't.

"Hi, Shaun."

He looks so cute with his gear on, his earpiece coiling around his scalp, radio buckled into his pants pocket. Cute in a crippled grandfather kind of way. He's pretending to fiddle with a piece of equipment, a black rectangle with red flashing lights. I'd probably be attracted to him if he weren't so nice to me.

"What's wrong? Sad about the last day?"

"Last day?"

I put my purse underneath the snack table with the vegan fruit roll-ups and salt-free rice cakes. It's always safe there. I see Brayden out of the corner of my eye, stocking a cart with miniature Fiji water bottles and plastic cups of kiwi.

"Yeah, today's the last day. Before hiatus, that is. We get three weeks off…no one told you?"

"PAs are kind of the last to know everything."

Brayden says this. Now he's pushing the cart in my direction.

"Why are you here so early, Brayden?"

Brayden is tall and blonde and was obviously molested at some point during his childhood. There are really no other words to describe him.

"I'm trying to get on Mr. Cherith's good side so he asks me back for next season. You should maybe think about doing that, too."

I'm more than used to Brayden's subtle verbal abuse: he never learned flirtation past a sixth-grade reading level. He's the type of guy to get in physical fights with his sister just so he can have an excuse to see what a woman's body feels like. Shaun rolls his eyes at me and places the black rectangle on his work table. It's no longer flashing red. I smile.

"Anyway, you bring these to Talia's room. I'm going to check if Mr. Cherith is in his office yet."

Shaun winks at me, and I head off, cart-first. Talia is one of tonight's guests: a thirteen-year-old Jewish popstar. I've seen a video of her online singing a clean version of Rihanna's "Bitch Better Have My Money," retitled as "Bubbe Better Have My Challah." It was alright. Got a bit too political for my taste.

Talia and her team enter as I place the last kiwi cup in the mini refrigerator. She dramatically sighs upon seeing me and I say nothing and quickly leave as an apology. I shift focus to the other night's guest: Xavier Diggory. He's a soap opera actor in his forties, and I've seen everything he's in. I'm hoping to get an autograph, or at least get close enough to know what he smells like. Maybe slip my number to his publicist, or at least make his publicist aware that I am single and looking. His team requested raisin-less oatmeal cookies and three cartons of orange juice, so I make a beeline for the Costco just a block away. I have to wait in a line of six people—all of whom are completely oblivious to the fact that I'm holding food that will go in Xavier Diggory's mouth and be digested in Xavier Diggory's stomach. I try to cut, saying it's an emergency, but the child in front of me tells me to fuck off. The man next to him—I'm assuming his father—simply nods his head in agreement.

On my way back into the building, I see Shaun. He's outside, smoking a cigarette. Earpiece still coiled, radio still buckled.

"Working hard or hardly working?" I ask.

I laugh, he laughs. He loves these kinds of non-jokes.

"Trying to avoid the mayhem before the show starts. Princess Talia is not happy."

"What? Why?"

My fingers are growing raw from the grocery bag straps. His fingers are pink and taut and stubby. They're like pigs in a blanket. I lick my lips.

"Something about a kiwi allergy. Guessing Brayden got his fruits mixed up."

He angles his lips downwards and to the left as he exhales—the smoke follows suit.

"Fuckin' Brayden."

"Fuckin' Brayden."

I head inside and set up Xavier's snacks. Then, I write some cue cards and print out some release forms. Most of my job, though, is running around, doing whatever the person closest to me asks. Getting their coffee, steaming a dress, getting their coffee, re-stocking the pen cabinet, getting their coffee, getting their coffee, getting their coffee. As I'm heading to the writer's room with a tray of three Americanos, four espressos, and one affogato, which I improvised on making because I don't actually know what that is, I see Xavier. I see his tight ass in eggplant-colored slacks, I see his curly silver locks. I don't actually see his face, but I can tell it's him. I could eat that ass, could have that hair for dessert. My hands are too full to linger—plus the writers asked for these coffees, like, thirty minutes ago.

The writers are four straight white men, one of whom is Mr. Cherith's son. Everyone calls him "Cherry" for short, but now that I'm thinking about it, he probably doesn't love that nickname. He also happens to be the only one who's nice to me. I use my foot to knock on the door three times—three kicks. Cherry opens the door, smiling and sweating and smelling like tuna salad.

"Here are the coffees," I say, "Sorry, I didn't know what an 'affogato' was."

"God damnit!" says the writer farthest away from me. He's writing the words **CHARADES OF AR-IANA GRANDE'S EX-BOYFRIENDS (BUT NOTH-ING RACIST)** on a whiteboard. Mr. Cherith usually improvises what he says on camera, but the guys are sometimes in charge of coming up with games and segment ideas. They're not very good at it. But, still, I'm intimidated by them in the same way I'm intimidated when I pass a group of teenage girls at the mall, so, yes, I'm frankly terrified of them. They all look at each other and snicker.

"Sorry, that was just a joke."

Cherry says this while actually making eye contact with me. I'm sure he's bullied for being a nepo baby—probably why he's so kind. I nod, set down the coffees, and leave. Mr. Cherith passes me in the hallway, and I smile and straighten my back. Or at least I think it's Mr Cherith. All I really see is a white blob surrounded by a pentagon of security guards. It's showtime. I get to the studio.

Mr. Cherith greets the audience, talks about himself for seven minutes, and then the first guest goes on. This is my favorite part, getting to see Shaun in action. His handling of software and pressing of buttons and saying technical words. Sometimes, he shouts, too. It's exhilarating. I switch my attention to the television backstage. Talia tries talking about Israel, but Mr. Cherith gracefully segues the conversation to scented glitter gel pens. After six minutes, we go to commercial as Talia heads to the stage to sing her newest release, "Single Goys (Put a Kippah on It!)." Conversion propaganda I believe. I mean, I'm close to convinced. Brayden comes up beside me, ruddy-faced, hair filthy with sweat. He's panting. Oh, God, he's panting.

"Where've you been?"

"Emily's sick today, so I've been doing some stuff for her. Just had to grab Mr. Cherith some of that hair gel he likes from Sally Beauty. She asked for it in the group chat."

Emily is Mr. Cherith's personal assistant and the only female friend I have in this place. She's so beautiful that you get angry seeing her do any kind of manual labor. She's sweet, too. She spit in Brayden's protein shake when he asked if I felt tired. She keeps talking about putting her two weeks in, and apparently has been for the last four years she's been working here.

"Oh. I didn't see."

"You should really check the group chat, Sienna."

He swallows back a mouthful of phlegm—or maybe it's vomit? He smells like lunch meat and hairspray and, well, vomit.

"God, did you run there and back?"

"Um, well—yes, actually."

One of the producers shushes us. I nod, straighten my back. Talia's performing now. Her face is as red and shiny as Brayden's. She's really giving it her all. I know child labor is wrong, but some of these kids are simply meant for stardom, or whatever this is. And hats off to her, honestly, for being able to squeeze an extra syllable in Beyoncé's chorus, while standing atop a six-foot rotating mechanical dreidel, I might add.

"Where's Brandon?" I whisper.

Brayden shrugs. I check the group chat—apparently, Emily requested me specifically to grab the hair gel. Whoops. I text her individually, asking if she needs anything else. I also update her on just how red and wet and lunch-meat-scented Brayden is right now. She leaves both texts on read. Talia finishes her song, and the audience claps, cheers, whistles. The cameras cut, and she speedwalks off stage, verbally assaulting her father and/or manager, whom she calls Eric. I hear the words "jackass," "kiwi," and "fired." Not too difficult to work out the message. Brayden's face crumples into itself, the kind of look a dog gets after licking its private parts in public. I look for Shaun. He's fiddling with equipment on his work table. His eyes widen.

"Fuck, I think—yeah, her mic is still attached. Sienna, could you go get it for me? I really can't go into her dressing room. Or I can, but, um, yeah—I really don't want to."

Brayden lights up.

"Oh, I can—"

"No, I got it."

I smile at Shaun and follow the four-foot-nine ball of rage, maintaining a close, yet safe, distance. Oh, God, she's ripping the hair right out of her skull—oh, wait, no, they're just extensions. Now, she's prying her fingernails off—oh, they're fake, too. I wonder how it feels to be more plastic than person at such a young age. Probably not great. Eric opens the dressing room door for her, and Talia slams it shut. I give it a couple of minutes, wait for her yells to subside, then knock three times, this time using my fist. Eric opens up, looking on the verge of tears.

"Um, hi, sorry—I just need Talia's mic."

And that was my mistake: saying her name, waking the beast.

"You! Come in."

I do as the thirteen-year-old girl says. The room is three times the size of my bedroom. Equipped with a flat screen, two mini fridges, and three couches. I stock it almost every day, but seeing her tiny girl body in a room this size is making my stomach turn. Does she even realize how lucky she is to be offered three couches?

"Did you bring me the kiwi?"

"No! Well, yes, but—"

"God. Everyone here is such a fucking imbecile."

Eric mouths the words "I'm sorry" to me. He fetches a Fiji water from the mini fridge and hands it to her, cautiously.

"Sorry, I just need—"

"I know what you need."

She starts unhooking and uncoiling the mic pack from her back, then pulls it out from her chest. She's wearing a white apron dress that stops around her ankles—the only thing age-appropriate about her. Or does it make her look like a child bride? Eric pops off the cap of a prescription bottle and feeds her an oblong blue pill. She swallows and chugs the water with her free hand.

"I know you think I'm a bitch. PAs are the worst of them all."

Eric laughs, nervously.

"Honey, she doesn't think—"

"Shut up!"

I laugh. I don't mean to, it just happens. Talia smiles, and Eric recoils and slinks away, feeding himself one of the oblong blue pills.

"You're new and—you know you have to be a bitch, right? Or else people take advantage of you. So get used to it, or find something else to do. That's my advice."

I laugh, straighten my back. She's going to be a great mother someday. I think I wish she were my mother right now.

"I didn't ask for advice."

She laughs. She laughs, big and loud and airy. She laughs as if she were a fifty-year-old woman dressed in a little girl mask. She laughs as if I said something funny.

"Here's your fucking mic."

By the time I get back, I see that the show is wrapping up. Mr. Cherith is bidding goodnight to the audience. Brayden is pounding down a mouthful of vegan fruit roll-up. Shaun is taking off his earpiece and unbuckling his pocket radio.

"Fuck, I missed it?"

Shaun smiles. He looks naked without his gear on, but also pure. Think: Benjamin Button as a baby.

"Who? Xavier? Yeah, yeah. They tried out a new segment that Cherry came up with. It's like strip poker, but with 'Finish the Lyrics.'"

"Wait, Xavier got naked?"

Shaun laughs.

"Um, well, pretty much. They got him down to his briefs."

"Is he in his dressing room?"

Shaun and Brayden look at each other and laugh. No matter how much Shaun is on my side, he'll always be a man first.

"No, uh, no. I'm sorry, little lady, but he left."

Fucking hell. That's what this job is—getting so close to everything you want, but never quite getting there. Mr. Cherith walks off stage, into our little nook of snack tables, wires, and heat exhaustion. The few seconds of the day that he's not either surrounded by cameras or gun-wielding goliaths. Very vulnerable when I think about it. Almost as if he trusts us. I look at him and smile, and he smiles back.

"Good morning, sweetie," he says to me.

He says it in a quick, reflexive manner, and it's obviously not morning, but I say it back anyway. It's the first words I've spoken to him, ever. He looks so different—from TV, I mean. Much shinier, much bigger, like a wax statue. Before I even think of it,

Brayden runs after him, intent on being the one to retrieve his mic pack and receive his much sought-after face time. I leave to shuffle the audience members out. It's ninety percent overweight moms and their sexually confused sons. I tell them "thank you," "have a nice night," "come back again," and pretty much rotate the three. They're usually still too starstruck to say anything back, just nod and smile giddily. But one mother comes up to me, a young mother with a son in a wheelchair. She begins to pull something heavy out of her bag—at first, I believe it to be a gun, but quickly realize it's a bottle. A champagne bottle.

"Thank you. Thank you so much. It was a great last show."

The son is crying. Happy tears.

"Please give this to Mr. Cherith, if you can. A thank you," the mother tells me.

"Of course."

I nod and take the bottle. The mother and son look at each other, excitedly, whispering and giggling as they walk and roll away, as if I myself am a celebrity they just spoke to. I guess this is the perk of the job—being able to make someone's week without doing all that much. The next person to walk out is a cataract-ridden woman in her eighties, dressed in a T-shirt with Mr. Cherith's face on it, who tries taking the bottle from me. I keep my grip firm and calmly point her to the nearest exit.

When I get back, everyone has pretty much dispersed—left. Workday over. Shaun is still here, attempting to separate two interlaced cords. Brayden is throwing out most of the uneaten food while covertly shoving some in his backpack.

"Well. That's it, boys. It's been a pleasure," I

say.

Brayden tosses on his backpack—it rides up to his shoulders.

"Sienna, I thought we could go out for drinks. To celebrate."

Oh, Brayden. He must know I cannot accept the sexual offer of a man wearing a backpack. Shaun fails at muffling his laughter in the corner.

"Um, maybe another day, Brayden. But, yeah, so—"

I stick out my hand for him to shake. He takes a moment before he gives in. His palm is sticky, gummy. He looks sad and wants me to know it.

"Alright. Well, then. Bye, guys. Bye, Shaun."

Shaun does a patronizing little salute goodbye. I laugh, and we watch Brayden's overgrown blonde bobbing head leave through the closest staircase.

"Whatcha got there?"

Shaun motions his head towards the bottle.

"Oh, champagne. A fan gave it to me to give to Mr. Cherith, but I—"

Before I can finish, he plucks the bottle from my hand.

"Got anywhere you need to be?"

I shake my head no.

"Then follow me."

He takes us to the roof. We walk a labyrinth to get there; one elevator ride, five turns, six flights of stairs. We walk, wordlessly. I think about making a joke about him leading me to my death, but I decide against it. It's just the sound of his heavy, wet breathing—like a drain emptying. I trust him, but not the way I trust my friends or my parents. I trust him with a blind vulnerability. I trust him like I trusted that young mother who I thought was going to pull a gun on me. I trust him, likely in the way Mr. Cherith trusts his unknowable employees. It could go horribly wrong, but I have no control either way, so I may as well lie down and take it. A collision hurts less when you don't tense your muscles. He inserts a key into a door emblazoned with the words "NO ACCESS."

"And here we are."

Shaun swings the door open and shines his phone's flashlight. I still can't see much, besides wide open space. Some big machinery and mysterious architecture, the kind that's supposed to be on roofs. And, of course, the skyline of murky gray rectangles and flickering yellow dots meant to make you feel small and unimportant. Not one star in the sky.

"How do you have access to this?"

He shrugs.

"Sometimes we record ADR here, so."

I walk forward—every step feels like its own little crime.

"Oh. Right."

There's a wooden anti-homeless bench facing the ledge—a three-seater. I sit on the right side, and Shaun in the middle. A metal fence lines the periphery, just tall enough to obscure my view sitting down, making it pointless. Shaun undoes the champagne bottle's dressing, then takes his big fat thumb and pushes the cork until a popping sound echoes. I scream, Shaun laughs.

"There we go!"

Shaun feeds the champagne's spilling pre-cum directly into his mouth. Some leaks out onto his stubbled chin, his lavender button-up. He's a fit guy—taut and compact. Even sitting down, I see little opportunity for protruding fat. He has two long, flimsy ears, each holding a small black gauge. He kind of looks like Wallace Shawn if he were fuckable. He hands me the bottle with a foamy smile. I chug.

We spend the next hour drinking and talking. I find out he's been married and divorced twice, with a child from each marriage—one boy, one girl. The second one was adopted because his wife was trans—he's really intent on letting me know his wife was trans. They're both teenagers now, the children, and he has a sneaking suspicion that they have a crush on each other, but he feels too awkward to bring it up. I find out he's forty-six years old and he likes making short science-fiction stop-motion films. He posts his films on a site called GalaxyGorge.com and has three hundred and thirty-seven followers. I tell him I'm really impressed. I tell him that I think I want to be a producer, but for the most part, I don't know what I want to do with my life, that I don't know if I have any real interests or hobbies, but maybe everyone thinks that. I tell him I only got this job because my mother is friends with Mr. Cherith's personal assistant. I tell him that I checked my email as we were walking up here, and I got a text from the personal assistant saying today is my last day, invariably. I tell him I got a text from Brayden saying he got the job for next season with a winky face emoji. I tell him I don't care, though, and that the only thing that sounds exciting to me is moving to a place I've never heard of, learning its history and culture and language, and making that place my new home, and that maybe I'll do that. A long silence ensues after that.

"Huh. So...how do you feel about the political climate right now? What the Senate is proposing is just absurd," he says, followed by a sour burp.

"Yeah, it's...crazy. It's definitely crazy."

He laughs. I take the bottle from his hands and chug the last sips. He laughs again, this time to himself.

"This is going to sound so weird, but...never mind."

I elbow-jab his ribs.

"No, what?"

"No, no, I can't—"

"No, you can't do that, you have to tell me now, you can't just do that!"

He swipes his hand across his mouth, hunches over so his forearms are perched on his knees. He looks back at me, and his eyes are like dark seaglass, his bottom lip wet and twinkling.

"Have you ever stuck a wine bottle up your pussy?"

I laugh, abhorrently. The kind of laugh that is both deep and shrill, and tears open your jaw vertically so you look like you're about to suck a monstrously large dick. He just smiles a very placating smile. A smile that makes me want to breathe deeply and touch his thigh as he plays with my hair. Or maybe that's just the champagne. Yes, it's the champagne. I clench my teeth, clear my throat.

"Um...I..."

"Sorry—it's just—well. Well, I was just thinking of my ex-girlfriend, she was really kinky and once she, well, she put a wine bottle up her pussy."

The moonlight is casting a salty blue sheen over the bald spot on the back of his head. Everything smells like how petroleum jelly feels. For a second, I think I hear someone trying to open the door. Is Xavier still here? No, no. He left ages ago.

"Thing cracked inside her. It was terrible, actually. I had to take her to the hospital. She needed three stitches."

He hiccups and places his old man's hand on my knee.

"Sorry, that was too much information, right? Ha. I'm a bit drunk, I guess. I think."

I remember to breathe, straighten my back.

"No, no, it's fine. It's funny—or, not funny, but…yeah."

He takes the bottle and pretends to chug even though there's nothing left—he pretends to swallow, too.

"So fucked up they didn't keep me on," I say, louder than expected.

"Yeah. It is. But I heard they only had the budget to keep on one, so…don't feel too bad."

Cars honking, teenagers screaming—everyone's on their way to do something, it seems. I think about maybe now making that joke about him murdering me. I decide against it once again.

"Yeah. Definitely nothing to do with the fact that I'm a woman and Brandon is black."

He laughs, pats my knee three times.

"Oh, God, no—don't start with that bullshit."

I laugh.

"Okay, sorry, sorry."

His hand is still on me. It's been there so long, I'm numb to what it feels like. I don't think I ever knew what it felt like; I can only see. His skin has a bluish-gray complexion in this lighting, his tendons like seizing worms, sun spots like chicken pox. His fingernails are well-trimmed, and his thumb is habitually fingering the crease behind my knee. I wonder if he thinks that's a pleasure spot. I mean, it does kind of feel good. I retract my thigh inward.

"Probably why he wasn't here today, though—Brandon, I mean. Probably heard they were only keeping one and didn't want to be a part of the fuckin' rat race."

Shaun shrugs and rolls his eyes.

"Anyway," I quickly add.

"Anyway," he echoes.

I wonder what I'd be doing right now if I had gone with Brayden. I wonder if we'd be fucking. I wonder if I even find him attractive. If the answer is no, then I wonder what it is that I am attracted to. That must not be for me to know.

"Stupid fuckin' Brayden," I say.

Shaun wields the empty bottle in the air, high and proud.

"To stupid fuckin' Brayden."

He uses his thumb to pull me closer, and then he kisses me. Shaun kisses me. Well, actually, he misses at first, lands on my chin, but eventually he finds his way. His breath is hot, hotter than I knew breath was allowed to be. His fingers, all of them now, are digging into the flesh behind my knee. The only thing that parts us is this handrail, and even that doesn't feel as real as I'd like it to be.

I have no real interest in explaining what happens next. You could likely picture it any way you want and still be right. Let's just say a champagne bottle was definitely involved, as well as his stubby sausage fingers. Once he's done, he zips up, wordlessly. He stands up, sighs, and cracks his fingers as he gazes at the horizon. All I can see are cold metallic grids.

I wonder what Brayden would be like as a father. I wonder how long it will take Mr. Cherith to notice I'm gone. I wonder if the writers know my name. Next month, they'll probably be like, "Hey, where's that Samara girl with my coffee?" and no one will feel it's necessary to correct them. I should ask Brayden out. I should call my mom more. This place makes too much sense. I need a new world, a world that makes no sense whatsoever. Shaun laughs and sticks his hand out for me to take.

"You comin'?"

I shake my head no.

"Okay, well, uh, you know how to get down?"

I nod my head yes.

"Cool."

He leaves, hiccuping and picking a wedgie on the way out. I turn back to the fence-laced night. I hear the desperate whine of the door opening and the raw slam of the door shutting. I put my hands out to see if my fingers are shaking, but, obviously, I already know the answer to that. The inside of my mouth tastes sweet, but acidic, like a cherry doused in vinegar. Like blood and Splenda. Like afterbirth and champagne. I feel like crying, but it doesn't feel useful if no one can see. Some stories happen so often that you're doing the world a disservice by continuing to tell them. I know this. My phone buzzes. It's on the ground. I pick it up and tap the screen. It's Jeffrey.

Hey
U up?
Wanna come over?

I text back, fingers still shaking, touch still raw.

I mean
Idk
I was just raped

He takes a couple of minutes to text before he responds.

Yep right
Got it
Go fuck yourself Sienna lol

www.ingramcontent.com/pod-product-compliance
Lightning Source LLC
Chambersburg PA
CBHW020140170726
47995CB00003BA/647